Vermont
State Facts

Nickname:	Green Mountain State
Date Entered Union:	March 4, 1791 (the 14th state)
Motto:	Freedom and unity
Vermont Men:	Chester A. Arthur, *U.S. president,* Calvin Coolidge, *U.S. president* John Dewey, *philosopher, educator* John Deere, *inventor*
Flower:	Red clover
Bird:	Hermit thrush
Fun Fact:	Montpelier is the only U.S. state capital without a McDonald's restaurant.

Trouble, Jennifer thought. ***This man is trouble.***

It was an aura that clung to him as he stood there staring blatantly at her.

"You're Jennifer Stansfield?" he asked, arching a dark brow quizzically.

She nodded, then found her voice—an embarrassingly breathless voice. "Who are you?"

He gave her a look that suggested she shouldn't have had to ask. "I'm Ben."

"What are you doing here?" she asked, deciding not to challenge his assumption that she should know him.

His wide mouth curved briefly in an unpleasant smile. "I'm here to cause you trouble, Jennifer Stansfield. A whole lot of trouble."

American

HEROES

AGAINST ALL ODDS

Saranne
DAWSON

Twilight Magic

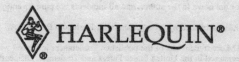

HARLEQUIN®

TORONTO • NEW YORK • LONDON
AMSTERDAM • PARIS • SYDNEY • HAMBURG
STOCKHOLM • ATHENS • TOKYO • MILAN • MADRID
PRAGUE • WARSAW • BUDAPEST • AUCKLAND

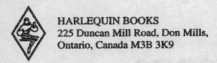

HARLEQUIN BOOKS
225 Duncan Mill Road, Don Mills,
Ontario, Canada M3B 3K9

ISBN 0-373-82243-X

TWILIGHT MAGIC

Visit us at www.eHarlequin.com

Printed in U.S.A.

About the Author

Saranne Dawson is a human services administrator who lives deep in the woods of central Pennsylvania. Her hobbies include walking, sewing, gardening, reading mysteries—and spending time with her grandson, Zachary.

Books by Saranne Dawson

Harlequin Intrigue

In Self Defense #286
Her Other Half #307
Exposé #356
Runaway Heart #472
Lawman Lover #503

Harlequin American Romance

Intimate Strangers #180
Summer's Witness #222
A Talent for Love #364
Bewitched #448
Deception and Desire #480
Twilight Magic #504

Prologue

Dust motes sparkled and danced in the flashlight's beam. The man's footsteps echoed eerily in the silence. Memories assailed him at every turn—some good, some not so good. And they were just *his* memories. After more than a hundred years, the old inn had piled up a lot more.

But there was one memory in particular on his mind this day; the one he least wanted to recall. The one, in fact, that he hadn't thought about in years, because he hadn't let himself think about it.

Now he no longer had the luxury of forgetfulness. Anger flared briefly, but the person at whom that anger was directed was beyond anger, and everything else.

That woman would be coming soon to claim her inheritance. His jaw clenched. Perhaps she'd find nothing here to interest her. It wasn't an unreasonable hope. But if she was one of the few who saw beyond the surface, who liked challenges...

Well, if she *was* that kind, she would have to be dealt with.

Chapter One

A creepy feeling of unreality swept through Jennifer the moment she saw the broken sign and the weed-choked driveway. But she turned into the driveway and proceeded through the woods that closed in on both sides. Then the woods ended abruptly, giving way to a wildly overgrown lawn—and her first view of the inn.

"No," she said softly as her brain denied the evidence her eyes revealed to her. A small, irrational part of her was still hoping that she'd gotten the directions wrong. But there couldn't possibly be two inns named Victoriana in this part of Vermont. Besides, in spite of the peeling paint, the sagging porch and the boarded-up windows, she could see that it was indeed the same place.

Without taking her eyes from the sight before her, Jennifer reached over and fumbled through her purse until she found the postcard. Her gaze went from the reality to the dream—a dream that had just become a nightmare.

She drove onto the circular driveway that surrounded a flower bed—or rather a former flower bed. A few daffodils still struggled against the weeds, their golden heads nodding in the breeze. Then she got out of the car and stood there, staring at the broken and rotted gingerbread trim around the edges of the porch roof and the sagging trellises that held dead vines. She raised her eyes to the whimsical turret, with its domed roof, its lacy ironwork and its broken weather vane, which was nonetheless turning slowly in the breeze. Behind the inn, off to one side, she could see part of an old carriage house with its own small cupola and weather vane.

Somehow, as she stood there staring at her inheritance, Jennifer felt a whisper of magic in the air—the magic that had once been Victoriana. She saw fresh paint and shutters, and wicker furniture on the porch, and trellises tangled with honeysuckle vines. She saw a velvet lawn, and beds of flowers. She saw a *challenge*.

There were certainly questions to be asked and answers to be demanded, but for now she simply stood there, hands planted on slim hips, and dared this reality to tell her she couldn't have her dream.

She walked over to the sagging front steps, convinced that she had to be seeing the worst of it, that the inside would surely be in much better condition. She tested the first step gingerly, then withdrew her foot quickly when it groaned and sagged still more. Considering the condition of the porch floor, she decided it was probably just as well that she couldn't get up there.

Instead, she made her way along the weedy brick walk that ran around the corner, her eyes busily checking the boarded-up windows. About halfway back—just beyond the end of the porch—she spotted what appeared to be a loose board. She'd have the key to the place soon, but still she felt an overwhelming need to reassure herself about the condition of the interior.

Carefully she stepped through the tangled mess that had once been a flower bed and grabbed hold of the loose board. It pulled free with a shrieking sound that shattered the stillness.

Cupping her hands around her eyes, Jennifer peered through the dusty window into what was apparently the dining room. In the dim light, she could just barely make out shrouded furniture, ugly flowered wallpaper and dark wainscoting.

She stepped back, somewhat reassured. It appeared that the inn's chief problems *were* on the outside, after all. The repairs would undoubtedly be costly, but if all that was required inside was some cleaning and painting—not to mention getting rid of that ghastly wallpaper—she could handle that.

Not even for a moment did Jennifer think about just walking away, selling the place for whatever she could get and picking up the pieces of her life somewhere else. If the Victoriana of her dreams didn't exist, she would just create it. And by the time she was finished, it would be even more truly hers.

She stared defiantly at the three-story structure. Okay, so she wasn't just going to walk in and start running the place as she'd planned. And there were certainly some questions that needed answering. But the magic was still here—and with it, the chance to plant her feet deep in the rocky soil of New England.

She wondered what she'd find inside. Could the sheets be hiding genuine antique furniture? Might there even be a crystal chandelier or two—and perhaps some Oriental rugs?

The sun slipped behind a cloud, and she stepped up to the window again, hoping she would be able to see better now. She started to cup her hands around her eyes as she leaned toward the window. And then a face peered out at her!

She screamed and stumbled back from the window. Her heel caught in the tangled flower bed, and she fell, twisting her ankle painfully and scraping her leg against the brick border.

With her heart pounding crazily, Jennifer sat there for a moment, rubbing her throbbing ankle and staring at the window. She could see nothing in it now. Surely the face had been a trick of dust and shadow. There couldn't be anyone in there. The inn was clearly abandoned, and she'd seen no vehicle around.

As she got to her feet, she thought about how isolated this place was. Then she heard a door slam somewhere at the back of the inn.

Visions of some deranged homeless man or some drug addict escalated her wariness to outright fear, and she began to run as fast as her injured ankle and her high-heeled shoes would permit.

"Hey! Wait a minute!"

Jennifer turned just as a man came running around the side of the inn. After the visions her mind had conjured up, the reality brought her to a confused stop. Which gave him enough time to reach her. He too stopped about ten feet away.

His deep blue eyes, fringed with dark lashes, held her captive as effectively as though he'd reached out to grab her. He was tall, with the rangy sort of build that suggests a natural athleticism that owes nothing to hours spent in a health club. He wore faded jeans and no shirt, which gave her far too clear a view of bronzed muscles and curling chest hairs. And those piercing eyes were set deep in a rugged face with a strong jaw and a cleft chin.

Trouble, she thought. *This man is trouble.* It was an aura that clung to him as he stood there staring blatantly at her. Every female instinct she possessed was telling her to get out of here before those eyes had finished undressing her.

"You're Jennifer Stansfield?" he asked, arching a dark brow quizzically.

She nodded, then found her voice—an embarrassingly breathless voice. "Who are you?"

He gave her a look that suggested she shouldn't have had to ask the question. "I'm Ben."

"What are you doing here?" she asked, deciding not to challenge his assumption that she should know him.

His wide mouth curved briefly in an unpleasant smile. "I'm here to cause you trouble, Jennifer Stansfield. A whole lot of trouble."

Their gazes locked, and she knew he meant what he said. She wasn't easily intimidated, but she was still off balance over her discovery of the inn's condition, and she hadn't forgotten their isolation. So she said nothing more, but instead turned and started toward her car, fearing that at any moment he would stop her.

But when she reached the car, she looked around and saw that he hadn't moved. He was just standing there, his hands jammed in the pockets of his jeans, watching her. She got into the car and drove away without a backward glance. But his image was burned into her memory—along with his warning.

BEN STARED AFTER HER until her car had disappeared down the driveway. Then he pulled his hands out of his pockets and turned back to the inn. Muscles rippled along his arms and across his chest as his hands clenched into fists. When his brain started to replay what had just taken place, he forced himself to relax, then smiled grimly.

She apparently didn't know who he was—but she would soon enough. And now that he'd seen her, he needed to rethink his strategy. A very interesting twist had been added to the whole damned mess.

He was staring at the inn, but what he saw instead was her: that pale blond hair, those widely spaced gray-green eyes, and that unmistakable aura of sophistication. He saw a challenge—and he'd never been one to run from a challenge.

"Ms. STANSFIELD, it's a pleasure to meet you, even though the circumstances leave something to be desired. May I extend my belated condolences on the deaths of your mother and stepfather?"

Jennifer shook hands with the attorney and murmured something appropriate as she took a seat in the charmingly old-fashioned office, which seemed to suit the courtly, gray-haired man. She was still rather shaken after the encounter at the inn.

Thomas Wexford made a steeple of his fingers as he regarded her across the width of a huge mahogany desk. "Have you given any thought to what course of action you wish to pursue?" he inquired.

"I definitely want to reopen the inn," she told him. Then she smiled ruefully. "I'm afraid I completely misunderstood the situation. I didn't know it was closed, but I'm willing to put whatever money is required into restoring it. It's a wonderful place."

She was certain about little else at this point, but was *very* sure about that. Now that the initial shock of the inn's appearance had worn off, Jennifer had actually begun telling herself what fun it would be to restore the place. And, thanks to her inheritance, she could afford it.

"It *is* a wonderful inn," the attorney agreed. "It was once the finest one in the area. But it's been closed since Edwin Walters retired, and that must be, oh…five or six years, I think."

Jennifer frowned. How could such a misunderstanding have occurred? "I just assumed it was still operating. Win said that his brother was managing it."

"Win?" Wexford asked with a frown of his own. Then he nodded. "Oh, you mean Edwin. No, his brother never ran Victoriana, although he *has* been acting as a sort of caretaker since Edwin left."

Jennifer tried to recall exactly what Win had said, and was forced to the conclusion that he must have said that his brother was "taking care of the place," or some such phrase, and she'd just assumed that meant he was running it.

"It seems to have deteriorated rather badly in that length of time," she said doubtfully.

"Well, New England winters are severe, and maintaining an old place like that is a never-ending chore." The attorney paused, then went on in a careful tone. "And I'm afraid that Edwin didn't really keep it up as well as he might have."

Jennifer said nothing, but his words shocked her. She thought about how fondly Win had spoken of Victoriana. She had the growing sense that something was very wrong. "Have you been inside—recently, I mean?"

"Oh, yes, I was out there only a few weeks ago with the estate appraiser. I have a complete list of its contents and their values right here for you." He indicated a folder on his desk.

"I peeked in a window, but I couldn't see much," she told him, as yet another image of the man named Ben formed in her mind. But she kept resolutely to the issue at hand. "Is it fully furnished?"

"Yes, indeed—and most of the furniture is antique. I'm not an expert, of course, but I believe the exterior is the worst of it, although there's much to be done inside, as well."

Then he regarded her with a frown. "You *did* receive my letter, didn't you? I sent it to your company's address in New York."

It didn't surprise her at all that she hadn't received it. "No, I didn't. I've been in Singapore for the past month and I didn't bother to have my mail forwarded. What letter do you mean?"

"Oh, dear. Then you don't know." His frown deepened.

"Don't know what?" she asked impatiently.

"Ben Walters is contesting his father's will."

Ben. Her mind replayed the entire scene—including his statement about causing her trouble. And now, of course, with perfect hindsight, she saw the resemblance to Win. If it hadn't been for those eyes, she probably would have seen it immediately. Win's eyes had been dark, but he'd had that same strong jaw and cleft chin.

It took a few seconds for all this to pass through her mind and leave in its wake the stunned realization that something was indeed very wrong.

"I didn't know that Win had a son," she told the attorney. "He never mentioned him." Win and her mother had both described him as a childless widower.

"Well, I'm afraid there was some, ah...estrangement between them."

"And this Ben is contesting his father's will?" she asked. "Can he do that? I don't understand the laws in these matters."

"I'm afraid that he's contesting it on the basis that his father was mentally incapable of making a will."

"But that's absurd!" Jennifer stated indignantly. "Win was fine until his stroke. And even after that, though he was physically impaired, and his speech could be difficult to understand, he was certainly of sound mind."

The attorney nodded. "Yes, I spoke to your attorney in Florida, and he told me essentially the same thing. He and Edwin were regular golfing partners, and he felt quite comfortable drawing up the will, even though, as you said, Edwin was difficult to understand."

Her mind registered the fact that Win had drawn up the will after his stroke, and not before, as she'd assumed. But that was the least of her concerns at the moment.

"I think I met...Ben." She described the man at the inn, using neutral words that didn't begin to describe the impact he'd had on her. As she spoke, she found herself hoping desperately and irrationally that he was some other Ben.

"That's him," the attorney confirmed. "He's just recently returned to the area."

"Is he *living* there?" she asked incredulously, although by this point she had nearly exhausted her capacity for being surprised.

"As far as I know, he's staying with his uncle—and his uncle has keys, since he's been acting as caretaker. Did he say anything to you, or cause you problems?"

Jennifer related what had happened, including Ben's warning. The attorney shook his head in disgust.

"Ben Walters has been trouble just about all his life. He and his father never got along. Ben was always in trouble of some kind. Edwin still sent him to college, though, but instead of appreciating the chance he was being given, he quit."

The attorney shook his head, dismissing the subject, then explained that there were several avenues Jennifer could pursue.

"The best solution would probably be to reach some sort of settlement out of court. In effect, you would pay him to drop his claim. But I suspect that might not be possible."

The implications of Ben's suit were just beginning to dawn on Jennifer. By claiming that Win was mentally incapable of making a will, he was saying that she or her mother had connived to get him to leave Victoriana to her.

"I refuse to pay him a cent," she said angrily. "How dare he lie like that?"

"I've taken the liberty of speaking briefly to his attorney, and it's my impression that Ben is unwilling to settle, in any event. He doesn't want money—he wants the inn."

"So we go to court," she replied defiantly. "How long will it take to get it settled?"

"Unfortunately, these things take time. My guess would be that it could take up to a year—perhaps somewhat less."

A year? "But there's no doubt that I'll win, is there?"

Wexford spread his hands. "We have a very good case—especially since the attorney who drew up Edwin's will knew him before he had the stroke. On the other hand, it's possible that they could subpoena medical staff from the hospital to back up their claim that he didn't know what he was doing or was incapable of communicating his wishes clearly.

"I must warn you, Ms. Stansfield, that it could get very unpleasant. Ben knows about your mother's previous marriages, and could use that to make her look, um...ac-quisitive."

Jennifer had to struggle hard to keep her temper in check. "It's true that my mother was married three times before she married Win. But she was already quite well-off."

"Were her previous husbands wealthy?"

"Yes, but she got no more from them than most women get when they divorce wealthy men." She tried hard not to be defensive, which was always difficult where the subject of her mother was concerned.

"Still, you can see how they might be able to use that," the attorney pointed out gently. "And there's another factor, as well. This may not seem to be a typical rural area, since it's a resort region, but it is, and local people are inclined to be traditionalists. Your mother—and, by extension, you—may be viewed as what we used to call 'gold diggers.' And besides that, you're an outsider, while Ben is a Walters, and the inn has been passed down from father to son ever since it was built in the 1880s. You can see how those things might influence a judge or jury."

Jennifer merely nodded. Her head was throbbing. What she really needed now was to get out of here and think about all this. She stood up and extended her hand to the lawyer.

"Thank you, Mr. Wexford. I need some time to mull this over, but I *do* know that I intend to fight him in court. So please proceed with whatever you have to do."

She told him where she could be reached, then took from him the keys to the inn and the inventory lists. After stopping at a drugstore for some aspirin, she drove back to the inn where she was staying. She was hungry and tired and felt as though she needed a shower. She lay down on the bed and waited for the aspirin to work—and her thoughts to stop spinning.

Too much had happened in too short a time. Barely two months before, her mother had been fatally injured in an auto accident as she drove home from the hospital following her husband's death. Then Jennifer had learned that her stepfather had bequeathed Victoriana to her. Believing the inn to be still operating, Jennifer had left her job with a major international hotel corporation—burning her bridges behind her in a rather spectacular fashion. A job she'd once loved had become one she hated, with a change of owners, and with her inheritance she saw the opportunity to put down roots and have something of her own.

Now here she was, the owner of a dilapidated, nonoperating inn that might be taken away from her by a man she hadn't known existed just hours before. Furthermore, both her mother and Win had clearly lied to her—perhaps about the condition of Victoriana, and certainly about the existence of Ben Walters.

And then there was Ben himself. Six feet two inches of lethal blue-eyed charm—determined, by his own admission, to cause her "a whole lot of trouble."

As she recounted these facts to herself, Jennifer was forced to smile ironically. If someone else had told her this tale of woe, she wouldn't have believed it.

Jennifer went back to the beginning, to the lie or lies told by her mother and stepfather. Now that she had some time to think about her conversations over the past few years with Win about Victoriana, she became convinced that she *hadn't* misunderstood him about the inn's condition. Several times he'd urged her to consider giving up her job and taking over the management of Victoriana. She could even recall his saying once that his brother was "getting too old to deal with it."

Suddenly she remembered Wexford's mentioning that the attorney in Florida had been a friend of Win's. She'd met him only once, after her mother's death. But if she had any hope of getting some answers, he might be a good place to start.

She found his number and called Florida. She'd promised to get in touch with him upon her return from Singapore, in any event; there were still some details to be settled regarding her mother's estate.

Fortunately, he was available, and after they'd exchanged the usual pleasantries, he asked if she'd seen Wexford yet. Jennifer told him everything—her ignorance about the condition of the inn and the existence of Ben Walters, and her meeting with Wexford. "Mr. Jacobs, did Win ever mention a son to you? I understand that you knew each other socially."

"We did indeed. We played golf together regularly. I miss those games. But no, I was as shocked as you were to learn that he had a son."

"Don't you think that's rather strange?"

"Well, it *does* seem a bit strange, frankly. But from what Wexford told me, the son's been a problem all his life, and I suppose Win had just washed his hands of him. What I *do* know is that Win intended that you should have Victoriana. He mentioned that to me several times. He was very fond of you, Jennifer, and I can remember his saying that if he'd had a daughter, he would have wanted one just like you. And he was definitely in full command of his mental faculties when he drew up that will.''

He paused a moment, then went on. ''I know this must be very difficult for you, but I hope you won't give up. It was Win's fondest hope that you'd take over the inn someday. In fact, he seemed almost obsessed with the idea. I recall his mentioning not long before he had the stroke that they'd received a letter from you and you seemed unhappy with your job. He thought he might be able to persuade you to leave it and take over the inn.''

''Did you know that the inn has been closed since he left Vermont?'' she asked curiously.

''No, I assumed his brother was running it, just as you did. He did mention once that it needed some work and he'd do that if you took it over.''

She thanked him and hung up, then sat there holding her still-aching head. But she did feel somewhat better after having confirmed that she wasn't the only one who'd misunderstood the situation. She was surprised, though, that the attorney had said Win had seemed obsessed with the idea of having her run Victoriana. In retrospect, she realized that he *had* brought up the subject repeatedly.

His mention of her letter and her unhappiness with her job brought up yet another problem. She hadn't just resigned; she'd marched into her boss's office and told him exactly what she thought of their methods of operation. At the time, she'd been certain she wouldn't need them again—not even for a reference. After all, she had her own inn now.

She lay back down on the bed with a groan. What on earth was she going to do? She certainly couldn't go back to Inter-Hotels after that little scene; neither could she expect a reference from them, despite the fact that her work had been highly praised. She couldn't even get a reference from Simon Beresford, the company's previous owner. That dear and wonderful man had died suddenly only two months after selling his hotels.

A year, Wexford had said. Despite his cautions, she still felt confident that she would win, because she was right. But what could she do in the meantime? She certainly had enough money to live on comfortably, and she supposed a lot of people would be happy to take a year off and travel. But she was tired of traveling. There was nowhere she wanted to go that she hadn't already seen. What she wanted was to settle down here and put her personal stamp on Victoriana.

She picked up a pillow and flung it across the room in an uncharacteristic fit of anger. Damn Ben Walters and his lies! How dare he mess with her life like this? No wonder his father had denied his existence!

THE NEXT MORNING, armed with a newly purchased flashlight and an inventory of Victoriana's equipment and furnishings, Jennifer set off to spend the day at the inn. She knew she might find Ben Walters there again, but her state of mind was such that she would welcome a confrontation with him at this point.

What business did he have going there, anyway? She should have insisted that Wexford get the keys from him—better yet, she should have the locks changed. Who knew what he was capable of doing? He might even have taken things, arrogantly believing he was entitled to them.

She drove up the driveway and around the side of the house, to the back. The front was boarded up, like the first-floor windows, and Wexford had instructed her to use the kitchen entrance.

She saw the motorcycle as soon as she reached the back corner of the inn. For one brief moment, she thought about driving away rather than facing that blue-eyed devil again. But her anger coalesced into a steely resolve, and she parked the car beside the bike.

It didn't surprise her one bit to discover that he had a motorcycle—and a very large one, at that. It was all shiny chrome and black paint, and looked as menacing as its owner. Although she hated to admit it, even to herself, it had that same quality of dangerous excitement, as well.

She heard a sound, and turned to see Ben Walters opening the door. At least he was wearing a shirt this time—and a leather jacket, as well. His thick, dark hair was unruly, as though he might have combed it with his fingers. And those blue eyes were once again piercing her like a knife, sending frissons through every part of her.

His gaze dropped to the papers she held, and a slight smile came to his wide, and very masculine, mouth. "Planning to see what all you've inherited?"

"Yes," she stated coldly. "And I'd like to know what *you're* doing here."

That insolent smile grew a bit. "Don't worry, I haven't taken anything. Why should I? It'll be mine soon enough."

"No, it won't! Victoriana is *mine,* Ben Walters. Your father left it to me—probably because he knew you couldn't be trusted with it."

She expected anger from him, but what she got instead was laughter—a deep, utterly masculine chuckle that seemed to vibrate within her, as well.

"It sounds like you've been checking me out. I guess I'm flattered, since that must mean you consider me to be a serious threat."

He had stopped just outside the back door, but now he started toward her, moving slowly, but with the natural grace of the born athlete. She stood her ground, her eyes locked on his. The truth was that she probably couldn't have moved if she'd wanted to. Ben Walters was doing very strange things to her.

He came *very* close to her, invading her personal space and filling the very air between them with a seductive danger. And then he stepped past her to his motorcycle.

He swung onto the seat with a lithe movement, then grinned and gave her a mock salute. "Have a nice day, Jenny."

Before she could respond to that, he revved up the motorcycle and roared off—without putting on his helmet, she noticed.

Jennifer was so angry that she could only barely keep herself from screaming. But at least half of her anger was directed at herself. There was no doubt in her mind that Ben Walters knew exactly how he'd affected her.

Although she certainly wouldn't give up her anger at him, she decided to give herself a break where her own emotions were concerned. After all, she had no experience with grown-up juvenile delinquents. Familiarity would surely breed contempt, wouldn't it? And she had a feeling she was going to become *very* familiar with Ben Walters before this was over.

She pushed open the door of the inn, wondering if it was written somewhere that every woman should encounter the likes of Ben Walters at least once in her life. The wrong man in the wrong place at the wrong time. Trouble with a capital *T*.

But before long, Ben Walters had slipped to the back of her mind as she lost herself in the dream of Victoriana. Despite the dust and the shabbiness and the inept decorating, the old inn lived up to her highest expectations.

Twelve-foot ceilings were edged with lovely plaster moldings, although some were crumbling. There was a real walnut wainscoting, dull from lack of care, in the dining room and in the small bar and library. The front doors, which had been boarded up from the outside, were etched and beveled glass, surrounded by small panes of jewel-toned stained glass and intricately carved wood. Even the registration desk in one corner of the lobby was of walnut, with beautiful burled insets.

When she began lifting the shrouds from the furniture, she found many fine antiques, although most of the chairs and sofas had been upholstered in ghastly fabrics. A number of Persian and Axminster rugs were rolled up and sealed in plastic. She worried about moth damage until she opened one and smelled mothballs.

The inn had twenty-four rooms and three small suites on three floors. The third-floor rooms were smallish—no doubt they'd once accommodated servants. And to Jennifer's delighted surprise, there was also a separate apartment on the second floor.

The living room of the apartment was set into the corner of the building that included the turret. Windows filled the curved space, and in front of them was a window seat with a faded and tattered cushion.

Jennifer was thoroughly enchanted with the apartment. She could easily imagine herself living here, relaxing in the cozy window seat while a fire blazed in the small marble-topped fireplace. The lovely antique furniture her mother had left her would be perfect for this place.

Tears came to her eyes as she thought about having her first real home. Ever since college, she'd traveled the world because of her work, living in hotel suites. She was thirty-one, and she'd never had a home of her own.

She finally left the apartment and continued her inspection, then went back downstairs and began to work her way through the inventory lists. The first thing she noticed was that there were two crystal chandeliers listed—very expensive chandeliers—but all she had seen were holes and dangling wires in the dining room and lobby.

Then she saw that the inventory also included four signed Tiffany lamps and a pair of Staffordshire dogs that probably belonged beside the big fireplace in the lobby. These items were missing, as well. She didn't have to check the list to know that they were the most valuable of the inn's furnishings.

With a renewed surge of anger, she thought about Ben Walters and his new motorcycle. No wonder he wanted the inn so badly; he obviously intended to sell it off piecemeal to pay for his expensive toys.

Thinking of him as a criminal did wonders for Jennifer's state of mind. She was confident that the police would be able to trace the items and recover them, and she was certain, as well, that Ben's thievery would end his claim to the inn.

Imagining the man behind bars also ended her unhealthy attraction to him. No matter how blue his eyes or how perfectly sculpted his mouth or how powerful that aura of essential maleness, the man was a common criminal.

Jennifer was so relieved that she thought she might not care too much if the lamps and the dogs were never recovered—although she really *did* want those chandeliers back. She turned to the inventory again, deciding to complete it and make certain she hadn't somehow overlooked the missing items. She would call Wexford as soon as she got back to town.

But when she had finished inside and walked out into the bright sunshine of a perfect spring day, she decided that Ben Walters's thievery could wait just a bit longer. She wanted to get a better look at the lake she'd seen from the second-floor windows. Along with the inn itself came nearly forty acres of land—including the lake, described in the deed as encompassing a little more than ten acres.

She followed the path that led through the woods and came to a clearing that had probably once been a lovely lawn stretching down to the water's edge. An old, rotting dock slanted down to disappear in the clear water. As with the inn itself, Jennifer saw not what *was*, but what *could be*—in this case, a velvet lawn with Adirondack chairs, and rowboats or even small sailboats tied up at the dock. The once and future Victoriana.

She walked through more of the grounds and discovered an overgrown rose garden with trellises that had broken and were now covered with weeds. In the center of the former garden was an old sundial, still intact, though its brass pointer was badly tarnished. Finally, at the edge of the front lawn, she found a jumble of wood that she was sure must once have been a gazebo—a rather elaborate one, to judge from the ruins.

By the time she left the inn, Jennifer was even more firmly under its spell—and very determined to see the Victoriana of her imagination become reality.

As soon as she got back to her room, she called Wexford, catching the attorney just as he was about to leave for the day.

"I have two questions," she told the attorney. "First of all, can I have the locks changed at the inn?"

"Yes, of course. Are you concerned about the keys Ben Walters has?"

"I certainly am." She told him about the missing items. "He must have taken them. I want the police informed immediately."

"Oh, dear." The attorney sighed. "I'm afraid it's my fault that you didn't find them. I should have told you. They're stored in the carriage house. They were put there when the inn was closed, apparently, and a strong padlock was put on the door. I suppose Edwin must have decided they'd be safer there. The key to the padlock is on the ring I gave you."

"Oh." Jennifer felt both relieved and disappointed. She was happy that the items were safe, but unhappy, too, because whatever else Ben Walters might be, he apparently wasn't a thief.

Chapter Two

"Thank you for seeing me on such short notice, Mr. Wexford," Jennifer said as the attorney ushered her into his office.

As soon as they were both seated, she took a deep breath. She could only hope that Wexford wasn't going to tell her how foolish her idea was. She began by explaining to him how she'd grown to hate her job, and then went on to give him a somewhat expurgated version of her final confrontation with her boss.

"So you see, that leaves me in a very difficult position. I'm confident that we'll win, but what am I to do in the meantime? I can't just sit around waiting for this to be settled. What I would like to do," she said, as calmly as possible, "is to begin the restoration work at Victoriana *now*, instead of waiting for the lawsuit to be settled. Is there any way I can do that?"

When the attorney didn't immediately say no, Jennifer allowed herself some hope. She had returned again to the inn, spending the day lost in dreams and plans, and she was desperate to find a way to make them come true.

After frowning thoughtfully for an unbearably long time, Wexford finally nodded. "It just might be possible, but it would require the approval of the executor and the judge—but basically, I think it would be up to Ben Walters. The judge and the executor, a retired banker in town who's an old friend of Edwin's, would almost certainly go along with it if Ben agreed."

Her hopes began a sickening slide toward despair. She'd thought—foolishly, she knew now—that perhaps Ben Walters could be kept out of it.

"He'll never agree, will he?"

"We won't know until we ask him. The inducement we can offer is that of getting the inn operational more quickly, which I'm sure must be what he wants, too."

"I know that I'd be taking a risk, but—"

Wexford cut her off with a wave of his hand. "If Ben agrees, we can structure the agreement between you and him in such a way as to guarantee that you won't lose the money you put into the inn if he should win the suit. So all you'd be risking is your time—and from what you've just told me, you're willing to risk that."

Jennifer nodded. But how would she feel if she spent the next six months or so working on the inn, only to lose it to Ben Walters and his lies? *Well,* she told herself, abandoning that unproductive line of thinking, *I'm not going to lose—so the question is moot.*

She asked if a meeting could be arranged with Ben.

"I'll contact his attorney and tell him you have something you'd like to discuss with him. I'll get back in touch with you as soon as a meeting is arranged."

"Thank you," Jennifer said, trying not to think about yet another confrontation with Ben Walters. "In the meantime, do you know a local contractor I could consult about the cost of repairs—someone with experience in restoration work?"

"Jim Thompson would be your man. He's the best in the area."

Jennifer thanked him, then accepted his offer to let her call the contractor from his office. She was able to reach Thompson, who agreed to meet her at Victoriana that afternoon.

She left the attorney's office thinking about the cruel twist of fate that had made a man totally unknown to her until three days ago the most important person in her life. Not to mention the fact that the man in question was a handsome, blue-eyed devil who did very embarrassing things to her treacherous body.

JENNIFER ARRIVED at the inn a few minutes before the appointed time to find the contractor's truck parked near the rear entrance.

As she got out of her car, a tall, gray-haired man came around the far side of the inn, carrying a clipboard.

"It's a real shame the way this place has been let go," he said after the introductions had been made. "I hadn't seen it in quite a while."

"I hope you're not going to tell me that it's not worth the cost of restoration," she said uneasily, worrying now that it might be in worse shape than was immediately apparent.

"Oh, no," he assured her quickly. "It's not that bad. In fact, I've worked on far worse than this. But it isn't going to be cheap."

"I'd already guessed that, but I don't have any idea just how much money we're talking about. Mr. Wexford said that you're the best in the area at this kind of work."

He reached into his truck and got a big flashlight. "Well, let's see what we have inside."

They began with the basement, which she'd visited only briefly. To her relief, he pronounced the boiler in excellent condition, but he expressed some concern about the wiring.

"I think the place was rewired sometime in the seventies. I'll check on that for you, because there's only one contractor I know of who would have taken on a job like that back then. The thing is, though, that there could be some damage from mice and squirrels if they managed to get in—and they probably did."

When they passed the wine cellar, he paused to examine the dusty bottles, and chuckled. "You could either have a small fortune in fine old wines here, or a cellar full of high-priced vinegar. This place once had the finest food in the area, you know, although Edwin let the dining room go like everything else."

"Did you know him?" Jennifer asked curiously, since he was the second person to suggest that Win hadn't run the place well.

"Not all that well," he admitted, rubbing the dust off a bottle and peering at the label. "But most people around here seemed to think that his heart just wasn't in it." He replaced the bottle and shrugged.

"I guess that can happen when a family's been in the same business for a long time. Some folks say that the place actually started to slide when Edwin's father was still running it. There are even folks who'll tell you that there's some sort of jinx on the place."

"Really?" Jennifer smiled. "I was actually wondering if it might have a ghost or two."

As they started back up to the first floor, his laughter echoed in the stairwell. "Oh, it does, it does—if you believe in that sort of thing. Have you seen the lake?"

She told him she had, and he went on as they came out into the kitchen. "Well, one story is that there's a ghost out there. Lots of folks claim to have seen her. Legend has it that she's the ghost of a young woman who drowned out there right after the place opened. Fell out of a rowboat, on her honeymoon." He chuckled. "It makes a real good story, anyway.

"Another tale is that old Caleb—that's Edwin's father—saw and heard things in the inn itself. Leastways, that's what he said when he'd had too much to drink." He grinned at her. "Could be to your advantage to have a ghost or two around. Might help to bring in business. Folks seem to like that sort of thing."

Jennifer smiled. "I think the ghost on the lake might be nice, but I'm not so sure about having them in the inn itself."

"Well, old Caleb's the only one who ever mentioned them, and from what I heard, he took to drink pretty bad in his later years, so I wouldn't put too much stock in it. He was quite a character. I remember him from when I was a kid. Big, good-looking man, quite the ladies' man in his younger days, and always fighting with someone. Well, what happened to the chandelier?"

They had gone through the dining room, and he was shining the flashlight beam on the hole in the ceiling. "Is the big one from the lobby gone, too?"

Jennifer explained where they were. She hadn't actually seen them yet. She'd been in the carriage house, but the missing pieces were sealed in boxes and she'd had no knife to open them.

"They're real beauties," the contractor told her. "The one in the lobby was made especially for the place when it opened, and then was converted from gas to electricity some years later." He ran the beam around the edge of the ceiling and made a note.

"Those moldings are in bad shape."

They went on to the lobby, where he examined the glass doors. "Looks like this is still in good shape, but that stained glass is going to need releading."

"Do you have people who can do that sort of thing, or would I need to bring in a specialist?" she asked as they moved on to the library. She knew how intricate and specialized such work could be—not to mention how costly.

He didn't answer for so long that she thought perhaps he hadn't heard her question. She was about to ask again when he directed the beam of his flashlight at the ceiling of the library, which was divided into large squares by dark wooden beams. Jennifer stared at it and gasped.

Thompson turned to her with a smile. "You didn't see them before?"

"No. It was dark in here, and I was more interested in the books."

She gazed in wonder at the murals painted on the ceiling. They were darkened with age and barely visible in places, but they appeared to represent various ancient Greek myths. One was a depiction of Prometheus bringing fire from the gods.

"Humph!" Thompson exclaimed as he aimed the light at one corner panel. "That one's going to take some real work. It looks as if a pipe must have leaked upstairs."

Jennifer walked over. The painting had been virtually destroyed where the plaster had crumbled.

"The others probably just need cleaning. Of course, that's easier said than done, when you're talking about frescoes. It takes a lot of skill and patience."

"Then I'll need a specialist for that, as well?" she asked, harking back to her earlier, unanswered question.

Thompson regarded her in silence for a moment before answering. "I had a man working for me who could do all of this—the frescoes, the leaded glass, plaster moldings, the trim around the porch, and more. In a lot of ways, he was a real pain in the butt, but I've never seen anyone better at this kind of work."

"But he isn't working for you anymore?"

"No, but he's just come back to the area...." He hesitated, looking suddenly uncomfortable. "Ms. Stansfield, I don't exactly know what's going on here, although I've heard some rumors. But I might as well say it. The man I'm talking about is Ben Walters.''

"Oh!" Jennifer was stunned. That overgrown juvenile delinquent with the motorcycle was a skilled craftsman? She hadn't given much thought to what he did for a living, assuming he was one of those shiftless types who moved from one low-skill job to another. Or at least that was what she'd *wanted* to think.

"The truth is that if it were anyplace but this, I'd tell you he's the one you should hire for the job. He's starting his own business, and this is right up his alley.''

"Then you wouldn't be interested in the job yourself?" she asked, her brain still spinning with this unexpected and unbelievable news.

"I didn't say that. I have a good crew. But to be honest with you, there's none of them as good as Ben is at this sort of thing. He stopped by to see me a couple of weeks ago, and I told him I'd send any restoration work I had his way.''

"But I thought you said he was a problem?"

He chuckled. "In my experience, most people with that kind of talent can be tough to deal with at times. It's as much an art as anything, you know—and most of them have an artist's temperament. 'Course, in Ben's case, he's got the Walters temper, as well.''

They left the library and went upstairs. Jennifer remained silent as she followed along after the contractor, paying scant attention now to his talk of plastering and plumbing. How many times was she going to have to revise her opinion of Ben Walters before the real man emerged? She was still trying to sort it all out when they reached the apartment.

Thompson frowned as he looked at the curved window seat. "Looks like someone must have made some changes here.''

"What do you mean?" Jennifer asked, drawing herself away from thoughts of Ben Walters with some difficulty.

He rapped on a wall. "I'm pretty sure there must have been a staircase here that led up to the top of the tower. There are windows up there, and that generally means there must have been a tower room originally.''

"Maybe the tower was unsafe," she suggested, though she was already thinking how wonderful it would be to have a room up there as a sort of hideaway.

"No, I doubt that. The stairs might have rotted, but the structure itself looks sound, at least from the outside. This place was built well. I suppose it's possible that the windows were put in just for effect, but in my experience, it's more likely there's a room up there. Folks liked that sort of thing back then."

They moved on to the third floor and then went up to the attic. Jennifer thought it must surely be the only attic in existence that was completely bare. While Thompson walked around, she stood at a window, staring out across the former lawn to the woods and thinking once more about Ben Walters.

Then, just as the contractor joined her at the window, they both saw a black pickup with white lettering on the side roar off down the driveway. The distance was too great for her to make out the writing.

"Is that one of your men?" she asked, since she couldn't imagine who else it would be.

"No," he said slowly. "That looks like Ben's truck to me."

"Ben Walters?"

He nodded. "Were you expecting him?"

"No, but I know he's been coming out here."

Thompson chuckled. "I imagine it might be more than just the inn that's bringing him here now."

She didn't ask him what he meant, because his chuckle made that rather plain. "I didn't know he had a truck. When I met him, he was riding a motorcycle."

"Got one of them again, has he? Doesn't surprise me. He always liked them, just the way he always liked trouble." He shook his gray head with a grin. "That boy's sure got a lot of his granddaddy in him. No doubt about that."

"You like him, don't you?" she asked curiously.

"He can be hard *not* to like—and that's what usually got him *out* of trouble."

AFTER the contractor left, Jennifer wandered down to the lake and stared out at the calm waters, which mirrored the sky and the dark forest. There was no sign of a ghost at the moment, but then, she probably didn't put in appearances during the day.

Jennifer sat down on the grassy bank and thought about what Thompson had said about Ben Walters. So now there was yet another irony in the situation: The best person to restore Victoriana was the man who was trying to take it away from her.

She couldn't decide whether this news was a plus or a minus as far as gaining his agreement to her proposal was concerned. He might very well agree—but with the proviso that he himself do the work. How on earth could she possibly work with him? From what Thompson had said, he was difficult under the best of circumstances, and these were very definitely *not* the best of circumstances.

And then there was the matter of her very unhealthy attraction to him. The truth was that she couldn't remember a time in her life when she'd felt such instantaneous—and dangerous—attraction to a man.

Still, what was the alternative? Sitting around waiting for the court to decide that the inn belonged to her?

Unwilling right now to choose between two equally unpalatable alternatives, Jennifer thought instead about the contractor's remark that he'd heard "rumors." It sounded as though Ben Walters might be spreading his lies all over town, which could cause problems for her. As Wexford had said, she was an outsider coming to steal something away from one of their own. Even though Ben was obviously something less than an exemplary citizen, she knew they'd still side with him.

She sat there for a long time, thinking about her increasingly uncertain future—a future that had, until a few days ago, seemed bright with promise. In fact, it was that promise of better things to come that had sustained her through the difficult loss of both Win and her mother.

Then she gradually became aware of a rising wind that began to ruffle the waters of the lake. The sunlight had dimmed, as well. She got up and turned toward the inn and saw, just before she heard the first rumble of thunder, that a storm was brewing.

By the time she came out of the woods near the back of the inn, the whole sky had darkened, and fat drops of rain were pelting her. She locked the back door of the inn, then ran for her car as the storm broke over her.

When she turned the key in the ignition, nothing happened. Confused, she tried again. Still nothing, except for a clicking sound that was barely audible over the sharp cracks of thunder.

At first, Jennifer was merely annoyed—but before long she realized the gravity of her predicament. A glance at her watch confirmed that she'd spent more time than she'd thought sitting beside the lake. By the time the storm passed on, it might well be dark. Then, just to make matters worse, her stomach growled, reminding her that she'd had no lunch.

She tried to start the car again, without success. "Damn!" she muttered as she leaned back against the headrest and thought about the road between here and town. The nearest house had to be several miles away, and she seemed to recall that it had looked empty—a vacation home, in all likelihood. And the road came to a dead end not far beyond the inn's driveway, so there was no source of help to be found in that direction.

It was growing steadily darker—whether just from the storm, or also from the approaching night, she didn't know. She could barely see the inn, only yards away, except when it was illuminated briefly by flashes of lightning. Then she realized that she didn't have her flashlight with her. She'd set it down inside somewhere, because Mr. Thompson had brought a much more powerful one.

Jennifer began to shiver. With the storm had come a sudden, sharp drop in temperature. The day had been pleasantly warm, so she hadn't brought a sweater or jacket with her, and both her pants and her shirt were wet from her dash through the rain.

With a sigh, she accepted the unpleasant prospect of spending the night here. At least there were plenty of beds and blankets. But there was no food and no water. Of course, there *was* the wine cellar. Her mouth twitched briefly with grim humor. At the moment, the thought of drinking herself to sleep was rather appealing.

What troubled her most was that no one would miss her and come looking for her. For years now, her work had been so full of responsibilities that any absence would have been quickly noted. She thought ironically about all the times she'd actually wished she could disappear like this.

She made one more unsuccessful attempt to start the car. Well, what had she expected? She might not know much about cars, but she *did* know that they didn't repair themselves.

So she sat there shivering, waiting for the storm to let up and wondering idly what could be wrong with the car. It was a rental, with less than two thousand miles on it, for heaven's sake, and there had been no warning that anything was wrong.

Then a sudden memory flashed through her mind.

She sat bolt upright as a chill shot through her that owed nothing to the falling temperature and her damp clothing. That truck they'd seen from the attic—Mr. Thompson had been certain that it belonged to Ben Walters!

Could he have done something to her car? The question provoked more icy chills. He'd seen it before, and must have known it was her car. She had no idea why he'd come out here today— but he would certainly have recognized Thompson's truck, as well, and guessed that she was thinking of hiring him. Could he have damaged her car in a fit of rage?

Jennifer swallowed hard. Was he just harassing her, or could he have something worse in mind? With the darkness and the storm as an ominous backdrop, her fears escalated. The best she could hope for was that he'd just had a fit of anger and was playing silly games—but the worst...

She drew in a ragged breath, then let it out slowly. The worst was that he was so determined to have Victoriana for himself that he would try to kill her and make it look like an accident. He might well believe that with her out of the way, no one would challenge his claim to the inn.

She shook her head, trying to deny that awful possibility. But the truth was that she knew next to nothing about him, and what she *did* know was far from reassuring. Both Wexford and Thompson had said he was trouble. His own father had disinherited him. And he was desperate enough to concoct lies in order to regain that inheritance.

But did all that add up to a man who would commit *murder*? She wanted very much not to believe that, but she kept thinking about all the times she'd read about murder being often a crime of passion, a temporary lapse of sanity.

She closed her eyes, then snapped them open again quickly when she saw those blue eyes with such startling clarity that he might have been there with her. Those eyes, and that firm, sculptured mouth, and that bronzed, muscular body. Was she unwilling to believe that he could kill her because she'd been attracted to him?

All the ghastly stories she'd ever read or heard about of women being attracted to such men ran through her brain—not to mention her oh-so-superior assumptions that *she,* Jennifer Stansfield, could never be guilty of such a lapse of judgment. But hadn't those hints of wildness in him been part of the attraction? Of course they had—but that wildness hadn't included murder! Just how big a step was it from being a lifelong troublemaker to being a murderer?

Finally the worst of the storm passed on, though a hard, steady rain continued to fall. Jennifer was so cold that her teeth were actually chattering, and she knew she had to go inside and find her flashlight and some blankets. Just as she'd feared, night had indeed fallen during the storm, and any thoughts she'd harbored about walking down the road to find help had quickly been banished. She would have to spend the night here.

She got out of the car and ran for the back door. She had to fumble with the lock for what seemed like hours before she finally got the door open and stepped inside into an even greater darkness. She stood there shivering, trying to remember where she might have left the flashlight.

After mentally retracing her earlier movements, she decided that she'd probably left it in the library. She'd been so entranced by the frescoes, and then so astounded by the contractor's revelations about Ben Walters, that she must have forgotten all about it. But the library now seemed at least a mile away, beyond a formidable obstacle course of shrouded furniture and rolled-up carpets.

Taking a deep, quavering breath, Jennifer began to feel her way across the dark kitchen to the padded doors that led into the dining room. After pushing them open, she stopped for a moment, until her eyes had adjusted well enough that she thought she could make out the dim shapes of sheet-covered furniture.

How long it actually took her to reach the library, Jennifer didn't know, since she couldn't even see her watch. But it felt like at least an hour before she had groped her way along the wall and at last touched the doorframe that she knew must be the entrance to the library. By that time, she had fallen once, stumbled several more times, gouged her side on the sharp edge of a table and banged her shins at least four times on various chair or table legs.

The good side to all this self-inflicted pain was that she'd been too busy trying to avoid it to give much thought to things that go bump in the night—or to the possibility that Ben Walters might return.

She stopped in the doorway to the library, trying to recall just where she might have set down the flashlight. Unlike the other rooms, the library contained several long tables and numerous chairs that had not been covered and were therefore completely invisible to her at the moment.

She shuffled slowly into the room, placing one foot carefully before the other. Each time she discovered a table, she made a slow, careful sweep of the top, saying a silent prayer that the flashlight would be here, and not up in the attic somewhere.

She screamed as something slithered over the top of her foot. When she jerked her foot away, it became entangled in something, and she stumbled back against yet another table. There were several crashes, and it took a few heart-stopping moments for her to realize what had happened. Her foot had become caught in the trailing cord of a lamp. The crashing noise—she hoped—was from the flashlight rolling off the table when she'd stumbled against it.

She dropped to her hands and knees and began to crawl cautiously along the floor. When she was almost ready to give up, her hand closed around the flashlight.

But her elation was short-lived, because when she flicked the switch, nothing happened. She shook it in frustration—and was rewarded by a welcome beam of light. It seemed far less bright than it had before, but at this point it still looked like an airport beacon to her. Clutching it, she stood up and started back to the lobby.

For some perverse reason, now that she had light, the darkness beyond the beam seemed far more threatening. And her fear that Ben Walters might return rushed back to engulf her once more. She stopped in the lobby and listened. Rain gushed from broken gutters, the noise so loud that she feared it would mask other sounds—such as that of a truck or a motorcycle.

Jennifer pushed those thoughts away and made her way upstairs, cold, tired and hungry. She took some blankets and a pillow from a linen closet and went into the apartment. She was surely no safer there than anywhere else at the inn, but she *felt* safer.

A short time later, she sat on the window seat, wrapped in musty-smelling blankets, her wet clothing hanging over some chairs to dry. The rain had slowed to a fine mist, and she thought again about walking down the road to find help. But that meant putting on her wet clothing, and also depending on the flashlight, which had gone out twice during her brief journey from the lobby. Staying here, however unpleasant and possibly dangerous, seemed a much better choice.

As warmth began to seep back into her body, Jennifer started to question her fear of Ben Walters. After all, she had no proof that he'd disabled her car, and no real reason to believe him capable of causing her harm. Even his presence here earlier wasn't so strange; he obviously came here often.

Thus reassured, she must have dozed off, curled up in the window seat, because when she opened her eyes and looked out, a nearly full moon was darting in and out of the clouds, at times casting a silvered trail over the distant lake. She stared out at the scene, feeling oddly peaceful.

The moon slipped behind some wispy clouds, and when it emerged again she saw something on the lake. She squinted to see better, but it wouldn't come into sharper focus. It looked like a slender column of some sort, drifting in a slow, meandering fashion over the dark surface of the lake. She decided that it must be mist, although it seemed strange that there should be just that one thin column. Then, abruptly, she remembered the contractor's talk about the ghost!

"There are no such things as ghosts!" she told herself firmly. "It's nothing but mist."

But she continued to stare out the window, unable to take her eyes off that pale, shifting object. It did, in fact, seem to be about the size of a person, although she couldn't be sure, because of the distance.

And then, suddenly, it was gone—vanishing, it seemed, in the blink of an eye. She waited, holding her breath, her eyes glued to the spot where she'd last seen it. But it didn't return. When the moonlight became stronger again, she saw only its glowing trail across the water.

She yawned and dragged herself over to an old sofa. She was just too tired at this point to consider seriously the possibility that she might have seen a ghost. And if she had, she trusted that it would remain out there on the lake, where it belonged.

Then she recalled the rest of Thompson's story, about Caleb Walters's drunken ravings. But she'd been in many old inns like this in the course of her work, and despite local stories about ghosts, she'd never seen or heard anything that couldn't be explained by the normal creakings and mutterings of old buildings. She'd left ghosts behind along with her childhood.

She fell asleep quickly, only to be flung into a series of disjointed dreams and nightmares. Images of men and women from another age were interspersed with darker, more threatening scenes, in which she was being pursued down seemingly endless dark hallways by someone she couldn't see, but definitely feared.

She awoke with a start, convinced that she'd heard something. Oddly enough, she experienced no disorientation; the moment her eyes opened, she knew exactly where she was, despite the darkness around her.

She sat up, clutching the blankets around her as she listened. Water still dripped from the gutters, but now there were other sounds that she couldn't quite identify.

"Mice or squirrels," she said aloud. As Thompson had said, they'd probably long since made the inn their home.

She was about to lie down again when she heard another

sound, more distinct, but still unrecognizable. She felt around on the floor until she found the flashlight. The beam was now very weak, and shaking it made no difference. But she used it to guide herself to the door of the apartment, then opened it and stood there listening carefully. Thoughts of Ben Walters crept once more into her mind—and so, too, did the fears she'd dismissed earlier.

Then her awakening fears coalesced into pure terror when she heard her name being called. The voice was distant, and it echoed weirdly, but it was definitely male. And there was only one person who could have come here now—Ben Walters!

She switched off the flashlight, and a moment later saw a faint, shifting light around the bend in the hallway. Whoever it was called out again, his voice much louder and more distinct this time. Despite the pounding of her heart, Jennifer could hear his footsteps on the stairs.

She backed into the apartment and closed the door with trembling fingers. The hinges squeaked slightly; the sound seemed very loud to her. She hadn't been able to lock the door earlier, but she tried again now. There was a click, and she thought—prayed—that she'd succeeded. But she knew the lock wasn't very strong.

"Jennifer? It's Ben Walters. Where are you?"

She held her breath. He must be very close now. She could even see a faint rim of light beneath the door. She whirled around, searching wildly for a way to escape. The doorknob rattled, and she drew in her breath sharply, barely managing to suppress a scream.

"Jennifer, are you in there?"

He was no longer shouting, and the low, cautious tone of his voice sent shivers through her that were only partly from fear. She stared at the door, seeing through it in her mind's eye, seeing him standing out there, actually feeling his eyes raking over her. She almost answered him. A part of her refused to believe that he could mean her any harm—that same part of her that even now was responding to the slightly husky quality of his voice.

But there was no earthly reason for him to be here now unless he *had* disabled her car and was now returning to kill her.

She had unconsciously backed toward the window seat, and now she spun around to look out. The side porch roof was beneath it—perhaps a six- or seven-foot drop. From there she could reach the ground. She flung off the blanket, dropped it on the window seat, then climbed up on it. As she fumbled with the latch of the casement-style windows, the pounding on the door became ever more insistent.

"Jennifer, open the damned door! It's Ben Walters! What—?"

Jennifer didn't hear the rest. She leapt out into the night after throwing the blanket out before her.

The cold struck her like a blow as she landed only half on the blanket, clad only in her bra and panties. Wrapping the blanket around her as best she could, she began to crawl toward the edge of the roof. She heard a crash behind her and knew that Ben must have broken down the door.

She was leaning out over the edge of the porch roof, hoping she could use the post to get to the ground, when the blackness around her was suddenly turned into near day-light.

"What the hell—? Jennifer, it's Ben Walters. Get away from there. That post is rotten!"

Just as he spoke, the edge of the roof shifted beneath her with a groan, and she saw the post begin to wobble. She backed up hurriedly, still bathed in the brightness of the flashlight's beam. The blanket she'd been clutching around her caught on something, perhaps a broken gutter, and when she tugged at it to pull it free, there was yet another creaking sound.

Then, with the blanket only half covering her, she turned to stare back at the window. Behind the blinding beam of the flashlight, she could just barely make out a large, dark figure.

"Crawl over to the middle of the roof and stay there," he ordered. "It'll be easier for me to help you down from the porch than to try to haul you back up here."

The light disappeared, and she was left alone in the cold darkness to consider her options. He was probably right about the posts; the whole porch was in bad shape. And she knew she couldn't get back up to the apartment alone. But there were other windows closer to the porch roof.

She scurried across the roof to check the closest window. The upstairs windows were shuttered, but not boarded up, as the first floor ones were. With cold, trembling fingers, she pried at the shutters, then realized they were latched from inside.

A feeling of utter helplessness came over her when she heard the back door slam and then saw the light from below. She was trapped!

He's Win's son, she told herself. Even if they didn't get along, how could Win have a son who was a killer? She clung to that thought.

She heard his footsteps, then saw the beam of light swing upward. "Jennifer, are you okay?"

He actually sounded concerned—didn't he? Despite the temperature, she felt a tiny curl of warmth inside her. "Yes," she responded in a husky voice.

"Okay, just stay away from the edges while I check these posts."

A moment later, she heard the sound of wood splitting, and then a muffled curse. "Ben?" she called fearfully, only belatedly feeling the unnerving rush of intimacy that accompanied her use of his name.

"I'm okay. The porch floor is rotten, too. Just stay put."

She huddled beneath the blanket, suddenly aware of her near nakedness as she heard him moving around beneath her.

The far corner of the roof was suddenly lit up, and he called out again. "Okay, this post looks like the best one. Come over here, but if it starts to shake, get back to the middle again."

She did as she was told, crawling cautiously across the roof, dragging her blanket, until she was within a foot of the edge. Then she inched forward carefully and peered over the gutter.

His face was lifted to hers, only three feet or so away, shadowed behind the beam from the flashlight that he had trained on her. Her blanket had slipped away, leaving her chilled flesh exposed to the cold night air. They stared at each other in a silence that grew more charged with each passing second until finally he spoke.

"I can't trust this railing to hold my weight, so I can't get up there to help you. Just turn around and ease yourself off the roof feetfirst, and I'll grab you.''

She resisted—not so much out of fear that he might harm her as out of fear of contact with him. "What are you doing here?" she asked, in as firm a voice as she could manage, given the fact that her teeth were chattering.

She felt as much as saw his smile in the shadows. "Do you suppose we could discuss that later? You're not exactly dressed for the weather, and I don't know how much longer this floor is going to hold me." She saw his smile as he raised his face still more. His white teeth gleamed in the flashlight's beam.

"Don't worry, I only attack women when the moon is full." He waved an arm toward the heavens. "It isn't quite there yet."

His low, mocking tone sent a rush of heat through her, momentarily driving out the chill and making her still more aware of her near nakedness. She reached back and tugged the blanket around her shoulders.

"Trying to climb down with that blanket around you will only make it more difficult," he said. "I know what naked women look like. I used to sneak a peek at *National Geographic*."

In spite of herself, Jennifer felt a smile tugging at her mouth. She moved back, out of his line of vision.

But his low, mocking tones followed her. "Okay, okay, so I'll be completely honest. I even looked at *Playboy*. I used to sneak it up to my room and hide it under the mattress."

She *did* smile this time, since he couldn't see her. Earlier thoughts of his "lethal charm" crept back into her mind.

He called her name.

"I'm coming," she told him, and tossed the blanket over the edge of the roof.

Feeling helpless and frightened, and hating it, she turned around and began to back toward the edge of the roof.

"Try to keep your weight off the gutter," he cautioned. "It could pull loose."

Keeping her body rigid—which wasn't difficult, under the circumstances—Jennifer pushed herself halfway off the roof, then let her bare legs dangle as she struggled to maintain a grip on the rough shingles. Then suddenly, strong and wonderfully warm hands seized her ankles in a firm grip.

"Now just let yourself go—slowly!"

Oh, she was letting herself go, all right, she thought as a bubble of semihysterical laughter welled up inside her. From the moment his fingers had grasped her ankles, she'd been letting go of her senses. Her reaction to his touch was as unbelievable as the rest of this incredible scene.

But she did as he ordered, and as she slipped slowly from the roof, his warm, hard hands slid up her bare legs, trailing curls of heat in their wake. Then his arms were around her waist, and she let go of the roof and dropped into his arms.

A blessed warmth surrounded her, sheltering her from the night's chill and heating her clear through. She wrapped her arms around his neck, inhaled the clean, masculine scent of him, and forgot about everything for a very long time.

A smile tugged at his wide mouth. Even in the semidarkness she could see suppressed laughter in his eyes. He held her easily, as though he were completely accustomed to such weight. The arms gripping her felt like bands of steel, and calloused hands pressed into her flesh.

"Thank you," she said huskily.

"You're welcome," he replied, a smile on his face and in his voice.

They stared at each other across a space of mere inches, and then his hooded gaze dropped to her mouth. Her lips parted slightly, either to protest or to receive his kiss. Such was her state of confusion at the moment that she didn't know which it was. His grip on her tightened slightly.

"Let's get off this porch. Just pick up the flashlight so I can see where I'm going." His voice held a trace of huskiness that belied his practical words.

She reached to take the flashlight from the railing, and her breast brushed against his arm. Only a thin scrap of silk separated them. Her skin tingled at his touch, and she drew away quickly— but not before she felt his quick indrawn breath.

He carried her down the side steps, then set her on her feet. She was barely able to hold back a sound of protest. The blanket lay at their feet, and he picked it up, then wrapped her in it before once again lifting her into his arms.

"Some of the bricks in the walk are broken," he offered by way of explanation when their eyes met.

She hadn't noticed any broken bricks, but the lie suddenly seemed necessary to them both. He carried her around to the back, where his truck was parked next to the rear door. By now consumed with embarrassment, she avoided looking at him. With each passing second, she became more aware of her foolish over-reactions, both to his appearance here and to his touch.

He set her on her feet beside the truck, but kept one arm wrapped loosely around her waist as he opened the passenger door. "Get in, and I'll get it warmed up."

She climbed in, shivering again now that she was deprived of his wonderful warmth. He got in quickly on the other side and started the engine.

"M-my clothes and p-purse," she said through chattering teeth.

"Right. I'll go up and get them, then lock up."

Jennifer watched as he disappeared into the inn. Already a tepid heat was pouring from the truck's vents. The clock on the dashboard read 1:10 a.m., and she began to wonder once more how he'd come to be here—unless, of course, he'd known that she'd be here because he'd disabled her car.

The sickening seesaw of her emotions tilted once again to fear. Maybe he *did* intend to kill her—but not here, where she'd be found. She thought about the long, lonely stretches of woods between here and town, and her hand edged toward the door handle. But it was too late. Ben reappeared at the back door, carrying her clothes and purse.

Chapter Three

"I guess you must have had car trouble."

Jennifer resisted the temptation to put her hand on the door handle. Ben had climbed into the truck, and he somehow seemed to have sucked in all the air. She couldn't breathe. He was so close—and so overpoweringly, uncompromisingly male.

In the light from the dashboard, she saw the dark stubble along his jaw, the sprinkling of dark hairs on the back of his hand as he turned the heat up higher. She saw the outline of muscles beneath the worn fabric of his jeans, and the shadowy cleft in his chin as he turned to her, seeming so calm, so completely in control.

She managed to nod. "It wouldn't start. I don't know what's wrong with it." Her voice was as taut as her nerves.

"I'll take a look. Are the keys in it?"

She nodded, and he opened the door and got out, letting in just enough cold air to remind her of her near nakedness beneath the blanket. She turned to watch through the rear window as he got into her car and tried to start it. Then he got out and raised the hood, playing the beam of the flashlight over the engine.

He returned to the truck and handed her her keys. Their hands brushed lightly, and once again the truck's interior was too small and too airless.

"It sounds like the starter," he said as he put the truck into gear. "Is it a rental?"

"Yes." Suddenly she hated him—hated the casual questions, the easy movements, the certainty of his control over the situation. She hated him almost as much as she hated herself for noticing all that.

She could talk to the mechanic. He would be able to tell if the car had been tampered with.

"Are you warm enough yet?" Ben asked, slanting her a quick glance that seemed to pierce the blanket she clutched to herself.

"Yes. Thank you." She was *too* warm, too aware of the heat of her own body.

He turned down the heat, then drove slowly down the driveway. When he reached down to shift gears, she moved her legs quickly—an unnecessary move, since they weren't even near the gearshift. He glanced at her again, and she saw the corners of his mouth lift briefly.

Then, suddenly, there was a clicking sound near her, and she jumped.

"Just locking your door," he said, giving her another of those brief smiles. "Don't worry. I told you before, I only attack women when the moon is full. You're safe for another night or two."

While she was still struggling to find an appropriate response to his mocking words, he went on in a calm, conversational tone. "You asked me what I was doing here. Tony, my attorney, called and said that you wanted to talk to me about something. I came out earlier, but I saw Jim Thompson's truck here, so I left. Then I kept trying to get you at the Willises'. Mrs. Willis told me she was expecting you back for dinner, but you didn't show up.

"She called me a little while ago and said she was worried because you still hadn't come back. Since I couldn't think of anywhere else you'd be at this hour, I decided to come out here. I thought you might have fallen through the porch or wandered off into the woods or something."

Jennifer simply stared at him, too surprised to say anything. It simply hadn't occurred to her that the Willises would be worried about her, even though their small inn had only a few guests at the moment. She was almost ready to believe him—until she belatedly spotted the flaw in his statement.

"If she was worried about me, why did she call *you* instead of the police?"

"Probably because she's known me all my life and she knew I'd been looking for you. Her son Rob and I were buddies all through school, and I've just hired her daughter Tracey for my crew."

"Your crew?" she echoed. This conversation seemed to be spinning away from her.

He glanced at her again. "I'm starting my own construction business. I just assumed you knew that."

"Yes, I did, but..." Her voice trailed off uncertainly.

"But you were surprised that I'd hire a woman? I guess Tracey's right. She said women are worse than men when it comes to things like that."

She hadn't really been thinking that, but since she didn't know what she *had* been thinking, she didn't protest. Instead, she thanked him politely for his concern and his trouble.

He turned toward her and ran his gaze slowly down the length of her blanket-wrapped body. Then he chuckled. The sound reverberated inside her, and she clutched the blanket still more tightly.

"The pleasure was all mine." He paused for just a beat, then arched a dark brow. "Or maybe it *wasn't* all mine."

She knew he was trying to provoke her, and she also knew that this wasn't the time or place for an argument—so she said nothing. After a few minutes, he turned on the truck's CD player, and soft jazz poured from the speakers. It was Earl Klugh, one of her own favorites. She even owned the same recording.

She waited for him to ask why she'd been so afraid of him, and what it was that she wanted to discuss with him, but he remained silent. When his silence persisted all the way into town, she decided it was just another game he was playing. He wanted her to apologize for having thought such terrible things about him—to put her on the defensive, and thereby present himself as the aggrieved party.

Or maybe, she thought as she gave him a covert glance, he *wanted* her to be afraid of him. Maybe he really *had* damaged her car, to set up this "rescue." Perhaps this was only the beginning of the trouble he'd threatened her with.

When they entered the town, he didn't take the route she had taken to the inn where she was staying, but she said nothing. She didn't know the town that well yet, and he did. He suddenly turned into the parking lot of an old-fashioned diner with a sign that said it was open twenty-four hours.

He turned to her after he pulled into a parking space. "I thought you might be hungry."

"I am. Thank you," she said, feeling very guilty about her uncharitable thoughts about him. Maybe she'd misjudged him from the beginning.

"What can I get you?" he asked. "They have great sandwiches, and good homemade soup."

"Oh. Anything will be fine." She had completely forgotten about her attire.

No sooner had he gone than two men came out of the diner. He'd parked the truck quite close to the entrance, and the lot was very well lit. The men passed within a few feet of the truck, and they stared at her unabashedly as they walked by. A moment later, their laughter floated back to her—and then she knew why Ben had shown such "consideration."

The lot was large, and he could easily have chosen a less conspicuous place to park. She felt her face grow warm—and then warmer still, when she saw several people inside the diner staring out at her through the big window.

She sat there seething, trying to ignore their continued glances in her direction. The men's laughter was still ringing in her ears. She imagined herself throttling Ben when he returned, but then she realized, just as he came out with a bag in his hand, that anger was what he wanted to see.

Another man came out with him, and he, too, stared at her before going on to his car. Jennifer felt ready to explode with anger, but when Ben got back into the truck and handed her the bag, she merely smiled at him and thanked him again, then dug into her purse and gave him some money. He waved it away.

"My treat," he said, giving her another of those damnable half smiles as he started the engine.

His treat, indeed, she thought indignantly, knowing that she'd provided considerable entertainment for him—at her own expense. By tomorrow, the whole town would be talking about it.

Oh, yes, she could see his game now. As Wexford had said, he would use her mother's many marriages to paint an unflattering picture of her, and now he might well have succeeded in creating an unsavory image of her, as well.

They pulled into the parking lot of the inn. The porch light was still on; Jennifer hoped that didn't mean that her hostess was waiting up for her. She was trying desperately to think of some acceptable reason why she should return clad in a blanket when Ben broke the silence between them.

"I'm going to be busy all day tomorrow. I'm starting a job, then I'll be coaching Little League after work. But if you want to come by after the game, we can go get some dinner and talk then."

Still preoccupied with her concerns about Mrs. Willis, Jennifer told him that would be fine. He reached behind her and got the bundle of wet clothes, then came around to help her out.

She was trying to hold the blanket around her while carrying her clothes and the bag of food. When he opened the door for her, she started to get out of the truck, and stumbled, propelling herself toward him.

He put out a hand to steady her, then stood there, too close, his eyes glinting with amusement. She knew what was going to happen even before he leaned toward her. Her brain told her to back off, to get away from him, but her feet would not move.

The kiss was so brief that it was over by the time she reacted to it. His lips brushed against hers softly, teasingly, and his tongue made a quick, tantalizing foray into her mouth. Then he withdrew.

"Good night, Jennifer," he said in a low, amused voice, and then he left her there.

She forced herself to walk with as much dignity as she could muster. Her mouth bore the imprint of his, and all her senses were filled with him. Beneath the blanket, her body felt cold and hot at the same time. But by far the worst and most humiliating part of it was the wanting, the hunger for more, the sense of having been tormented and then cheated—and the certainty that he *knew* she was feeling all that.

She was struggling with this knowledge, and with her burdens, as she tried to open the front door. Before she did, Mrs. Willis was there, opening it for her and then glancing out to see Ben's truck driving away.

"So Ben found you," she said. "What on earth happened?"

"My car broke down," Jennifer told her. "And I got caught in the rain. Thank you so much for being concerned about me. I would have had to spend the night at the inn if you hadn't called Ben."

"Oh, my..." The woman clucked. "You must have been scared to death."

Jennifer just smiled, thinking that she hadn't been—until Ben Walters showed up.

"I know *I* wouldn't want to spend a night out there," Mrs. Willis went on. "I'm not superstitious or anything—and I'm sure it'll be lovely when it's reopened, of course," she added quickly.

"Oh, so you've heard about the ghosts, too?" Jennifer asked, even though ghosts were about the last thing on her mind at the moment. Her problem wasn't with ghosts, it was with a very much alive man.

"Oh, my, yes—but don't let that trouble you. It certainly didn't hurt the business before, and those stories have been around for years. My father always said that the only ghosts Caleb Walters saw were at the bottom of a bottle."

She shook her head sadly. "I'm afraid Ben's grandfather took to drink in his later years—and that's when he started to let the place go downhill. Everyone thought Edwin would put things right again, but he only let it get worse. My husband said once that it was almost like they wanted to be rid of the place. But if they'd wanted that, they should have sold it."

Jennifer was far less interested in past members of the Walters family than she was in the present one, but she was too tired and too hungry to pursue the conversation. So she thanked the woman again and hurried up to her room.

BEN CROUCHED between home plate and first base, keeping an eye on the kids and thinking about his own Little League days on this same field. Little League and high school football and track were about the only things he hadn't been thrown out of at some point. He'd liked them too much to let that happen.

His grandmother had called him a hellion. His mother had said frequently, and with many sighs, that he was a true Walters. His teachers had either said he was stupid or called him a genius who was easily bored. Parents—especially those with daughters his age—had said he was "wild" and "headed for trouble."

But Ben had never paid much attention to any of the talk. He was who he was. He knew, and had always known, what he wanted and what he didn't want.

His weakest hitter struck out, and the team started out into the field. Ben stood up—and saw her. A smile tugged at his mouth.

He stared down at his hands, remembering the chilled, smooth flesh he'd held, the soft, heavy undersides of her breasts brushing against his arm, the faint scent of some elegant perfume.

He smiled again as he thought about the faint tremors he'd felt in her when he kissed her. The lady was definitely seduceable, although he didn't expect it to be easy. He'd had her at a big disadvantage last night, and he knew she'd be determined not to let that happen again.

He lifted his hand briefly to acknowledge her presence. She returned the wave with a toss of her blond curls. Pretty hair. Pretty woman. Her hair, and those big gray-green eyes, reminded him of her mother—but, thankfully, the rest of her didn't.

JENNIFER RETURNED Ben's wave and then found a seat in the bleachers. She saw numerous heads turn her way, but tried to ignore them even as she wondered how many of them had heard about her sitting in his truck last night wrapped in a blanket. She had no experience with small towns, but if what she'd heard was true, they probably *all* knew.

She tried to keep her eyes off Ben, but it didn't work. And every time she looked his way, she was inundated by memories of last night: his rough, warm hands gripping her legs, his lips brushing so softly against hers, that annoying half smile that she was sure could so easily become an endearing trait.

Still, she was convinced that she was well armored against any further sensual assaults. They had business to discuss, and she had long years of business experience behind her—including, she reminded herself firmly, dealing with men just as attractive as Ben Walters.

Maybe so, a nagging little voice whispered as she found herself staring at him yet again. But they had been attractive in a different way. They had been polished, urbane men who played the game by rules she understood. Ben was rough and earthy…and probably disdained *any* rules.

She couldn't help noticing how good Ben was with the kids—always ready with a pat or a hug or a word of encouragement. It didn't fit with her image of him. In fact, she was rather surprised to find someone with his reputation coaching Little League at all. Maybe they'd been unable to find enough coaches.

The game ended with Ben's team the victors, and he was swallowed up by a crowd of kids and parents. Jennifer stood there alone, feeling isolated from all this community activity and wondering if that had been his intention when he suggested she meet him here. After the episode at the diner, she distrusted everything he did.

Finally he broke loose from the crowd and came toward her, walking with the loose, easy gait unique to the naturally fit and the perfectly self-assured. He was wearing jeans and a T-shirt with the team's name on it, a matching cap pushed far back on his dark, tousled head.

Little curls of heat uncoiled themselves inside her as she felt again that powerful, primitive male-female attraction. The situation felt absurdly, embarrassingly intimate—almost as though they were lovers. He'd held her nearly naked body in his arms, and yet she barely knew him.

As he approached, he smiled at her, and his deep blue eyes made a slow, deliberate sweep of her. *Rakish* was the old-fashioned term that came unbidden into her mind. Ben Walters had the unmistakable air of a man who has always taken his appeal to women for granted.

"You got your car fixed?" he inquired as they started toward the parking lot.

"Yes, and you were right—it *was* the starter." She didn't tell him that the mechanic had said it couldn't possibly have been tampered with. Apparently that particular model was prone to starter problems.

He paused beside her car, not standing particularly close, but still managing somehow to make it seem as though he were.

"I probably should have arranged to meet you somewhere," he said. "I need to go home and take a shower and change."

"I can go to a restaurant and wait for you there," she offered, thinking that he'd just confirmed her suspicions. He'd wanted her to come here to show her that he was a part of this community—and she wasn't.

"Okay, or you can come over to Harry's with me. He's my uncle, by the way. I'm staying with him until I get my own house built."

She accepted the invitation, because she wanted to meet Win's brother. Maybe there was even a chance that he could provide some answers to her questions about Win.

She followed Ben's truck through a quiet residential neighborhood of old but well-cared-for houses. His uncle's home was in a cul-de-sac—a big white frame Federal-style place with black shutters and a black wrought-iron eagle over the lacquered red front door. Slightly behind and off to one side of the large property was a small carriage house that had been converted into a garage.

"Your uncle has a lovely home," Jennifer commented as they walked up to the front door. "Has it been in his family long?"

"No—not by local count, anyway. My father bought it after he and Mom were married, and Harry came to live here after his wife died. He didn't want to stay in his own house any longer. I own it now, but he has a life interest."

Jennifer couldn't help taking note of the strange juxtaposition of the formal "my father" with the more intimate "Mom."

"So you grew up here?" she asked, feeling a pang of envy. It wasn't that she hadn't lived in lovely homes herself—but she hadn't lived in any of them for very long.

"That's right," he said, suddenly stopping and reversing his steps. "Come here. I'll show you my first construction project—or what's left of it. I've got to work on it one of these days."

She followed him around the side of the house, caught somewhat off guard by his apparent friendliness. As soon as they reached the rear, she saw a tree house nestled in the wide branches of a huge old tree at the back of the big yard. They crossed the yard and stood there staring up at it. The paint was peeling, and it sat slightly askew.

"I took the steps out," he told her. "Some of the neighborhood kids were climbing up there, and it's not safe now."

"How old were you when you built it?" she asked, envying him more and more for the wonderful childhood he must have had, despite his disagreements with his father.

"Ten. I built it all by myself, too."

He lowered his gaze, and their eyes met, but this time it was he who quickly looked away. Then he abruptly started toward the house. She was left with the impression that he regretted having shown it to her.

He ushered her into the house, then called his uncle. Jennifer was surprised to see that Ben more closely resembled his uncle than he did his father. Perhaps it was because the two men were the same height and had similar builds. Win had been both shorter and heavier.

Ben introduced them. If Harry Walters was surprised to meet her, he gave no outward indication. His greeting was polite—not unfriendly, but reserved. When Ben excused himself to go upstairs, Harry asked Jennifer if she'd like a drink. He offered iced tea or "something stronger," and Jennifer chose iced tea. She wanted to be very sure she kept her wits about her this evening.

The first thing she saw as she entered the living room was a baby grand piano in one corner, its closed lid covered with photographs. While her host went to get the iced tea, she walked over to examine them.

The first one that caught her eye was clearly the oldest: a sepia-toned picture of a family posed in front of Victoriana. Jennifer stared at it, feeling for the first time the true enormity of Win's decision to give the inn to her, an outsider. Her gaze traveled involuntarily toward the stairs as she thought about the broken link in the long chain of ownership.

Harry returned while she was still examining the photograph and trying to guess what color the inn had been originally. It was impossible to tell, but she thought it might have been a shade of tan.

"That was taken when the inn first opened," Harry said. Then he pointed out his father, a toddler sitting in the lap of a handsome, smiling woman.

"It's a wonderful place," Jennifer said carefully, knowing she might be stepping into a mine field. She had no idea how Harry felt about her inheriting the place, but she doubted that he approved.

"It *was*," he acknowledged. "But Eddie let it go."

It took a moment for her to realize that he was referring to Win, and then she wondered at the lack of disapproval in his tone. Given the family's long history with Victoriana, she would have expected him to resent his brother's failure to keep it up.

"Did you live there when you were growing up?"

He nodded. "In that apartment on the second floor. It was bigger then. Eddie turned most of it into guest rooms, since he didn't live there."

"It's a lovely apartment," she said, then recalled what the contractor had said about the tower. "Is there a room in the tower that was closed off at some point?"

Harry wasn't facing her at the moment, but she thought he seemed to stiffen at her question. Perhaps he resented her nosiness—or maybe he just resented her, period.

"Dad had it walled off," he replied after a moment. "It was drafty in the winter, and it made the living room cold."

"Oh. That's too bad. The view from up there must be lovely."

"There's only those two little windows, and they're up pretty high," he said. "Are you thinking about moving into the apartment?"

His first acknowledgment of her ownership made Jennifer wary. She thought about lying, then decided against it. Whatever Harry or Ben might think, she had a right to be there.

"Yes, I've been considering it. I'm staying at the Willises' at the moment."

"Pretty lonely place for a woman alone," he remarked neutrally.

"I suppose so, but it would be convenient—and I don't scare

easily." Her gaze shifted again to the stairs, and she wondered what Ben would have had to say about her bravado. Then she remembered that strange sighting on the lake and told Harry about it. Ghosts seemed like a safe enough topic.

The older man nodded. "Might've been her. But like you said, it could just as easily have been mist."

"Have you ever seen her?" Jennifer asked curiously.

"Oh, I've seen her, all right. I know you young folks don't believe in such things. Ben doesn't, at least. But she's there."

"I heard there are ghosts inside the inn, as well."

"Could be. Dad claimed to have seen them, and even Eddie said the place gave him the creeps sometimes. It's not a good thing for you to live out there alone," he said, shaking his head. "Not good at all."

Jennifer said nothing. She couldn't decide whether he was simply being old-fashioned or just didn't want her there. She turned her attention to the other photos and saw two familiar, though much younger, faces.

It was a picture of Win as a young man, with a delicately pretty young woman who was obviously Ben's mother. Ben himself was perhaps three years old, sitting on the floor between them as they posed on a Victorian love seat.

Her gaze went back to the sepia photo, and she held it up. "Ben really looks a lot like his grandfather," she said. In fact, the likeness was so remarkable that they might have been the same person.

"He sure does," Harry agreed, reaching to pick up a picture at the back. "Here's his granddaddy when he was about Ben's age."

The picture was a formal portrait of Caleb Walters alone. With allowances for differences in hairstyle and clothing, it was Ben. "That's amazing," she said sincerely.

"Ben's a lot like Dad in personality, too," Harry remarked. "Dad was his own man, that's for sure. No one could tell him what to do. Ben's always been like that, too."

If his words were intended to be a warning, Jennifer didn't need one. She didn't know Ben Walters well yet, but she didn't doubt that he was his own man. For about the hundredth time, she questioned the wisdom of the proposal she was about to make to him.

"THIS FOOD IS EXCELLENT," Jennifer told Ben. She was already wondering if she could steal the chef away when Victoriana re-opened. Then she met the blue eyes of the man seated across from her and reminded herself that he stood between her and that dream.

Their conversation thus far had been polite and rather stilted—the conversation of two strangers thrust together unwillingly. From the moment he'd come back downstairs, Ben had been cool and remote.

She'd been quite surprised when he'd appeared in well-tailored slacks and a handsome suede jacket worn over a subtly striped silk shirt. He wore no tie, and somehow managed to achieve that same impression of disregard for his appearance that she'd noted before. She knew many men who could put together such a look with great care, but Ben seemed to shrug into it, giving it no more thought than if he were wearing jeans and a T-shirt.

He'd ordered wine with considerable expertise, and when she was unable to resist commenting on it, he'd given her a brief smile and told her that he'd learned about wines from his grandfather. She was left with the very strong impression that he was enjoying confounding her image of him.

The truth was that she didn't know what to think about him. In fact, it was impossible for her to think clearly about him at all when he was present.

The hostess had offered them a choice of tables, and Ben had chosen one in a corner, almost hidden from view of the other diners by a brick wall topped with lush plants. It was perfect for a quiet business discussion, but it also felt entirely too intimate, being lit chiefly by two candles in unusual wrought-iron holders.

From the beginning, the air between them had seemed to hum with an electric tension that made her conscious of every word she spoke and caused her to dissect his conversation, as well, seeking hidden meanings. She sensed a peculiarly primitive quality to their encounter, on two different levels. First, there was that undeniable male-female attraction, and second, there was a sense of two predators circling each other warily, waiting for signs of weakness. All of it was barely concealed beneath a fragile layer of civility.

He had not yet asked why she wanted to talk to him, having apparently decided to leave it up to her to raise the issue. She continued to put it off as they talked and ate, still not convinced that she'd made a wise decision. But she could find no way out now, since he knew she had something to say. She'd almost begun to hope that he'd save her from herself by refusing to go along.

When the waitress brought coffee, Jennifer knew it was time to get down to business. She kept herself outwardly calm, although inside she was anything but.

"Mr. Wexford told me about your suit, of course," she began, this time forcing herself to meet his unrelenting gaze. "And he also said that you weren't willing to consider any settlement short of sole ownership of Victoriana."

She paused for a moment to see if he would refute that, but he merely nodded, sipping his coffee and watching her.

"Well, that's your right, of course, and I can certainly understand your feelings about the inn...."

She was about to continue when he suddenly spoke. "No, you can't. But go on."

There was no sarcasm in his tone, but what *was* there seemed even worse: an implacable hardness that was visible in the slight tightening of the muscles in his firm jaw. She bristled inwardly, and came very close to telling him what she thought about his behavior and his lies.

Instead, she continued smoothly, "The reason I wanted to talk to you is that I'm hoping we can at least agree on the one thing I think we both want—the reopening of the inn as soon as possible." She waited a moment for some affirmation, but when none came, she pressed on.

"Would you be willing to let the renovations begin while the question of ownership is settled in court? Mr. Wexford says that if you agree, both the executor and the judge will probably agree, as well, and we can come to some sort of arrangement about the money."

She stopped, and for the first time she felt she could read his thoughts. He was clearly surprised, even though he covered his emotions within seconds.

He leaned back in his chair and regarded her with a hooded expression. "Why are you in such a hurry about it?"

She wasn't prepared for the question, although she realized too late that she should have been. She'd told him earlier that she was on vacation from her job.

"I really love the place, and I want to see it come to life again."

He shook his head slowly. "There must be another reason."

Jennifer hesitated, hating his smug certainty. "I don't really like my present job very much," she said after a pause. "I'm ready for a new challenge."

"So if I agree to this, you intend to stay here? And do what? It's going to be months before the place will be ready to open again."

"There's a lot I can do," she stated defensively. "I'll supervise the renovations, and I can do some of the work myself. It has to be cleaned and painted, and all that terrible wallpaper has to be replaced, and—"

"My mother chose that wallpaper," he said, narrowing his eyes threateningly.

Oh, God, she thought. Don't tell me this whole thing will fall apart because he agrees with his mother's deplorable taste in wallpaper. She thought about trying to soften her words, but instead she looked him straight in the eye.

"It's terrible. There are wonderful reproductions of Victorian wallpaper available now—and that's what the inn should have."

To her amazement, his mouth began to twitch—and then he laughed. "You're right. I loved her, but she had really awful taste. The same goes for the upholstery. Can you do that, as well?"

She smiled, unbelievably relieved that this particular hurdle had been surmounted. "Not all of it, but I might be able to do the dining room chairs, at least. They should be easy enough."

It occurred to her then that she sounded almost like a job

applicant. And she resented the mockery she heard beneath his light tone.

"So that's why you had Jim Thompson out there."

"Yes. I needed to get some estimate of the costs involved, and Mr. Wexford told me he was the best in the area."

"He was. He isn't anymore, because I'm back. I used to work for him."

"Yes, he told me that." Where, she wondered, is the line between self-confidence and arrogance? She wasn't sure in his case.

"And he probably also told you that I can be a real pain in the butt when it comes to restoration work."

She smiled in spite of herself. "As I recall, those were his exact words."

"He's right. I am. I'm also the only one who's going to touch that place."

"Well, I'm certainly willing to consider hiring you. Jim Thompson *did* highly recommend you."

He continued to lean back in his chair, and his blue eyes bored into her. "Maybe I didn't make myself clear. What I mean is that if I agree to let the work go ahead, *I'm* the one who's going to be in charge of it."

She just stared at him. Now she knew where that elusive line was—and he'd definitely crossed it. If he thought he was just going to take over...

"It's *my* money that will be paying for it," she pointed out coldly.

He shrugged. "So what? You could have all the money in the world and still not be able to make Victoriana 'come to life,' as you put it. That takes skill—and *I'm* the one who has that. I can always wait until it's mine, then borrow against it to do the work."

"You're making a pretty big assumption," she replied angrily.

"Victoriana *will* be mine," he stated, suddenly leaning forward so that his face was uncomfortably close to hers across the small table. "So you'd better give some thought to whether you want to waste your time and money on something that will never be yours."

"I'm willing to take that gamble," she responded icily. "I'm going to win in court, because your father wanted me to have Victoriana, and I can prove that. Besides, even if you manage to persuade a judge or jury that your lies are true, I'll still have the pleasure of seeing Victoriana as it should be. And, of course, I'll get my investment back, as well."

"You'll get it back, all right—but on *my* terms."

"For someone whose stake in this is tenuous at best, and based on vicious lies at that, you're making a lot of demands, Ben."

"Right. Take them or leave them. I can wait."

The waitress appeared just then to refill their coffee cups, but Jennifer asked for the check instead. She feared that if she remained here any longer, she'd be tempted to throw something at Ben.

"I'll have to think about this," she told him. "And talk it over with Mr. Wexford."

"Take all the time you want. I'm not going anywhere."

He finished his coffee, the very picture of self-satisfaction. She sat there fuming, but trying hard not to let it show. The inn was hers. The money to renovate it would be hers. But *he* was demanding to be the boss.

She knew she had only herself to blame. She should never have told him she was unhappy with her job, thereby letting him know just how eager she was to get this project started. If she'd only thought it through more carefully, or allowed Wexford to handle it. But she'd wanted to deal with Ben herself—and for the worst possible reason, at that.

"I would think," she said into the silence, "that you'd be more reasonable about this, Ben. After all, I'm sure you could use the business right now."

He gave her an insolent grin. "Yeah, Ms. Moneybags, that's true. But I'm *not* a reasonable man. I've picked up a couple of small jobs already, and there'll be more, because I do good work. I'm not starving, and I have pretty simple tastes."

She glared at him, hearing the clear implication that they were very different in that regard. Fortunately, she was saved from making an intemperate remark by the return of their waitress with the check.

The young woman started to hand it to Ben, but Jennifer plucked it from her fingers, fully expecting him to protest. Instead, he merely smiled that damned superior smile of his as she handed the waitress a credit card.

Jennifer could honestly not recall a time when she'd been so irrationally angry with someone. Certainly she had reason enough to be annoyed with him, but it went far beyond that. She'd dealt with many difficult people over the years, but Ben Walters had a unique talent for getting under her skin. And, worst of all, he knew it and enjoyed it.

As soon as the waitress brought the charge slip, she signed it and rose from her seat. Then she walked out of the restaurant, pausing only to compliment the hostess on the excellence of the food.

She started to push open the door, but just then Ben's long arm reached around her to open it for her. They brushed against each other, and she recoiled as though she'd been burned—which wasn't far from the truth. Angry as she was, he still had the power to summon a sensual response from her body.

He followed her through the lot to where his truck was parked, beside her car. She ignored him completely—or rather gave the appearance of doing so.

"Here," he said, handing her a card. "I had my own phone installed at Harry's. There's a machine. Just let me know what you decide."

"Thank you," she said with exaggerated politeness, reaching for the car's door handle just as he did the same.

Neither of them moved. His hand rested lightly on hers, and their arms brushed against each other. She didn't want to turn to look at him—but she did.

His face was close to hers, scant inches away. She could feel the heat emanating from him—or was it from her? The moment felt frozen in time, yet laden with whispers of what must surely be coming. His gaze dropped slowly to her mouth, and his own lips curved slightly and parted a bit. It was a kiss that didn't happen—and yet it felt to Jennifer as though it *had*.

There were probably a million things he could have said, but his total silence was far more eloquent than any of them. That silence said he remembered that other kiss—and knew she wanted more. A promise and a threat, inextricably linked.

BEN GOT INTO HIS TRUCK, chuckling to himself. The lady had a temper, but she carried it off with class. He wondered just how much it was going to take to break through her formidable self-control.

She'd caught him by surprise tonight. He hadn't expected her to be so eager to get to work on the inn. But he was nothing if not resourceful, and it hadn't taken long for him to see how he could turn the situation to his advantage.

Year after year, he'd watched Victoriana deteriorate, and there had been nothing he could do about it. His father had refused to put any money into it. In his dreams, he'd done the job many times—and now, sooner than he'd expected, he was going to get to do it in reality. That is, if she agreed to his terms.

Ben remembered her now as she'd looked sitting across the table from him, fighting the chemistry between them—maybe even shocked by it. She'd been cool, poised and elegant, even as her emotions ran amok in those big gray-green eyes of hers.

He wondered what he'd see in those eyes when he made love to her, what it would be like to watch that poise shatter into passion. It would happen; it was only a matter of time. And if she agreed to his terms, it wouldn't be much time, either.

And that brought him back to the question of why she was so eager to get to work on the inn. What about her job? She'd said she didn't like it, but he was sure she hadn't told him the truth. Maybe she'd quit her job already. He was curious enough to look into it.

There was no way he was going to let Jennifer Stansfield become an obsession. Ben Walters didn't operate that way. Besides, the stakes in this battle were too high—and they were getting higher still.

Chapter Four

"I'm calling about a Ms. Jennifer Stansfield. She lists InterHotels as her current employer."

"Ms. Stansfield is no longer employed here, sir."

"Ah, well, maybe I didn't make myself clear. My name is Ben Walters, and I own an inn in Vermont. Ms. Stansfield has applied for a position as manager. Is there someone I could speak to regarding a reference?"

"One moment, please."

After an extended pause, another voice came on the line. "This is Robert Graham. You're calling for a reference for Jennifer Stansfield, Mr. Walters?"

"Yes. I own an inn in Vermont. Ms. Stansfield has applied for the position of manager, and naturally I want to be sure I hire the best person."

"Well, frankly, Mr. Walters, in that case, I would strongly urge you to look elsewhere. I cannot in good conscience recommend Ms. Stansfield. We had, ah, some considerable difficulties with her."

"I see. Do you mean you fired her?"

"I'm afraid so. Her attitude was entirely inappropriate."

"Well, thank you for the information. I guess I'll have to look elsewhere."

Ben dropped the receiver back into its cradle. The guy sounded like a real jerk. He wondered if she *had* been fired, or if she'd just had enough of him and quit. But it didn't really matter. The man had confirmed his suspicions—and more. Not only didn't she have a job, but she was also going to have a tough time finding another one. Of course, she wasn't exactly a candidate for food stamps, but he suspected she wasn't the kind to be content living off an inheritance, either.

A phone call to his attorney confirmed what Jennifer had said—if he went along with her plan, the judge would, too. The call also produced another interesting bit of information. Wexford had told Tony, his lawyer, that Jennifer had come to Vermont believing the inn was operating.

What that suggested to him was that she'd probably quit her job and told off that jerk in the process—then come here to find out she couldn't just move in and take over Victoriana.

But why had she believed it was operating, when it had been closed for five years?

"PLEASE DON'T take offense at this, Ms. Stansfield, but Ben Walters has always been very, um, attractive to women, and I would hate to think that you might be letting, ah, personal considerations lead you into a wrong decision."

Jennifer stifled the sharp reply that was on the tip of her tongue. It was clear that Wexford was truly concerned for her welfare, and given her tumultuous feelings toward Ben, she couldn't honestly protest that concern.

"Basically, you'd be giving him carte blanche with your money."

"I know that, but even Jim Thompson said he's the best man he's ever seen at this kind of work. And, as I told you before, I want to get started as quickly as possible."

She left the attorney's office knowing he was frustrated with her, and knowing, too, that she was equally frustrated with herself. But she'd made her decision, and she was determined to stick with it.

Furthermore, she hadn't needed to hear from the attorney that Ben Walters had always been attractive to women. It had taken her no more than two or three seconds to figure that out. But if Ben thought he was going to seduce her into handing over Victoriana, he was making a very big mistake.

Through the early years of her job, when Simon Beresford still owned the company, Jennifer had seen many places like Victoriana restored to their past glory. Her job had been to supervise the work, hire and train the staff, then manage the inns and hotels for a time before moving on to the next place. And each time she'd promised herself that one day she'd have such a place for herself. That was why Win's stories about Victoriana had gained such a hold over her.

Win. She thought again about his lies. Even if he hadn't wanted to talk about his son, why hadn't he told her the truth about Victoriana? She sighed. She supposed that was a question that would remain unanswered for the rest of her life.

Instead of going to her car, she decided to walk around town for a while. The day was very pleasant, and she had precious little else to do while she waited for the attorneys to draw up the agreement. After so many years of a hectic career, she felt disoriented and useless—yet another reason she'd been willing to make concessions to Ben Walters.

She strolled along, pausing now and then to peer into shop windows. The town had quite a number of upscale shops, thanks to its location not far from the Killington ski area. Those shops stood side by side with homey little stores that served the local population and stubbornly resisted any tendency toward trendiness.

Then she came to a church she'd passed before—one of those quintessentially New England churches of white frame, with a tall steeple, utterly beautiful in its simplicity. The doors stood open, so she walked in, then stood admiring the austere charm of the sanctuary, which was decorated only by several lovely stained-glass windows. No one was around, but she could hear the sounds of hammering and the whine of power saws coming from the basement.

She left the church and opened the old iron gate to the adjacent cemetery, drawn by what were clearly some very old tombstones. Years ago, as a schoolgirl, she'd gone on a field trip to just such a cemetery, and she'd been amused by the inscriptions on the tombstones of centuries past, not to mention the grotesque decorations, such as winged skulls, that people had favored then.

As she looked around, two things caught her attention almost simultaneously: a familiar name on a tall monument that was surrounded by smaller gravestones, and an equally familiar truck parked next to the rear door of the church, its bed piled high with lumber.

She remembered the sounds she'd heard coming from the church basement and recalled Ben's statement about already having found some work. As she stood there uncertainly, her gaze flicked back and forth between the truck and the name Walters in bold letters on the monument. Her usually keen common sense told her to get out of there and avoid a confrontation with him now. Their attorneys could handle the agreement, and she had no need to see him until it was a fait accompli.

But she stood where she was, her body beginning to tingle with the expectation of seeing him again. Finally she started over to the Walters plot, thinking she would just take a quick peek and then leave—never mind the fact that she knew she was behaving like some silly schoolgirl.

The oldest grave in the large plot dated from 1810. She stared at it, thinking about Ben's claim on this town—and on the inn. Before she could let guilt be added to her tangle of emotions, she began to scan the other markers.

Win himself wasn't buried there. Her mother's dying wish had been that they both be buried together in Florida, where they'd lived throughout their five-year marriage.

Then her gaze fell on the most recent grave: that of Elizabeth Walters, who had died not quite five years ago. Jennifer frowned, then began to check the other markers. The next most recent was over twenty years old, that of Caleb Walters, Ben's grandfather. If she hadn't already discovered that Win had lied to her, she wouldn't have felt the slight uneasiness that began to stir inside her. Perhaps Ben's mother was buried in her own family's plot, although that seemed rather unlikely. But if Elizabeth Walters was Ben's mother...

Jennifer suddenly had a strong sense of being watched, and spun around to see Ben standing about ten feet away. The expression on his face sent a chill through her. As their eyes met, she was suddenly sure that he hated her.

For all her considerable social skills, Jennifer could think of nothing to say. She wanted simply to walk away, but he was blocking the path. His eyes, which remained locked on hers, were the color of ice reflecting a winter sky. With each slowly passing second, the tension between them grew stronger, sizzling with anger and yet still crackling with a sensual undercurrent.

Why was he so angry about her being here? Desperately seeking a way to defuse the situation, and also wanting to lay to rest her disquiet over the grave, she gestured toward it.

"Was Elizabeth Walters your mother?"

He nodded, but his expression didn't change, and his gaze didn't waver. She could actually *feel* the tension in his body, even though he'd come no closer.

Jennifer's brain grappled with the impossibility of the date on the tombstone. Was she wrong about when her mother had married Win? No, she knew she wasn't. But she couldn't think about that now, not with him standing there. She tried to smile.

"I was thinking about how deeply rooted some families are. Mine never was."

The words rushed out in a thin voice that she barely recognized, one she was sure must sound false to him. He still said nothing, and his expression didn't change. She decided to try another tack, retreating into the relative safety of business. Surely he'd be happy with her news.

"I've just spoken to my attorney, and I told him that I'm willing to agree to your requests. He'll be in touch with your lawyer about drawing up an agreement."

"They weren't requests," he stated, coldly and succinctly.

"All right, I agree to your *demands,* then," she replied, in a carefully calm voice. She was determined not to get into another battle with him now, when he seemed so tightly wound that he might explode at any moment.

"Don't expect me to thank you," he said after a moment. "*You're* the one who wants to get started right away."

"And so do you, Ben," she replied, unable to keep a trace of exasperation from creeping into her voice. "You can surely use the work, and having a restored Victoriana to show off to potential customers would certainly be helpful to you."

The anger seemed to drain from his face—but it was replaced

by an unpleasant smile that was no better. "I'm not as desperate as *you* are. I have a job, and you don't. InterHotels fired you, and you'd have a tough time getting a job without a reference."

The anger that had left him now took root in her, as though it had traveled through the charged space between them. "That's not true! I resigned. Where did you get that information—or is this just another of your lies?"

"Lying must be contagious, then," he stated with another unpleasant smile. "I called InterHotels and told them I was considering hiring you to manage my inn."

She exploded. "How dare you do something like that? And what makes you assume that what they told you is the truth?"

"If you resigned, why wouldn't they give you a reference?" he asked, his tone challenging.

"I don't have to explain myself to *you*, Ben Walters," she replied coldly, although she had to quell an urge to do just that. Instead, she walked across several graves to get past him, then hurried from the cemetery without looking back.

BEN WATCHED her walk away. Her body was rigid and less graceful than usual. He was surprised to find that he wanted to run after her and apologize. Instead, he jammed his hands into the pockets of his jeans and turned to his mother's grave. He could almost see her standing there, shaking her head in disapproval.

Then he turned around again and caught Jennifer standing near the gate, staring at him. The moment their eyes met, she turned her face away and started around the front of the church. The sunlight gleamed in her golden curls, and he caught a quick glimpse of her long, tanned legs as the breeze briefly lifted her skirt.

The bitterness in him drained away, leaving in its wake a hunger that jolted him with its fierceness, a hunger that he was just beginning to realize could be *very* dangerous.

He started back to the church, wondering if it was possible that she didn't know what had happened. Something troubled him about her reaction to his confirmation that the grave was his mother's.

Well, it didn't matter. He'd gotten what he wanted—or at least the first part of what he wanted.

BEN AND TWO OTHER MEN walked into Wexford's office just as Jennifer finished reading the agreement. His only concession to the formality of the occasion was an old tweed jacket worn with a chambray shirt and his usual jeans. Somehow, though, instead of seeming underdressed, he managed to make the other men appear overdressed.

Jennifer was fully prepared for this encounter, but that didn't prevent her feeling those all-too-familiar surges of electricity.

Introductions were made, chiefly for her benefit, since it was clear that the men all knew each other. She shook hands with Ben's attorney, a young man who made no attempt to conceal his interest in her. Then she was introduced to Win's executor, a retired local banker whose interest was of a more restrained and benign nature.

"You've already met Ben, of course," Wexford said.

She nodded. Ben said nothing, but his eyes remained on her as he took a seat across from her. His gaze left hers only long enough to travel slowly down to her bare, crossed legs, which she realized were far too well displayed below a slim vented skirt. She managed to resist the temptation to uncross them and tug at the skirt.

She was far from willing to forgive Ben for his behavior, but she *had* done some serious thinking about their future working relationship. She knew she had to find a way to work amicably with him, even if it meant biting her tongue and reining in her temper, which he seemed to provoke as no one else ever had.

The first step she'd taken toward that end was to order the book that was the bible of Victorian restoration work. The large, expensive tome had arrived this morning, and it was out in her car. She intended to give it to Ben as a peace offering, and she also hoped it would become a mediator in the disputes she was sure were coming.

The attorneys insisted upon going over the agreement verbally, despite the fact that everyone present had already read it. So Jennifer was forced to sit there trying to avoid Ben's stare while appearing not to. Wexford's voice became a barely noticed background drone as she alternated between returning his gaze measure for measure and feigning interest in the proceedings.

Then, finally, it was over, and she rose to sign the agreement. When she backed away from the desk and turned, she collided with Ben, who had gotten up to affix his signature.

His hand gripped her arm briefly to steady her, and she murmured an apology, all the while staring fixedly at the open neck of his shirt, which was so close that she could see the throbbing of his pulse and smell the clean odor of wood shavings.

"*I'm* not sorry," he said, in a voice so low that she thought only she could hear.

But as she returned to her seat, she saw that Mr. Collins, the executor and Win's old friend, was glancing speculatively from her to Ben. She was sure he'd heard his remark.

The two lawyers remained behind to discuss another matter, while Jennifer, Ben and Mr. Collins left the office. Jennifer wondered if she might be able to talk to Win's friend in private and find a way to raise the subject of Win's lies, but the man stopped to chat with Wexford's secretary, whom he apparently knew well.

So she left the building with Ben, determined to start their new partnership in a strictly businesslike manner.

"When do you think you'll be able to begin work?" she asked, trying not to let her eagerness show, for fear that that might prompt him to delay things.

He pushed open the outer door, then stood aside to let her pass. She managed to do so without any more physical contact, though she was excruciatingly aware of his closeness.

"The job at the church will probably be finished next week, and then I have a remodeling job that will probably take another week or so. But I'm interviewing a couple more people, and once I've hired them and gotten them started, I should be able to spend most of my time at the inn. Then, when they finish, they'll come, too."

He paused, then said in a noticeably gentler tone, "I know you want to get started right away, and I do, too—so I'll hurry it along as much as I can."

His words and tone had an impact on her all out of proportion to their actual meaning. They felt, in fact, not unlike a caress, and made her aware of being completely at the mercy of his shifting emotions. But she reminded herself of the necessity of establishing a good working relationship with him, and then remembered her gift. She reached into the car and got it out.

"I have a present for you, Ben—a sort of peace offering."

He glanced at it and smiled. "I guess it would be ungrateful of me to refuse it, but I already have a copy."

"You do?" she asked in surprise.

He nodded, and his eyes glinted with amusement. "Believe it or not, I *can* read."

She felt herself flushing, and quickly averted her face, but he hooked a finger beneath her chin and forced her to look up at him. Her fingers gripped the book tightly, holding it up between them. The breeze blew her hair across her face, and he brushed it away, then trailed one finger lightly across her cheek to the corner of her mouth before dropping his hand.

"I think maybe we should call a truce. You agree that I'm not some backwoods hick, and I'll agree that you're not a complete snob."

Then he gestured toward the book, which she still clutched to her chest. "You might want to keep that for yourself, so we can quote it at each other every time we disagree. And if that doesn't work, we can always throw them at each other," he added, with a low, deliciously masculine chuckle.

She laughed and lowered the heavy book. "Loaded books at ten paces? All right, I agree to the truce, but I never thought of you as a backwoods hick."

He let the silence grow just long enough to let her know that he knew exactly what she *did* think of him, but the challenge in his eyes remained unspoken.

"Why don't we have dinner together tonight? I'm busy all day, but we've got a lot to talk about."

"Thank you. I'd like that."

He told her when he'd pick her up, then left quickly. Jennifer had the impression that, for all his seeming confidence, he'd been nervous about something. Had he expected her to refuse, even though it was clearly a business invitation?

As she got into her car, Jennifer wondered for the first time if the attraction between them could be making *him* nervous. But she dismissed that thought quickly. She could not afford to let herself believe that anything Ben Walters did or said had any purpose other than to seduce her into giving him Victoriana.

WHEN THE PHONE RANG, Jennifer had virtually every piece of clothing she had brought with her spread out on the bed and chairs in her room. She glanced at her watch. It was a bit early for Ben to be arriving, and when she picked up the receiver, the faint hiss on the line told her right away that it was probably her father.

She greeted him distractedly, her gaze continuing to rove over her wardrobe. Nothing seemed right. It was the classic situation, but she'd never faced it before.

He was calling from Moscow this time. Since her mother's death, he'd been contacting her far more frequently, and while she appreciated his interest, it was too little and too late.

James Stansfield was a career diplomat who had advanced steadily over the years to one of the highest positions in his field, deputy secretary of state for trade affairs. He was a casting director's dream of the perfect diplomat: tall, elegant, gray-haired, firm-jawed, with cultivated speech that bore no trace of any regional accent.

She brought him up to date in as few words as possible, finding it difficult, as always, to discuss her mother with him. He regarded his brief marriage to her as the only mistake he'd ever made, which never failed to make Jennifer defensive, even though his complaints about her mother were certainly justified.

When she had finished recounting the situation, there was a long silence on the line while he digested the information. James Stansfield—ever the diplomat—never spoke in haste.

"I agree with you that Edwin probably never mentioned a son because he was ashamed of him," he said finally. "But it *does* seem strange that he didn't tell you the truth about the inn, especially since he apparently wanted you to have it. I can't help thinking that you haven't gotten to the bottom of this yet."

Jennifer certainly concurred with him on that point. She hadn't told him about Win's other lie, that he'd been a widower when he married her mother. It wasn't relevant to the situation in any event.

"I also agree with your attorney that signing the agreement may not have been wise," he went on. "It seems likely that this Ben isn't very reliable. Otherwise, his father would surely have left the inn to him."

"Parents are not automatically right," she replied rather acerbically.

He laughed. "So they aren't. No one has better reason to know that than you."

How very true, Jennifer thought, although she doubted he was referring to himself, as well as to her mother.

"Well, my dear, you must do what is best for you, and I agree that it seems very unlikely that he could win his suit. Would you like me to make some inquiries about another attorney? I'm sure I could find someone who's an expert at this sort of thing."

"Thank you, Father, but no. I think that would only prejudice the case. I'm already an outsider here, and if I brought in an outside attorney, as well, there could be a lot of resentment. I'm satisfied with Mr. Wexford."

She winced as she thought about him calling his old Yale buddies, then sending in some Boston Brahmin, or a partner in one of New York's elite firms.

"Perhaps just on a consulting basis?" he suggested.

After some discussion, she managed to persuade him that Wexford could be trusted to handle the case alone. Things were helped along considerably when she told him that Wexford was a Harvard graduate. She'd noticed the framed diploma on his wall.

After she hung up, Jennifer shook her head sadly. Was it possible—now that she was long past needing him—that her father was beginning to take his paternal duties seriously? Well, at least he wasn't likely to show up here; rural Vermont was a bit off the beaten path for a world traveler like him.

The phone call had at least taken the edge off her increasing nervousness about her dinner date with Ben.

She'd been searching her wardrobe for something that wouldn't seem too sophisticated. Ben's remark about her being a snob had stung. She wasn't a snob, but she knew that her life-style before she'd come here could easily create that impression. And so, too, could her wardrobe, which consisted mainly of clothes bought in Europe.

She decided now on the first outfit she'd taken from the closet: a sage-green raw-silk skirt and matching silk moiré blouse. The style was simple and classic, and the color brought out the green in her eyes. Then she fastened pearl studs in her ears and studied herself in the mirror. She'd pulled her hair back in a French braid, but now she wondered if she should just have left it in its usual style. She certainly didn't want to give Ben the impression that she'd spent a lot of time preparing for this date, which was really just a business engagement.

There was, she thought wryly, just a tiny inconsistency in wanting to look your best for someone bent on seduction for nefarious purposes. Fighting fire with fire had never seemed to her to be a very prudent course of action.

She gathered up her creamy lightweight wool blazer and went downstairs. Voices floated in from the front porch, and she found Ben there, swinging in the wonderful old porch swing as he talked to Mr. Willis. He was wearing a handsome wool jacket with fashionable pleated trousers and another open-necked silk shirt, and Jennifer was once again struck by how easily he managed this kind of transformation.

The old inn, the swing, even the fatherly Mr. Willis, combined to flood Jennifer with a strange nostalgia for something that had certainly never been part of her own life. Then she saw that Ben was watching her quizzically as he continued to push the swing, and she schooled her features into a polite smile and apologized for having kept him waiting.

"No problem," he assured her as he brought the swing to a halt and stood up. "Mr. Willis told me you had a call from Moscow."

She heard the unspoken question, and realized that she'd told him nothing about her own family. She didn't want to do so now, either.

"It was my father. He's with the State Department."

Ben handed her into his truck, then began to question her about her father. It wasn't a subject she wished to discuss, so she responded briefly, knowing she probably sounded rude.

"Deputy secretary, huh?" Ben whistled appreciatively as he put the truck into gear. "That's pretty impressive."

Jennifer laughed in spite of herself. "So is he, believe me. But we haven't exactly been close."

He said nothing, and it occurred to her that he might be thinking about his own father. She wanted badly to question him about Win, but given the estrangement between them and Win's bequest to her, the subject seemed too dangerous now. Besides, if anyone could understand a reluctance to discuss one's parents, it was surely her.

She slanted a glance at him as he drove through town, then looked away quickly when he suddenly turned toward her. But she could feel his smile, that slight curve of his lips that told her he knew what was going on.

To break the growing tension between them, she asked him about his work at the church, only belatedly realizing that she might already be treading on dangerous ground, given their confrontation there.

But his voice was calm and matter-of-fact as he told her that he was converting part of the basement into a day-care center.

"It's my family's church, so I'm basically doing it for the cost of the materials and my crew's wages, but it's giving me a chance to see what kind of work my new employees can do."

Then he told her about a remodeling job he was about to start for an old high school friend, and before she realized where they were headed, Ben was turning onto the road that led to Victoriana.

"Are we going to the inn?" she asked, knowing there were no restaurants out here.

He nodded. "I thought we'd stop there first. I have something to show you."

He was silent until they stopped in front of the inn. "It's hard for me to look at this place objectively," he said as he stared at it. "I still tend to see it as it was during my grandfather's time."

Jennifer saw an opening, and she took it, but very cautiously. "Why didn't your father keep it up?"

He was silent for so long that she was sure she had shattered the fragile peace between them. But then he turned to face her. His expression and voice seemed determinedly neutral.

"My father hated Victoriana. I'm surprised he didn't burn it down at some point."

Jennifer started to protest, but then clamped her mouth shut as he drove on to the rear of the inn. There was something in his movements that warned her not to carry this discussion any further. She reminded herself that she was determined to make their partnership work—even if that meant not having answers to the questions that were tormenting her.

He unlocked the door, and they walked into the dark kitchen. Then he crossed to the dining-room doors and pushed them open. Jennifer let out a soft cry of surprise as she followed him into the dining room. The boards had been removed from the windows, and the room was flooded with light. Near the windows was a table set for two, its surface polished to a gleaming finish and set with lovely old china and silver. In the center of the table was a crystal bud vase that held a single rose, flanked by slender tapers in matching crystal holders.

Delicious aromas filled the air, and she shifted her stunned gaze to the long sideboard. It, too, had been uncovered and polished, and it held covered serving dishes, and a silver bucket filled with ice and a bottle of champagne.

Jennifer was overwhelmed—both by the work that had gone into this and by the thought behind it.

"This is *my* peace offering," Ben said, sweeping his arm around the room. "All it requires is a little imagination, so that you don't notice the cracked moldings and the worn carpet and—"

"Stop!" she said, laughing. "It's *perfect!*"

He arched a dark brow. "If you think *this* is perfect, lady, you're in for a very big surprise."

His tone was light and teasing, but the gleam in his eyes said something very different. He drew out a book of matches and lit the tapers, then went over to the sideboard to pick up the bottle of champagne. Jennifer watched him, suddenly aware of their isolation, and noticing more than ever the sheer animal magnetism of this man as he moved around the room, dominating it effortlessly.

She also realized that she was rooted to the spot, as though any movement on her part might somehow propel her into a dark magic from which she might not escape—and might not *want* to escape. Seeking to dispel that magic, she walked over to the sideboard and lifted the lids from the dishes.

"This looks delicious! Where did you get it?"

He explained that his cousin and her husband owned a catering business. Then he poured them each a glass of champagne and handed one to her. Their hands touched briefly, and she forgot about the food, the room, and everything else. His eyes met hers, and he touched his glass lightly to hers. The crystal chimed in the heavy silence.

"To our partnership," he said softly, his gaze holding hers easily, effortlessly. "To your money and my skills, which are going to bring Victoriana to life again."

Those words freed her from his mesmerizing gaze. She resented the implication that her only part in this was her checkbook.

"Does that mean that you intend to pay no attention to what *I* want?" she asked him challengingly.

He regarded her in silence for a moment, filling that space with a volatile mixture of threat and promise. Then he smiled lazily. "You'll get *everything* you want," he said as he raised the glass to his lips.

Then, just as the various meanings of that statement settled in, he shrugged, as though he knew exactly when to draw back. When he spoke again, his tone was businesslike. "It's just that I don't know how much you know about restoration work."

"I *do* know something about it," she replied, eager to get the conversation back onto safer ground. "Simon Beresford, the man I worked for before he sold out to InterHotels, bought up old inns here and in Britain and France. He hired experts to restore them, then sent me in as manager to start them up again. I always went in while the work was still under way, so that I could work on marketing and hire and train the staff."

Ben appeared to be listening, but his gaze was focused too intently on her mouth, creating the impression that he was merely humoring her. "You liked your work then," he said, making his words a statement rather than a question.

"Yes. I loved it. Simon didn't believe in cutting corners."

"And InterHotels did," he stated, in that same tone.

She nodded, moving away from him and pausing to sip her champagne. "They didn't just cut corners—they cut everything. That's why I left them."

"So you *did* quit?"

She turned to face him and, somewhat to her surprise, began to laugh. Perhaps the champagne was already going to her head—or perhaps it was only that his tone suggested that he had believed her all along.

"Oh, I quit, all right—and in a rather spectacular fashion. I marched into the office of the vice president for management operations and told him in no uncertain terms exactly what I thought of InterHotels."

Ben chuckled. "I'd say you made quite an impact. I could hear his blood pressure going up as I talked to him." He cocked his head to one side and stared at her beneath half-lowered eyelids. "I wonder when *I'll* get to see your temper on display."

His tone was teasing, but she chose to consider his words seriously. "Maybe you won't—at least if you're as good as I've been led to believe."

"I am," he replied, his wide mouth curving briefly.

"Then we shouldn't have any problems, should we?"

He waited until she heard her own words echo with hidden meaning. "We'll have problems, all right—but maybe not about work."

He gestured toward the doorway that led into the lobby. "Let's walk around, so I can tell you what has to be done."

They carried their champagne with them, and Ben picked up his flashlight again. Some light spilled into the lobby from the dining room, creating a twilight effect. Ben moved the flashlight's beam around, pointing out the work to be done. Gone was the teasing, seductive tone, replaced by something she found even more seductive: the voice of a man who loved his work and took great pride in it—and in this place.

He told her that he'd spent the past five years working on restorations in various parts of the country, many of them for charitable trusts that couldn't afford to pay much but offered a wealth of experience.

"Everywhere I went," he said, in a soft voice that made it sound as if he were musing to himself, "I kept thinking about Victoriana, about coming back here to use what I was learning."

Into the pause that followed, she poured her silent questions: Why did you have to fight with your father? Why didn't he understand how you felt about this place? Why do we have to be locked in this battle that only one of us can win?

But just as she was about to risk the peace between them by asking those questions aloud, he turned the light on the dangling wires of the chandelier and asked if she'd seen it.

"No," she replied, grateful to be rescued from what would surely have been disaster. "I know it's in the carriage house, but I didn't open the box."

"It was taken apart to be stored," he went on. "That's something I'll be happy to turn over to you."

She laughed. "Just what I always wanted—a crystal jigsaw puzzle. Are there instructions?"

"No, but I know there are some pictures of it." He started toward the library. "Have you seen the frescoes?"

"Yes. Can you really restore them, too?"

He nodded, stepping back to let her precede him into the library. He played the beam of light over the ceiling, and they both stared up at them, standing close together in the semidarkness.

"That one in the corner is almost completely ruined," she said, pointing in that direction.

"Don't remind me," he groaned as he shone the beam on the crumbling ceiling.

"But how can you restore it, when there's almost nothing left to see?"

"I'll start from scratch. I know what it was."

She moved over to stand under it. There was too little left for her to guess what it might have been. "What was it?"

"Venus and Adonis," he said, a smile in his voice. "X-rated, too. It was my favorite when I was a kid—for purely artistic reasons, you understand."

Jennifer laughed. "As I recall, that myth ended rather badly for Adonis."

Ben lowered the beam and shrugged. "Maybe he thought it was worth it."

The flashlight's beam was directed downward, bringing the surrounding darkness closer and casting his face in shadow. Jennifer felt as though they were treading along the edge of a volcano that could erupt at any moment, set off by a glance, a look, a word.

BEN READ her thoughts easily as they stood there, encompassed by darkness. He'd set out to seduce her, and he knew he'd succeeded. But what should have been triumph became instead a wariness. *His* feelings weren't supposed to be involved here—at least not beyond the obvious pleasure of having her.

He led her back to the lobby, and then to the dining room, where they filled their plates and carried them to the candle-lit table. He opened a bottle of wine he'd brought up from the cellar and sniffed at it.

"I think we're in luck," he told her. "If the rest of it is still good, we've got the beginnings of a great cellar."

He let the wine breathe for a few minutes, then filled their glasses, realizing belatedly that he'd said "we." That thought only added to his sudden uneasiness.

Beyond the windows, the sun was sinking down behind the dark woods. Its red blaze, and the flickering candlelight, bathed Jennifer in a breathtakingly beautiful glow. Ben, who sometimes painted, wanted very much to paint her as she was now: soft and vulnerable, touched by desire, yet not quite willing to give in to it.

He could admire the other side of her, as well: the polished, sophisticated businesswoman. That part of her challenged him, but the woman he saw now was reaching deep into him and touching something that had never been touched before.

What the hell is going on here? he asked himself. Just who was being seduced? Was it possible that she had the same plan he did—to seduce him into giving up his claim to Victoriana? That thought shocked him—and made him realize just how little he really knew about her.

"This food is excellent," she proclaimed, suddenly looking up at him and catching him studying her. Her statement ended with a slight catch in her voice.

"Do they have a restaurant, as well, or just a catering business?" she asked, quickly reverting to a more normal voice and concentrating on her food again.

"Just catering at the moment, and they're doing it from their home. But their business has grown to the point where they're going to have to find some other place, so they're thinking about opening a restaurant, as well."

Jennifer stared thoughtfully at the kitchen. Ben, who was still thinking about her, was slow to realize what was on her mind. Then he followed her glance and nodded.

"They might be interested. We could talk to them about it." There he went again with that "we" stuff, as though they really were partners, and not two adversaries who'd only agreed to work together for the time being.

"A really good restaurant could do wonders for this place, you know. There's a high markup on food and beverages, and we'd even have a built-in clientele from their catering business. A lot of inns survive during the off-season because of their restaurants or bars."

He noticed that she'd reverted to that businesslike tone again, and was surprised to find that he, too, was willing to return to that relatively safe ground. But it wasn't easy to stay there. The contrast between the candle-lit intimacy of the scene and their talk about the work that lay ahead created a sensuality all its own, heightened by glances that met and slid away into small silences.

"You said you could re-create that fresco," she stated after he explained the process of cleaning them. "So you're an artist, as well?"

Ben felt uncomfortable, as he always did when this particular subject arose. "Yeah, I do some painting occasionally."

"But if you can re-create that, you must be very good," she persisted.

"Those frescoes all came from prints in a book. All I have to do is to copy the original."

"I see." She smiled. "So it doesn't suit your self-image to think of yourself as an artist."

"No, it doesn't," he stated succinctly, thinking about all the arguments between his mother, who'd wanted to encourage his talents, and his father, who'd been determined not to have an artist for a son.

Thankfully, she dropped the matter. But the next subject she brought up caught him by surprise.

"Would you have any objections to my moving into the apartment here?" She hurried on to say that she knew it wasn't part of their agreement, but it would be very convenient, and she needed a place to live. Ben thought she sounded as though she expected him to refuse her—so, of course, he didn't.

"I have no objections. I can probably have it ready for you in a couple of weeks—unless you want the bathroom and kitchen remodeled."

"No. Maybe later, but they'll be fine for now."

"You'll be awfully isolated out here," he pointed out, thinking about that "maybe later," and how she, too, was feeling the weight of the uncertainty that hung over them.

"That won't bother me," she assured him.

Their eyes met, and the memories of that other night here filled the small space between them. Ben also thought about the advantages of having her live here. He'd be working in the evenings often enough....

"I think I might have seen the ghost on the lake that night," she said, smiling. "I forgot to tell you about that."

"Ah, the infamous lady of the lake," Ben said, chuckling.

"Have *you* seen her?"

"No, because she doesn't exist. It's a lake—and lakes have mist."

"How unromantic of you," she chided him with a smile. "Jim Thompson said she's supposed to be the ghost of a woman who drowned on her honeymoon."

"Maybe her husband changed his mind and decided to get rid of her."

She laughed. "He also said that your grandfather claimed there were ghosts in here, as well."

"I've heard that, but not from Granddad. Are you sure you want to live here?"

"Things that go bump in the night don't bother me."

"Is that so?" he asked challengingly. "Then why is it that I seem to remember a woman in her underwear crawling around on the porch roof?"

She blushed. "I wasn't running from a ghost that night."

"What *were* you running from, then?" he asked softly.

She surprised him by giving him a very level look. "I was running from a man I thought intended to...hurt me. If you recall, when we met, you said you were going to cause me a lot of trouble. I saw you out there earlier, when Jim Thompson was here, and I thought you did something to my car."

"I assume you know now that I didn't—and that that wasn't the kind of trouble I had in mind."

She nodded, and a silence fell between them again as they finished their dessert. Ben's thoughts remained on that vision of her on the roof, and the feel of her later in his arms—cold, smooth skin that begged to be warmed. He wanted her way too much for his peace of mind.

When they had finished, he suggested they go up to the apartment so that he could see what needed to be done. Guided by the flashlight, they walked through the lobby and up the stairs, the darkness pressing against them.

JENNIFER KNEW the moment they walked into the apartment that it was a mistake to have come up here. She remembered the smallest details of that night, but most of all she remembered the feel of his warm hands on her chilled body, the protective strength of his arms as he'd carried her—and the hunger that had stayed with her ever since that night.

As Ben talked about plastering and repairing a rotted window frame, and some tile work in the bathroom, they moved around the apartment, staying close together in the beam of the flashlight. Then he walked over to the window from which she'd fled that night and stared out, bringing back a fresh wave of memories that she knew he must be reliving, as well.

In a voice that sounded, even to her own ears, far too bright, she told him what Thompson had said about the tower, and that his uncle had confirmed that there was indeed a room up there.

Ben turned to her and nodded. "I never saw it myself. Grand-dad closed it off when Dad was little. We could open it up again, if you like."

"That would be nice, but it can wait. The important thing is to get the inn ready to reopen."

They left the apartment and started toward the stairs. Jennifer paused at the top and stared down into the dark lobby, seeing it as it would be soon. The words came out before she could stop them.

"I really do love this place, Ben. I think I fell in love with it the first time I saw it, awful as it is now."

When Ben said nothing, she hurried down the stairs, embarrassed, and not really understanding why. He followed her back to the dining room, still silent.

"Should we take this out to your truck?" she asked, gesturing toward the food.

"No, leave it. I'll take care of it tomorrow."

He put out the candles, then walked toward the kitchen. She followed, certain now that her words had changed something. Had he thought she was making a plea for him to give up his suit? Whatever the reason, an evening that had seemed so right had now gone wrong.

When they reached the truck, he put out a hand to open the door for her, then stopped. She turned toward him questioningly, and her arm brushed against his. She couldn't stand the silence.

"Thank you for this, Ben. It was wonderful."

He said nothing for several heart-stopping seconds—and then

he leaned toward her, very slowly. Her lips parted of their own volition, already feeling the imprint of his. But it didn't happen. Instead, he kissed the curve of her neck, his mouth and tongue tracing slow, fiery lines along the taut cord and then along the rim of her ear and behind it.

A moan poured from her mouth, which he had yet to claim. At the sound, he drew her against him, molding her to his length as he very slowly found his way to her lips, meeting them softly at first, and then with increasing demand.

Jennifer's fingers entwined themselves in his hair as she arched into him, wanting more, needing more, and ignoring the warnings of her brain. Whether this was right or wrong simply didn't matter. No man had ever made her feel this hunger.

She met his demands with her own, moving against him, feeling his hard body respond to hers and knowing that he shared her need. It seemed they could not get enough of each other as they strained against the barriers of their clothing, unable to control the forces they'd unleashed—and not wanting to.

Jennifer was lost in the wonder of him, in the way he tasted, in his clean, masculine scent, in the thick crispness of his hair and the taut muscles that trembled beneath her fingers.

He drew away from her slightly, then stared down at her as he held her face imprisoned in his hands. She turned her mouth into his hand and kissed his callused palm. He groaned and began covering her face with kisses before reclaiming her mouth again—but with a tentative softness this time.

Ben was shaken to the core by the feelings she'd aroused in him. Who was doing the seducing here? What had happened to his plan? He lifted his face from hers briefly and stared up at the inn, thinking about all the beds in there, and about the silken skin beneath her silk blouse.

He wanted her—not because of Victoriana, but because their bodies seemed to have been made for each other. Her curves fitted themselves to him perfectly. The firm, full breasts that were crushed against his chest were made to fill his hands. He felt out of control, lost in her softness. And he knew that even when he'd had her it wouldn't be enough.

He loosened his grip on her, sensing that the moment had come when she, too, was beginning to question what was happening here. They were both breathing raggedly as they stared at each other. In her eyes, Ben saw passion being replaced by wariness, and disappointment sliced through him. He wanted to carry her inside and make love to her now, before either of them had time to think.

"We'd better leave now," she said, in a husky voice that made his nerve endings tremble.

"Right." He opened her door and helped her into the truck, then went around to get in himself.

JENNIFER UNDRESSED in her room and slipped a silk nightshirt over her head. She was so incredibly aware of her body, as though every nerve ending had been rubbed raw and left aching. Scenes of the evening replayed in her mind in a tumbled fashion—Ben's half smile, his low chuckle, the quiet intensity in his voice when he talked about his work, the fire of passion in his blue eyes, the feel, taste and smell of him.

She wanted Ben Walters. She wanted him so badly that she'd come dangerously close to ending the battle then and there, giving him the inn in return for the pleasure of his lovemaking.

She was stunned as she thought about it now, in the safety of her room. Men had simply never been all that important a part of her life. She had traveled too much to establish any long-term relationships. And then, of course, there had always been that fear that she might turn into her mother, a creature totally dependent on the affections of men.

He's only seducing you to get Victoriana, an inner voice whispered. She couldn't let herself believe there was anything more to it. There was too much at stake for her to engage in self-delusion.

Chapter Five

"I told them they can start tomorrow," Ben said, gesturing toward the four teenage boys.

For their sake, Jennifer struggled to control her anger. *She* was the one who was supposed to be in charge of the work on the grounds.

"I don't have the equipment they'll need," she stated, trying to regain control of the situation.

Ben shrugged. "I'll get it this afternoon." He then told the kids to be there at eight o'clock the next morning.

As soon as they had gone, Jennifer turned on him angrily. "How do you know they can do the job? Did you interview them? And what about references?"

Ben regarded her with that damnable half smile that never failed to send curls of heat through her. She knew that he knew it, too.

"I don't have to interview them, and I don't need references. I know who they are, and they'll be fine. They all need the work, and I wanted to let them start as soon as possible."

She hated his calm, reasonable tone—and she hated the memories that assaulted her at times like this, memories that pointed up still further her past foolishness with Ben Walters, and reminded her that she could so easily let it happen again.

It had been like this for two weeks now. They worked together, held endless discussions. To all outward appearances, it was a smoothly functioning partnership. But when their eyes met, she saw the fire there—banked for now, but ready to reignite.

She glanced at her watch. "The movers shouldn't be here for at least another hour. I'll go get the equipment they need."

He fished his keys out of his pocket. "Take my truck. You'll never get it all in your trunk."

She took the keys and walked away, certain she'd heard criticism of her choice of cars. After she'd bought it, he had suggested that she should have let him help her make the choice, as though she were incapable of buying a car herself!

She drove into town, letting go of her anger only reluctantly. Whose fault was it, really, that Ben seemed to have invaded her life with all the subtlety of a tornado? Could she blame him if she couldn't seem to control her wayward thoughts? Not once in the past two weeks had he tried to repeat that scene the night of their dinner at Victoriana.

But he didn't have to try, did he? All he had to do was to be himself, surrounded by that aura of masculine sensuality, to turn her into a bowl of quivering Jell-O.

At the garden center, she bought shovels and rakes and other equipment, then paused to look at mowers and garden tractors. But she knew nothing at all about them, so she decided—reluctantly—to let Ben deal with that.

Part of what was bothering her was how completely he seemed to have taken over. She tried to find fault with what he'd done, but couldn't. If he hadn't already taken over her thoughts, not to mention her dreams, she might not have resented it so much. But since she seemed to have lost control of herself, she desperately needed to control *something* in her life.

When she returned to the inn, the moving van had just arrived, and she quickly cast off her bad mood. For weeks she had looked forward to moving into the apartment. She led the movers upstairs, opened the door—and froze.

The beautiful, expensive wallpaper she'd so carefully put up herself lay in a crumpled pile on the newly refinished floor, only a few shreds still clinging to the wall. For a moment she simply could not believe her eyes. Then one of the movers peered over her shoulder.

"What happened here?" he asked incredulously.

Jennifer just shook her head and walked into the living room.

She began to pick up the shreds of wallpaper, then stopped and went into the bedroom, where she'd papered one wall in a lovely pattern to match the new bedspread for her mother's wonderful old brass bed. It, too, had been stripped away, and the drapes she'd hung the day before had been cut to shreds.

She fought tears as the men began to carry in the furniture. Who could have done such a thing—and why? It seemed such a personal violation. Ben had offered to put up the wallpaper for her, but she'd insisted on doing it herself. She'd worked so hard to match the complicated pattern perfectly.

"Jennifer?"

She turned to find him standing in the bedroom doorway, frowning. "What happened?" he asked, gesturing toward the stripped wall and the ruined drapes.

"Maybe *you* can answer that!" She flung the words at him as she swiped angrily at the tears that were streaming down her cheeks.

He stared at her in silence for a long moment, then started toward her. She backed away when he reached for her, but even as she did, a treacherous part of her wanted to seek solace in those arms. He stopped, and the light went out of his eyes, leaving them a cold, flat blue.

"Whenever you're ready to discuss this rationally, you know where to find me," he said, then turned and walked out.

She gathered up the paper and tried not to think about why he would have done such a thing. When the movers had gone, she called the store to order new wallpaper and drapes, then slipped out the back door and went down to the lake.

The viciousness of it continued to shock her. There was no way Ben could convince her that this was the work of vandals. Even if someone had managed to get into the inn, why would they have picked her apartment as a target? Ben had all sorts of tools and woodworking equipment downstairs in the lobby that would surely have attracted their attention.

Her eyes filled with tears again. How could he hurt her like this? She felt so...*betrayed*. And she felt foolish, too, for having liked him and trusted him—and more. When he'd appeared in her bedroom, she'd wanted so much to fling herself into his arms.

How could she have been so dumb? How could she have been so wrong about him?

She remembered the threat he'd issued the first time she met him. He'd said then that he was going to cause her "a lot of trouble," and she'd very conveniently forgotten about that as she let him seduce her. And that was just what he was doing, wasn't it—seducing her? He didn't even have to touch her. It was all in a glance, a smile, that lean, hard body, his undeniable maleness.

As she sat there in the weeds, staring out across the lake, her hurt and anger turned slowly to determination. If he thought he was going to use a combination of seduction and fear to force her to leave, he was in for a surprise. She would repaper the walls and buy new drapes and get a new lock for the apartment. She would *not* let him drive her away from here.

But regardless of her determination, she couldn't help thinking about her situation. She was so isolated out here—as he himself had pointed out. If this was only the opening salvo in a campaign to get her out of here...

She broke off her thoughts abruptly when Ben silently dropped down beside her. But she ignored him, continuing to stare out at the lake—or rather she *pretended* to ignore him. Then, suddenly, he reached out to grab both her hands and draw her around to face him. She glared at him, lifting her chin defiantly and pulling her hands free at the same time.

"Jenny, you can't believe I'd do something like that," he said softly.

"I don't like to be called Jenny," she replied frostily, even though the way he said it felt like a caress.

"All right. *Jennifer,* you can't really believe I'd do something like that."

They locked gazes until she finally looked away. He seemed genuinely hurt; she could actually feel it. But how could she know what he was capable of? For all she knew, he might have practiced that look before a mirror, knowing she'd be bound to accuse him. Still, despite her determination not to be ruled by her foolish emotions, she *wanted* to believe him.

"If you didn't do it, then who did, Ben? This wasn't any ordinary act of vandalism. This was...personal."

He heaved a sigh and ran his hands through his thick hair. "I know it was, and that's what bothers me most. Ordinary vandals would have damaged my saws. I checked the windows and doors and can't find any sign of a break-in, either. Ted said you were still here when they left yesterday. Are you sure you locked up?"

"I'm very sure." But she wished she weren't, because then maybe she *could* believe it was just some particularly nasty vandal.

"Okay, two things. First of all, we change the locks—and only the two of us will have keys from now on. And secondly, I'll redo those walls for you as soon as you get new paper."

"I've already ordered it, and I'll do it myself. And I'm going to have a new lock put on the apartment."

He was silent for a moment, still wearing that hurt look that hurt her, as well. If he'd remained silent one moment longer, she knew, she would have been asking him to forgive her for suspecting him.

"Look, I know you want to move in now, but don't you think it'd be better if you stayed at the Willises' for the time being?"

"Why?" she asked challengingly as her suspicions returned.

"Because whoever did it might come back. Do you realize how alone you'll be out here? The police are miles away." He paused for a moment, then went on. "Look, I guess I can understand how you'd blame me. You're right. The act was personal, and it was directed at *you*."

"That's right. Now, you tell me, who else could possibly have anything against me?"

He got up and then stared down at her through narrowed eyes that still looked wounded. "I don't have anything against you—at least not personally."

"Oh, of course not, Ben. You're just spreading lies and trying to take Victoriana from me—not to mention trying to seduce me into giving it to you. And since that didn't work..."

His eyes became slits of blue ice, and he bent down until his face was very close to hers. Her gaze was fixed on his wide mouth, but she didn't draw back.

"So it didn't work?" His lips curved slightly. "I suppose you haven't given a single thought to that night since then?"

Without waiting for her answer, he straightened up and walked away.

Jennifer sat there, angry, hurt, humiliated, frustrated, and a few dozen other things. Well, she'd asked the question, hadn't she? How could she complain when it was answered? At the moment, she was too hurt at discovering that he'd deliberately seduced her to give any rational thought to his guilt or innocence in the vandalism.

She returned to the inn to find Ben on the phone in the kitchen, trying to persuade a locksmith to come out right away. He didn't turn around when she entered, but she could feel his eyes on her as she walked through the kitchen and then went back up to her apartment.

The moment she saw the ruined wall, anger got the best of all the other emotions churning inside her. This was a day she'd looked forward to for two weeks—and now her pleasure had been stolen.

Ben knocked on the door as she was rearranging the furniture for the third time. She opened it, but said nothing.

"I thought maybe I'd move into one of the rooms for the time being," he announced after a few moments.

"That isn't necessary," she replied coldly as she picked up a small carton to carry it into the bedroom. He was in her way, and as she started to walk past him, he reached out to take it from her. She held on to it tightly, making it a barricade between them.

"I don't need your help, Ben. I've been taking care of myself most of my life, and I've gotten to be very good at it."

She strode past him and went down the hallway to the spare room, torn by the implications of his offer. She wanted him here, and she didn't want him here. She didn't trust him—and she didn't trust herself, either. And if he was actually living here, she'd have no way of avoiding him.

Of course, she thought wryly, it didn't make much difference, did it? Even if he wasn't here, she'd be thinking about him, and dreaming about him. There were two Ben Walterses: the man she knew she shouldn't trust, and the passionate lover who invaded her daytime fantasies and her nighttime dreams.

When she turned, Ben was standing in the doorway.

"What did you mean by that?" His tone was full of curiosity, and almost tentative.

"By what?" she asked, confused.

"Why did you say that you've been taking care of yourself most of your life?"

Although surprised by the question, she certainly wasn't about to discuss her childhood with him. She was beginning to understand that she dared not show any vulnerability to him, lest it be used as a weapon against her.

"I just meant that I'm nearly thirty years old and I've never been married or lived with anyone," she replied, in a tone meant to signal an end to the discussion.

He stared at her for a long moment, then nodded. "Okay, so maybe I overreacted. I just wanted you to know that if you're worried about being here alone, I'll be glad to move in."

"Thank you, but that won't be necessary."

THE PHONE RANG that evening while she was in the tub. Her machine was on in the bedroom across the hall, and she heard it click on—but there was no message.

Don't let this happen, she warned herself as fear prickled her spine. *It could be a wrong number, or just someone who doesn't like machines.* But she knew there was another possibility: that whoever had damaged the walls was calling to see if she was there.

She'd been so busy all evening that she hadn't once thought about her isolation here—but now, of course, she did. The silence seemed oppressive. Envisioning the dark inn around her only heightened her sense of aloneness.

The phone rang again just as she was about to get into bed. Chills ran up and down her spine as she reached for it, then drew back at the last second to let the machine take the call. Her brief message seemed to take forever. Then, after the beep, she heard a familiar voice.

"Jenny—Jennifer—are you there?"

She picked up the receiver quickly, then sat down on the edge of the bed, achingly aware of her nakedness. "I'm here, Ben."

"Is everything okay?"

"If it isn't, I'm not likely to know about it. I'm so tired they could tear the place down around me and I wouldn't wake up."

He chuckled. The sound rolled softly out of the phone and flowed through her like liquid fire.

"You've made me feel a whole lot better," he said.

"I have?"

"You said *they* could tear the place down, so I'm assuming that you've decided I'm not guilty."

She hesitated. It was true that she no longer blamed him, though she didn't trust her reasons for it. "I'm sorry, Ben. I didn't really think you'd do such a thing, but I was so upset..."

"I'd still feel a whole lot better if you'd let me come over."

Jennifer looked at her nakedness, glanced at the turned-down bed—and almost said yes. Then she shook her head to rid it of those tantalizing fantasies.

"I'll be fine, but thank you."

"Sleep well, then." His voice was a low drawl that echoed through her mind as she curled up in bed alone.

THE CLOCK READ 1:20 a.m. when Jennifer awoke suddenly, certain she'd heard something. Her heart thudded noisily in her chest as she tried to listen. Then she heard it again: a distant, muffled sound, coming, she thought, from somewhere downstairs, at the back of the inn.

Perhaps because she'd just been awakened from badly needed sleep, Jennifer was more angry than fearful at this point. She knew she was safe in the apartment. A strong new lock had been installed, with an additional chain lock on the inside.

She got quietly out of bed, straining to hear any repetition of the sounds. Then she walked around the dark apartment, peering out each window in turn. Unfortunately, the apartment had no windows that faced the rear.

She considered leaving the apartment to find a room that faced the back. But by now caution was overtaking her anger, and when she heard nothing more, she began to wonder if the sounds had been made by mice or squirrels or some other animal outside.

There was definite evidence of a skunk's having visited on several occasions.

She returned to the front windows. There was no moon, and the light Ben had rigged up temporarily on the driveway side of the front porch shone only feebly into the vast darkness.

Just as she was about to turn away, she saw something move in the shadows just beyond the reach of the light. She peered into the darkness, and thought again that she saw something moving away from the house, down the driveway—something about the size of a man. It occurred to her that if someone *was* out there, he had to have a car nearby. So she opened the window and listened carefully for the sound of an engine, scanning the darkness for headlights.

Unfortunately, the spring peepers were in full chorus, filling the night with their rhythmic, throbbing sound. Although she thought she heard the distant sound of a car's engine, there were no headlights. By the time she finally closed the window and returned to bed, she was wondering if she'd imagined the whole thing.

Maybe she was subconsciously seeking a reason to have Ben move in. She'd spent much of the evening wondering if she'd been too hasty in rejecting his offer, telling herself that she might need his help—and knowing that what she really needed and wanted was *him.*

"I'D RECOMMEND A SHOTGUN," the burly man behind the counter told Jennifer.

"Why?" she asked, frowning at the impressive weapon he held.

"Because shotguns scare people, and that's what you want it for."

"Yes, but I think I'd prefer something smaller—a handgun. I want something I can easily keep hidden and can get quickly. And something I can actually shoot, if necessary."

An hour later, Jennifer left the shop with a new .22-caliber revolver. The owner had a target range out behind his rural shop, and he'd spent most of that hour showing her how to use it, all the while trying to find out why she wanted it. She felt like a female Rambo, and she was appalled at how easy it was to buy the gun—but she didn't regret her decision.

When she'd awoken that morning, Jennifer had thought long and hard about the night before, and she had become more and more convinced that someone *had* been out there. If there had been only the noise, or only the shadow she thought she'd seen, she might have dismissed it. But to her way of thinking, two possibles added up to a probable—especially when she knew there had been an intruder before.

She didn't really believe Ben was responsible for either incident, but in the absence of any other suspect, she couldn't afford to rule out the possibility.

What it had come down to, finally, was that she had only herself to depend on—a situation she'd grown quite accustomed to long ago. Even if she could have ruled out Ben as a suspect, she still wouldn't have wanted him moving into the inn. Their relationship was already too explosive, too fraught with tension.

Before returning to Victoriana, she stopped to make some other purchases, then hid the gun, the box of ammunition and the cleaning kit in the bags. She didn't want Ben to know that she'd bought a gun, since he would certainly insist upon moving in. She also hadn't told him about last night, justifying her silence on the admittedly dubious grounds that she wasn't sure anything had actually happened.

When she walked into the inn, she found Ben at work in the lobby, where he'd set up his woodworking equipment. He was starting to make the lovely gingerbread trim for the edges of the porch roof. All of it had to be replaced, and he was carefully re-creating the exact pattern of the original work. He'd told her that these designs were often unique to the individual craftsman, acting as a sort of signature.

He didn't see her, so she stood there for a few moments watching him. He worked smoothly and competently, with an intensity that belied his otherwise laid-back nature. She admired his dedication to his work, and his pride in it, and she found herself wondering how she would feel about him if it weren't for the lawsuit that stood between them.

He was so very different from the other men she'd known, but maybe it was that difference that attracted her. She'd thought—or hoped—that the physical attraction, that undeniable chemistry between them, would lessen with constant exposure, but she realized now that she'd been wrong. Instead, the better she got to know him, the more powerful that attraction became.

BEN STRAIGHTENED UP and reached for another piece of wood—then stopped when he saw her. She seemed startled, as though she might have been standing there for some time, watching him. And she might well have been. He always lost himself in his work.

She walked toward him with a smile. She was wearing jeans and a T-shirt, but the jeans were the loose-fitting, baggy type, and the T-shirt was big enough to fit him. She wore very little makeup, and her hair was in a French braid. A deliberate attempt, he thought, to disguise her desirability. Did she think he had no memory of that body covered with nothing but scraps of silk and lace?

She leaned over, close to him, to examine the piece of trim he was working on.

"No problems last night?" he asked.

She looked up from the trim. "No." Then she shrugged. "Or if there was, I slept right through it."

She was lying, he thought. Then he quickly backed off from the sudden impression. How would he know if she was lying or not? His brain seemed to stop functioning the moment she appeared. But she definitely seemed nervous as she stood there clutching a big shopping bag.

"I still think it'd be a good idea for me to move in," he told her, wondering why he didn't insist upon it. Was it because he really was having second thoughts about his plan to seduce her to get the inn?

She hesitated for a moment, then shook her head. "I don't think that would be a good idea, Ben."

"Oh? Why not?"

She looked at him with those big gray-green eyes, outwardly calm, but with nervousness darting about just beneath the surface.

"Because it would cause problems—problems neither of us needs right now."

"Maybe it's just the kind of problem we *do* need. Or maybe it would solve the problem we *already* have."

Her eyes met his just long enough to tell him that she knew exactly what sort of "problem" they had, and then she shook her head and walked away.

Ben watched her climb the stairs. In his mind, he followed her to her apartment, to that big brass bed. In his mind, her attempts to hide that smooth, curvy body from him did no good at all.

A few minutes later, when he came dangerously close to slicing off his thumb, he decided that their "problem" had to be resolved—and soon.

"IS THAT LUNCH, or just an appetizer?" Ben asked, staring dubiously at her container of yogurt.

Well, so much for having a peaceful, solitary lunch, Jennifer thought as he dropped down beside her at the edge of the lake.

"It's lunch," she replied, holding up an apple. "Along with this."

He dug a thick sandwich out of his bag, then ran his eyes over her. "Well, I guess I shouldn't complain, since the results are worth it—even if you *do* seem to be making a real effort to hide it."

"Hide what?" she asked, confused.

"What's underneath all those baggy clothes you've been wearing lately," he replied as he unwrapped his sandwich. "Fortunately for me, I have a very good memory."

*Un*fortunately, she did, too. To cover her embarrassment, she lashed out at him. "Ben, I think it's time for you to stop the innuendos."

"Oh?" He arched a dark brow in amusement. "What would you suggest we do instead?"

She lowered her gaze to her yogurt. Confronting him about this was a mistake. She'd encountered such situations a few times in the past, and had found that clearing the air was the best possible way to deal with unwanted attention from men. But she hadn't been attracted to those men. She hadn't spent too much of her waking time—not to mention her sleep—dreaming about blue eyes and demanding lips and callused hands and—

"I suggest that we both keep our minds on our work," she stated firmly.

"Right. Well, you might want to start thinking about what color to paint the exterior. We'll be ready to begin in about another week."

Jennifer couldn't quite hide her surprise at his willingness to follow her "suggestion." The laughter in Ben's eyes confirmed that.

"Ignoring the obvious isn't so easy, is it?" he asked softly.

It certainly wasn't, but she was determined to try. "I saw that old sepia photograph at your uncle's house, but it was impossible to tell what colors it was painted originally."

"The Victorians had some pretty strange tastes. I've looked at that picture, too, and my guess is pumpkin."

She burst out laughing. "Pumpkin?"

"It was actually a pretty common shade back then. I don't know what *they* called it, but that's what I call it."

"I call it disgusting," she said with a grimace. "Let's not get carried away with this authenticity business. I think maybe a cream, or a nice soft beige or taupe."

Ben said that he'd get some samples, and then they went on to talk about the rest of the work. She commented that the girls she'd hired were making progress with the cleaning and the boys were working hard on the grounds.

"They all seem to be working out very well," she remarked. "I was afraid they'd require so much supervision that I'd get nothing else done."

Ben grinned. "They'll be fine—as long as we keep them separate."

"Oh? Do you know something I don't?"

"No, except that it's spring and they're kids. Isn't it nice to be all grown up and past that kind of thing?"

Jennifer laughed. "Actually, I never went through that as a teenager. When I was twelve, my mother packed me off to a girls' boarding school. Then, in summer, I went to a girls' camp."

"Did you like it?"

She shrugged. "I got used to it. Besides, I didn't have any choice."

"My folks used to threaten to send me off to military school—the middle-class version of reform school."

"Were you really that bad?" she asked curiously.

"No—or at least not by today's standards. I was just very good at walking along the edges of the rules. I still am."

"Yes," she said with a smile. "I've noticed that."

"It's a real talent, knowing just how hard to push and knowing when to quit. I have great instincts for that."

She bit into her apple and said nothing. Suddenly he leaned over and bit into the other side while it was still in her mouth. From a distance of mere inches, his eyes taunted her. She responded by drawing in a sharp breath—and choking on a piece of apple. He withdrew quickly and thumped her on the back.

"That was a pretty good example, wasn't it? Would you like me to use the Heimlich maneuver? I've had first-aid training." He moved behind her and encircled her with his arms.

"No, thanks," she gasped. "I'm fine."

"You don't sound fine," he murmured, bending close to her ear. "But you smell fine." He briefly drew an earlobe between his teeth. "And you taste fine, too."

"Ben!"

"Hmm?" He released her earlobe and began to run his tongue along the curve of her neck.

"I thought you agreed that we should keep our minds on our work," she said, her voice embarrassingly husky.

"*I* never said that, you did. And whoever said you shouldn't mix business and pleasure got it all wrong. Although I *did* damn near slice off my finger because of that a while ago."

"You what?" She drew away from him, and he slid around to sit beside her again.

"I was watching you when I should have been watching what I was doing. Maybe if you started wearing clothes that didn't leave so much to the imagination, I wouldn't be risking my life imagining."

She laughed. "Is there logic in that?"

"Absolutely." He stood up. "Well, let's get back to work. How about dinner tonight? You could cook for me. I'm easy to please."

"I'm certainly glad to hear that, since I can't cook," she replied dryly, knowing she shouldn't agree to dinner, but would anyway.

"All right, if you want to risk your health, I'll cook," she said.

He made a mock bow. "Thank you. Then, after dinner, I'll show you how I spent my *mis*spent youth."

JENNIFER WISHED the sounds of the shower running didn't reach her here in the kitchen. Her cooking skills were poor enough without the distraction of knowing Ben was only a short distance away, naked in her shower.

He had worked late, then asked if he could shower and change in her apartment. It was interesting, she thought, that he'd just happened to have a change of clothes with him. If she were inclined to be suspicious, she might have thought his seemingly spontaneous "invitation" was anything but. The truth was, though, that she liked having him here. She considered him to be her very first guest in her new home—never mind the fact that he might be responsible for making it no more than a temporary home.

The absurdity of their situation was becoming more and more apparent. Here they were, working together and edging closer and closer to becoming lovers—and all the while they had lawyers fighting a surrogate battle for them.

The sound of the shower stopped, and the pages of her cookbook blurred temporarily as Jennifer imagined him in there, drying himself off, rubbing a towel over his hard, muscled body.

She had just put the coq au vin into the oven and was starting to work on the lyonnaise potatoes when he appeared in the kitchen doorway.

"I thought you said you couldn't cook," he stated, frowning at the stacks of cookbooks on the counter and in a carton.

"I can't. I just collect cookbooks."

He came over to examine them. His presence filled the small

space in the kitchen immediately. "Would you like a shelf for them?"

"Yes, that would be nice, whenever you have the time."

He pulled one of her Sabatier knives from their wooden block. "Nice knives for a noncook."

"Wherever I went, I bought things that I thought I might need when I finally settled down," Jennifer explained. If he didn't leave soon, she would be in danger of slicing off one of her own fingers.

As soon as she put down the knife, he kissed the nape of her neck, sending a shudder through her. He chuckled softly, his breath fanning across her sensitive skin.

"Ben, if you want dinner, you'd better get out of this kitchen."

"If you're offering a choice between dinner and—"

"I'm not."

"Then I'll go down to the cellar and find some wine."

She breathed a sigh of relief when she heard the door open and close. Then she returned to her cooking, a silent battle raging within her. Somehow, somewhere, a line had been crossed without her being aware of it. Had it been this afternoon, when he'd used the excuse that she might be choking? Had it been just now, with that casual but devastatingly erotic kiss on the neck? Or had it been more gradual, a slow wearing away of her meager defenses as she got to know and like him?

Whenever it had happened, however it had happened, the unthinkable now seemed inevitable. Sooner or later, the plaintiff and the defendant, to use their attorneys' words, would become lovers.

She could not allow it to become inevitable. But when Ben returned, he put an end to her argument with herself with one glance of those blue eyes.

He poured them some wine, and they carried it outside, where they sat down on the newly rebuilt front steps and stared out over the broad lawn. The boys had mowed the grass, and while it was scarcely the green-velvet carpet she wanted, it was at least neat. She was hoping to nurse it back to health, in order to avoid the expense of having it dug up and replaced.

She and Ben talked about work, about schedules for various

projects, about everything but themselves and the tangled mess of their lives. Beneath their conversation ran the low hum of sensuality, filling the silences and making her excruciatingly aware of his knee, which rested lightly against her leg.

Dinner provided more of the same. He complimented her skills, then insisted on helping with the cleanup in the kitchen. Night had fallen while they'd eaten, and Jennifer thought about the long evening ahead. She knew she should plead work, or tiredness, or anything, to get him out of here—but she didn't want him to leave. And then he reminded her of his promise this afternoon to show her how he'd misspent his youth. She'd been curious about that comment at the time, but then had forgotten all about it.

"We can stop by Harry's first, and I'll get you that photo album I mentioned," he said. It contained many pictures of the inn taken before his mother had redecorated.

When they arrived, Harry was sitting on the front porch, and he invited Jennifer to join him while Ben went up to the attic to find the album. She had been rather surprised at Harry's failure to show up at the inn, but it quickly became apparent that he'd been keeping up on the progress of the work through Ben.

"Heard you had some trouble out there," he said.

"Yes. Mr. Walters, can you think of anyone who'd do something like that—maybe someone who doesn't want to see the inn reopen?"

He shook his head. "Doesn't make any sense to me. Like Ben said, it sounds more like someone doesn't want you there. But I guess you're planning to stay?"

She said she was, and he was silent for a few minutes.

"Even in a quiet place like this, we can get some bad types. Just a few weeks ago, a young girl was raped while she was baby-sitting for some folks who live just outside town. Big old house, sitting there all alone."

"Did they catch him?" Jennifer shuddered, but she couldn't believe it was the same man. Rapists weren't likely to go around tearing wallpaper off walls.

"Nope. She never even got a good look at him. He was wearing a ski mask."

"Well, no one is going to scare me out of Victoriana. We put good locks on all the doors, including the apartment."

"Are you still planning to open up that tower room?" Harry asked.

"Yes, but Ben has more important things to do now, so it'll be a while. I think it could be quite nice, though."

She began to talk more about the work at the inn, but Harry seemed to have lost interest. She was glad when Ben returned with the album. Harry's silence had a brooding quality that she found disturbing. She guessed his manner was the result of her ownership of the inn—something that surely couldn't please him any more than it did Ben.

"Is your uncle glad that Victoriana will be reopening?" she asked Ben as they drove away.

"That's hard to say. Harry's just never been all that interested in the inn."

"What did he do before he retired?"

"He was an accountant. He lived in Boston until his retirement. Then he came back here, and my aunt died not long after that."

She noticed that they were leaving the town behind, houses giving way to farms and isolated rural properties. "Where are we going?" she asked curiously. She couldn't imagine what it was that he intended to show her.

"Back in history," he said, giving her a grin. "Or at least it will be for me. Actually, it's sort of past and future together."

"Is this a riddle I'm supposed to figure out?" she asked teasingly.

"No, it'll all become clear very soon," he replied as he downshifted the truck.

The road had been climbing steadily for the past mile or so, and now he turned onto a gravel road flanked by stone pillars. In the center of each pillar was a cement square with something written on it, but in the darkness, Jennifer couldn't make it out. She could see the dim shapes of scattered houses, most of them either small A-frames or chalets. All were set on fairly large lots, with thick pine copses in between. There were no lights on in any of them.

"Are these all vacation homes?" she asked as he drove slowly past them.

He nodded. "I think there may be one or two that haven't been sold yet."

Then, suddenly, he came to a stop in front of a bright orange metal gate that blocked the road. The road narrowed beyond it and continued steeply uphill. Ben got out of the truck and unlocked the heavy padlock on the gate, then pushed it aside. They drove through. The thick forest pressed against the narrow road, and she saw no more houses anywhere. Her curiosity grew, but she said nothing.

When they had gone perhaps a mile, the road ended abruptly, just as the woods ended, as well. Before them was a house under construction, nothing more than a foundation and a partial framework. Abruptly she recalled that Ben, or someone, had mentioned that he was building a home for himself somewhere in the area.

"Is this *your* house?" she asked as he turned off the engine.

"Uh-huh. I'd planned to get it finished this summer, but that was before I knew I'd be working on Victoriana. I'm still hoping to get it under roof before next winter, though."

"I don't understand. What did you mean when you said you were going back in history?"

Instead of answering, he got out of the truck, then came over to help her out. Her eyes had adjusted by now to the darkness, and thanks to a nearly full moon and a brilliant carpet of stars, she could see well enough to follow him as he walked alongside the foundation.

Jennifer drew in a sharp breath as they both stopped. Less than twenty feet from where they stood, the ground beneath them ended in a sheer cliff. Beyond that, twinkling in the darkness, lay the town, nestled in its valley.

Ben pointed off to the left. "On a clear day, you can see all the way to Killington. It's over there."

"What a beautiful spot for a house," she exclaimed, turning from the view to look at the structure.

He turned, too. "This side will be all glass—with a deck, of course."

"How much land do you have?"

"A little under eight acres. This was part of my grandparents' farm. Mom inherited it, and she sold off the farmhouse and the land next to it. Then she sold the land where those vacation homes are to a developer. She kept the rest for me."

"So that's what you meant about history?"

He chuckled. "In a way. I told you I'd show you where I misspent my youth. This is it."

"I don't understand."

He turned to her with a grin. "Are you sure you didn't spend your teen years in a convent, instead of just a girls' school?"

When she still looked nonplussed, he chuckled and shook his head. "This is where I used to bring my girlfriends. It was also the scene of some great keg parties. There was just an old logging road then, but Granddad always had a locked gate across it, so we had a lot of privacy. I got stuck up here on one memorable occasion, which is why Wexford doesn't like me. His daughter was with me."

They both laughed. "I guess I *did* miss out on a few things," Jennifer admitted. "About the only place I even saw boys was at well-supervised dances."

Instead of commenting on that, he went back to the truck and returned a moment later with an old quilt.

"Better late than never," he said teasingly as he spread it out on the ground.

"Ben, I think we'd better go back."

He chuckled. "You even *sound* like an echo from the past. My line goes like this—'is that what you *really* want?'"

"And if they said yes?"

He shrugged. "Then we went back. I wasn't very discriminating—not with all those raging hormones."

She stood there staring at him, feeling aroused and foolish and angry in equal measure. He sat down on the quilt and put out a hand to her.

"I've become *very* discriminating, Jenny-Jennifer."

She took his hand and sat down beside him, maintaining a small but all-important distance. He continued to hold her hand.

"There seems to be a lot of electricity in the air," he said with a smile in his voice. "Maybe there's a storm brewing."

"Ben, we *can't!*"

"We can't what?"

"We can't become lovers!"

"Why not? Our partnership is working out well enough, and I'll bet you didn't think that would work, either."

She couldn't think of any response to that except to shake her head. He dropped her hand and turned to stare out at the town far below.

"Are you sulking?" she asked, unable to see his expression in the darkness.

He laughed. "No, I'm being a gentleman. I found out long ago that that usually works. My buddies always started pawing girls the minute they got them alone, and ended up getting nowhere. It's ironic, isn't it, that I got my reputation because I was always a gentleman?"

"Always?" she asked, laughing.

"With girls, anyway. I got into other trouble from time to time. And, of course, the motorcycle and the black leather didn't help my reputation much, either. Have you ever ridden one?"

"No, and I don't intend to. They're dangerous."

"Motorcycles aren't dangerous. It's just that they're often owned by idiots with something to prove. So tell me, Jenny-Jennifer, where do you find all that self-control that means you can keep your hands off my very desirable body?"

Since she couldn't very well deny his "desirability," she merely laughed.

"There isn't anyone else, is there? Some three-piece-suited type who's going to show up and force me to knock him on his well-tailored butt?"

"No, there's no one," she replied, smiling.

"Well, that's good, because I'm getting too old to fight—even over you."

His final words echoed in the silence that followed as they sat there side by side in the darkness. She wanted to leave, and she didn't want to leave. She couldn't deny that there was a certain eroticism to being here in his "past"—but she felt an aversion to it, as well, as though she were nothing more than the latest in a long line of women in his life.

She'd been staring out at the view, but suddenly she became aware of his gaze on her and turned toward him.

"Maybe I shouldn't have told you about my past," he said, staring at her intently. "I just thought that since we're grown-ups now, we could laugh about it."

"We can."

He reached out to touch her mouth with one finger. "Then smile, Jenny."

She did smile, and he leaned toward her, very slowly, until his mouth was so close that she could feel his breath mingling with hers. And there he stopped.

The temptation was irresistible. She closed the tiny space between them, drawn like a magnet to his waiting lips. But his mouth remained totally passive against hers, and she started to draw away. Then his hand came up to grasp her head. With his lips still clinging softly to hers, he lowered them both to the quilt.

They lay on their sides, his arms loosely around her waist and hers encircling his chest. Their lips and tongues explored lazily, belying the urgency they both felt. Trapped in the heat of their desire, neither noticed the increasing wind that swirled around them.

A part of her waited tensely for him to move beyond the kisses, forcing her into a decision. But it didn't happen. His arms remained loosely around her waist, and only in her fevered imagination was she pulled against his hard body. His mouth teased her lightly, then became more insistent, then withdrew to her ear, her eyelids, her throat, before returning once again to their sensual assault upon her lips.

They might have been there for mere minutes, or for an hour. Jennifer lost all awareness of time—all awareness of anything but his warmth and his kisses. The tension began to drain away from her as she understood that they would go no further this night.

Gradually the intervals between their kisses became longer, and they simply lay there holding each other, in a silence that had a strange sort of peace to it, as well as a tacit understanding that they should enjoy these moments and not look beyond them.

"Cold?" he asked huskily as the wind blew still stronger.

She shook her head, not trusting her voice.

He kissed the tip of her nose. "If you were, I'd be insulted."

She smiled, and he planted soft kisses at both corners of her mouth.

"I'd ask if the cat got your tongue," he murmured, "but I know it's still there." To prove it, he caught it between his teeth and tugged gently.

She laughed. "I thought men always complained that women talk too much."

"That's *afterward*. We haven't got to that yet."

He kissed her again, then stood up and drew her to her feet. Still half-lost in a sensual haze, she stumbled against him, and his arm circled her protectively.

"Sorry to rush you, but if we stay here any longer, I won't be responsible for the consequences. There must be something in the air up here."

"I think you're right." She smiled, turning to stare at his future home. "It could be a dangerous place to live."

"Not for *me*, it won't be," he replied against her ear.

BEN GOT INTO HIS TRUCK and drove around the side of the inn, then stopped for a moment to stare up at the illuminated apartment. He could be up there now, finishing what they'd started. Instead, he'd walked her up to the apartment, given her a quick kiss, and then left before she could ask him in or he could invite himself.

He put the truck in gear again and drove slowly home. For the first time in his life, Ben Walters wasn't sure exactly what he was doing. He'd set out to seduce her, and he'd succeeded. So why was he running away?

Face it, fella, he told himself. You're running away because you want her every bit as badly as she wants you—and you're going to go on wanting her even after you've had her. You're out of control. This one's a keeper—except you know you *can't* keep her.

Victoriana and Jenny. He might be able to have one of them, but not both. For the first time, he wondered if there might be a way out of this mess.

Chapter Six

Jennifer's head jerked up the moment she heard the noises downstairs. She set aside the books of wallpaper samples she'd been leafing through and listened. It was early evening, not yet full dark, and the fact tempered her fear somewhat. Still, she listened carefully.

Then she heard the distinctive whine of Ben's power saw and relaxed—relatively speaking, that is. Fear had just been exchanged for emotions of a different sort.

She picked up the sample books again, but the patterns blurred before her eyes. The thin scream of the saw built to a crescendo, then stopped, only to start up again a moment later. She closed the books and set them on the floor.

Feeling drawn to him, as always, she left the apartment and walked toward the stairs. But when she reached the landing, she stopped. His back was to her as he expertly maneuvered a piece of wood to create the delicate gingerbread work for the porch roof. It was an extraordinarily difficult and time-consuming task, and she marveled at his determination to do it himself, rather than buy precut trim. He insisted on matching the original work. His crew had taken to calling him "the gingerbread man."

Jennifer smiled and went back to her apartment. This afternoon, when she'd been doing some grocery shopping, she'd bought a package of gingerbread mix, intending to present it to him and his crew tomorrow. Instead, she decided to make it now. It was, admittedly, a silly thing to do, and she didn't even know if he liked gingerbread, but she hoped it would break the tension between them.

In the four days since he'd taken her out to the site of his new house, they hadn't been alone once. It was true that they'd both been very busy. Ben likely had had a Little League game one of those evenings, and he had probably been working on his house the other evenings. But it was also clear that he was avoiding her, or at least avoiding being alone with her. She'd felt him watching her, and had caught him at it on more than one occasion.

She mixed the gingerbread and put it in the oven, then made some lemon sauce to go with it. Then she went back to the wallpaper books with renewed determination.

She'd initially planned to wallpaper all the guest rooms, except possibly the smaller rooms on the third floor. But after totaling up the cost of the expensive Victorian-reproduction paper, she had decided to scale back her plans and paper only one wall in each room. Ben's estimates thus far had proved to be very accurate, while her own were climbing out of sight.

When the timer went off, she was surprised. It seemed that Ben wasn't the only one who could lose himself in his work. She'd even managed to tune out the whine of the saw.

She cut two large squares of gingerbread and put them in bowls, then poured the warm lemon sauce into a small pitcher. After fitting it all onto a tray, she started once more toward the stairs.

She was halfway down the stairs, balancing the tray carefully, when he looked up, then pushed his protective goggles back into his thick, dark hair and smiled. The smile became a laugh when he saw what she'd brought.

"I wonder where you got *that* idea," he said, eyeing the gingerbread hungrily. "I don't suppose you'd happen to have any milk?"

"Of course. I'll get it now."

When she returned with two tall glasses of milk, they both sat down on the wide stairs. Jennifer thought about how good it felt to be with him. Only when she *wasn't* with him did she think about their problems.

Was it the same with him? she wondered. Did he regret his decision to fight her for the inn, or was he still hoping to persuade her to hand it over to him? And what did he feel for her...apart from the obvious? Although, now that she thought about the way he'd been avoiding her, perhaps the obvious wasn't so obvious anymore. Maybe he'd decided to depend on the courts to give him what he wanted, and not risk any entanglements with her.

He broke the silence to ask if she'd gotten an estimate from the landscapers yet, and she fell gratefully into a business discussion, as eager as he apparently was to avoid the real issues between them.

"Yes, and it's even worse than I expected. I've decided to do it myself, with the boys' help. Ben, I haven't had a chance to ask you about it, but I saw that picture of the gazebo in the book you gave me. Are you planning to rebuild it?"

He nodded, giving her an eager, boyish grin. "That's going to be my favorite part of the restoration. Did you like it?"

"I *love* it! I've never seen one so elaborate. But I suppose that's why you're looking forward to it."

He chuckled. "It's going to be a challenge, all right—but it'll be worth it. Did you know that there was an herb garden next to it?"

"No. The picture showed only the gazebo."

"It was terraced with railroad ties. I can still remember what it smelled like."

Jennifer thought about those pictures, and about the gazebo, and everything else that had been let go in this magical place—and the words came out before she could stop them. "I still don't understand why Win let this place go. He seemed so proud of it...." Her voice trailed off when Ben looked up at her sharply.

"Win?" he echoed.

She tried for a casual shrug. "That was what my mother called him."

Ben finished his gingerbread and drained his glass of milk in silence. She regretted her outburst, but felt an equally strong urge to continue this conversation, which they should have had long before this time.

"He wasn't proud of it, he hated it. I told you that."

"But, Ben, he talked about Victoriana so much." Then she rushed on, telling him how she hadn't even known it was closed, let alone in such deplorable condition. She was well aware of just how dangerous this conversation was, but she was also determined that it should take place. And perhaps Ben was, too.

"I asked Harry once why Dad hated the place so much, but all he said was that Dad just wasn't cut out to be an innkeeper. But I never heard him say he wanted to do anything else." He paused for a moment, then went on in a quiet, musing tone. "Mom told me that after Granddad died, Dad suddenly got the idea to tear the place down and rebuild it." He stopped again and looked around. "I don't think he hated being an innkeeper. I think he just hated Victoriana."

"Do you think it could have been because he hated growing up here? The family lived here then, didn't they?"

Ben nodded. "That could have been it, I suppose, because he refused to move in after Granddad died. The two of them never got along. Mom told me that sometimes she thought Dad really hated Granddad, and I thought so, too."

"It sounds as though your father might have had a pretty unhappy childhood, Ben," she said carefully.

"Maybe he did, but so what? Are you trying to excuse what he did?"

She was startled at his sudden burst of anger. "What do you mean?"

Ben, who was sitting several steps below her, stared up at her intently for a long, tense moment. Then he shook his head. "You really don't know, do you? I can believe *they* never told you, but I figured Wexford had."

"T-told me what?" she asked as a chill swept through her.

Ben got up and took a few steps away from her, then turned. His face was expressionless, but he clenched his fists briefly before jamming them into his pockets.

"Your mother and my father had an affair. Then he left Mom. She died a couple of months later."

He spoke the words in a neutral tone that somehow made them sound even worse than if he'd shouted them in anger. Jennifer made a strangled sound of protest, and he glared at her.

"You don't have to believe me. Ask Wexford. He may not have told you, but he knows. Everyone in town knew about it." He stopped abruptly, then went on again in that deadly quiet voice. "I caught them together—here, on the couch in the office! Later, I found out that Mom and I were the only ones in town who didn't know about it.

"My mother hadn't been well for a long time. Dad moved out, and he and your mother stayed in one of the suites until he could close the place. At that point, they stopped any pretense of discretion. You can imagine what that was like for Mom. Or maybe you can't, if you've never lived in a small town."

Ben stood there staring at her, his eyes dark with pain and anger. She wanted to reach out to him, but couldn't. She could see herself through his eyes: the daughter of a woman he had surely hated.

Even though she wasn't at all sure that her legs would carry her, Jennifer got to her feet, then half ran, half stumbled, up the stairs and down the hall to her apartment.

She wished she didn't believe him—but she knew her mother. Living for the moment, and somehow managing to justify behavior that would have left most people guilt-ridden, had been the only constants in her mother's life. Her relationship with Win hadn't been her first adulterous affair; just such an affair had ended her marriage to Jennifer's father.

Throughout her life, Jennifer had instinctively tried to separate the mother she loved from the woman whose behavior she deplored. But never before had it been so difficult.

"I guess we should have had this conversation when we first met."

She lifted her head and brushed the tears from her eyes. Ben came slowly into focus as he stood there in the doorway, carrying the dishes she'd left downstairs.

"They told me he was a widower," she said, in a voice that was just barely above a whisper. "When I saw your mother's grave, I knew they'd lied. I should have guessed the truth then."

He said nothing as he walked in and then took the dishes to the kitchen. By the time he returned, she had managed to regain some control over herself.

"I loved my mother, Ben, but I didn't agree with a lot of her behavior. I just tried to separate the two."

He remained standing in the middle of the room, his hands once again shoved into his pockets and his eyes avoiding hers. "You're lucky you could do that—separate the two things. I couldn't. He called me and wrote to me, but I hung up on him and I threw away the letters without reading them. Whenever I think about him now, what I remember is the look on his face when I walked in on them." He gave a mirthless laugh. "It's a great picture to have as your last memory of your father."

"I didn't even know you existed," she blurted out, only belatedly realizing that she could be causing him additional pain. "He told me he didn't have any children."

"That doesn't surprise me," Ben said bitterly. "He knew how much I loved this place, so he gave it to you to punish me. What I don't understand is why he didn't just sell it. Harry told me that someone wanted to buy it a few years ago and made a good offer. But when he got in touch with Dad, he refused to sell it."

Jennifer told him about all the times Win had tried to persuade her to take over the inn. "But he must have known that if I took him up on it I would find out about their lies. It doesn't make sense."

Ben nodded, but made no comment. He seemed lost in thought for a few moments, then looked around the room. "Have you got anything to drink? I think I could use something."

She gestured toward the kitchen. "In the cabinet over the sink. Help yourself."

He returned with his drink and sank into a chair. He seemed pensive, but more in control now. He sipped the amber liquid and regarded the glass appreciatively. "This is the best Scotch I've ever had."

"It isn't sold in the U.S. I bought it in London. Your father liked it."

He stared at the glass. "Mom and Dad had one of those marriages that would probably have ended in divorce years ago if they'd been a generation younger. But most people their age just stuck it out. Mom was sick a lot, and I guess that didn't help. She had a miscarriage before she had me, and a difficult pregnancy with me, and then she couldn't have any more children. That never seemed to bother Dad, but it sure bothered her.

"They never really fought that I know of, but there wasn't a whole lot of love, either. Still, that didn't excuse what he did. He'd made a commitment to her, and he didn't keep it—even though he must have known what his leaving would do to her."

"My mother could be very persuasive, Ben. And she was a terrible flirt. She actually flirted with several men I brought home to meet her, men young enough to be her sons. And when I told her about it, she honestly didn't believe she'd done it."

Ben nodded. "Yeah, I can believe that. She came to see me after I caught them, and she acted that way toward me, too. I've never come so close to hitting a woman in my life. She kept saying that she wanted us to be friends, as though she couldn't understand why I wouldn't want that, too."

"That sounds like her. The sad thing is that she really *didn't* understand. She had this crazy ability to disconnect any actions of hers from their consequences for others. When she sent me away to boarding school because her latest husband didn't like kids, she really convinced herself that it was *my* decision."

A silence fell between them as they sat there, wrapped in their private pain, wanting to say something but unable to find the words.

Then Ben stood up. "I'm going back to work for a while, if the noise won't bother you."

She stood, too, assuring him that it wouldn't. She knew he was seeking relief in the best way possible for him.

He paused at the doorway and turned to her. "I'm sorry, Jenny."

"Me too."

But neither of them was exactly sure what it was they were sorry for: the behavior of their parents, the mess they'd inherited—or the impossibility of their feelings for each other.

"READY FOR a lunch break?"

Jennifer turned over another clump of weeds to lay bare the dark earth below, then leaned on the spade and wiped her sweaty brow. As if on cue, her stomach rumbled loudly.

Ben laughed. "I'll take that as a yes." He held up a large bag. "My treat. Sherri and Tom made us some of their New York deli-style sandwiches."

"Are they still planning to move in next week?" she asked, wondering what having them here was going to do to her waistline. Of course, if she continued to work this hard, she could probably afford the extra calories.

"Uh-huh. Everything's ready for them. The electricians just finished putting in the new lines for the microwaves. And they've ordered new menus and business cards with the change of address. I drew a sketch of Victoriana on it for them."

He dug in his pocket and brought out a folded piece of paper with a pen-and-ink drawing of the inn. Beneath it, the name of their business, The Moveable Feast, was written in a lovely flowing script.

"That's really good. Did you do the script, too?"

He nodded. "I bought a book on calligraphy a couple of years ago."

She shook her head with a smile. "You really are a man of many talents, Ben Walters."

Her tone was light, but it faltered slightly as their eyes met. Things had definitely changed between them—but into what? The difference was subtle and difficult to put into words.

In some ways, they had become much closer, bound by their conversation last week, by sharing a painful history that hadn't been mentioned by either of them since that night. But in other ways they seemed further apart than ever. They spent their days working together companionably, but didn't see each other except for work. Ben was cautious; she was wary.

Jennifer had come to feel a great deal of anger toward Win for having used her as a means to punish his son unfairly. She also felt betrayed by someone she had once considered a surrogate father.

More than once she'd been ready to offer Ben half of Victoriana, but each time she'd drawn back. Not because she was unwilling to share it with him, but because she feared he would reject the offer—and her, as well.

The one thing she could not do was to give up the inn altogether. With each passing day, she fell more and more under its spell. She had never worked so hard in her life, and never before had her work seemed so worthwhile. Besides, if she walked away from Victoriana, she would be walking away from Ben.

One of the many ironies of her life just now was that while she was so very eager to see the work completed, when it was, either she or Ben would probably be gone. After consulting with Ben's attorney and the court, Wexford had told her that the matter would probably come before the judge in the fall session.

"Let's go down to the lake," Ben suggested as they walked back toward the inn. "Then, after lunch, you can look at some paint samples. We should be ready to start painting tomorrow, weather permitting." He gestured toward the side of the inn. "Let me show you what I have in mind now."

His crew had been scraping away the peeling paint, and he pointed to a spot near the end of the porch. "See that?"

She bent to peer at the spot, and then, as comprehension dawned, she straightened up quickly. "Oh, no! I don't care how authentic it is—it's horrible!"

Ben stood there looking at the spot, his dark head cocked to one side. "Oh, I don't know. Olive green with dark red trim might be kind of nice. And we *did* agree that we wanted everything to be authentic."

"You aren't serious, are you?" she asked warily. He certainly *sounded* serious.

"It's a shame color photography didn't exist back then, so we could see the full effect."

She didn't need a picture. She could imagine the "full effect" quite easily. "Did you find traces of the red trim, too?"

He nodded. "In a couple of places. They were definitely the original colors. Since then, it's always been white."

She stared at the spot in mute horror. *Was* he serious? Surely he couldn't be.

Then he burst out laughing. "Come on, let's eat. And just so I won't spoil your lunch, I agree that we'll have to compromise on this. It looks like the color of split-pea soup. I've hated split-pea soup since I was a kid. Even my dog wouldn't eat it—and he ate anything."

"Are you telling me that if you didn't have a thing against split-pea soup, the inn would be wearing it?"

"We could always replace the weather vanes with giant revolving soup cans," he suggested. "That might even get us into *Architectural Digest.*"

"Andy Warhol meets Victoriana. Sherri and Tom could get to work on a recipe for the house specialty."

"Let's not get carried away. I'm planning to eat here regularly."

Ben took her hand, and they started toward the lake, laughing. The gesture seemed so spontaneous and natural that she wasn't sure he realized what he'd done as he continued to talk about the Victorians' penchant for strange colors.

After days of cloudy weather and rain, this day had dawned bright and beautiful, with the warmest temperatures they'd had yet. The forest around them was redolent of damp earth and sharp, bittersweet pine. There was no place Jennifer wanted to be other than here in this place with this man.

The name for that feeling was whispering on the breeze: *love.* She glanced over at Ben and found him watching her with eyes as blue and warm as the sky above. His hand tightened briefly around hers, but he said nothing.

They sat down on the grassy slope at the edge of the lake. It had recently been mowed to a neat, if not exactly weed-free, carpet.

"You haven't mentioned our lady of the lake again," he said, gesturing toward the breeze-ruffled water.

"That's because I haven't seen her again. But I look each night."

Ben passed her a huge sandwich and a can of soda, then opened a container of kosher dills. "And there've been no more incidents," he said thoughtfully.

"No. I hope you're not suggesting that the two things are related," she said in a teasing tone.

He remained serious. "It's strange that whoever it was came just that one time—and did what he did."

She thought about admitting that there had been a second incident, but the longer they went without further problems, the more likely it seemed that she'd only imagined that one. The noises could have been any number of things, and she'd never been sure she'd seen anything out there in the darkness.

"Maybe the inn has more than one ghost after all," she said, in an attempt at lightness, "and it didn't care for my choice of wallpaper. The new paper has arrived, so I guess I'll find out when I put it up again."

She decided she was going to put it up tonight. When the wall was covered again, she could forget the entire incident. She knew the intruder couldn't have been Ben, but the memory of her suspicions came back to torment her every time she looked at the ravaged walls.

She looked over at him to find him watching her with an amused expression.

"You know, I thought your part in all this—besides the money—would be to walk around dressed for success, telling everyone else what to do. I never expected to find you scrubbing down walls or digging a garden."

"I'm not surprised. After all, you *did* call me a sophisticated snob, or some such thing."

"That's the way you looked to me, Ms. Jennifer Stansfield."

She smiled. "Well, to be honest about it, I never *have* done work like this before, so your image was pretty accurate. But I'm happier now than I've ever been."

Her last words came out without forethought, because they were the truth. But, once spoken, they hung there, taunting her. She knew just how ephemeral this happiness was—and how very dangerous it would be to believe it.

Ben said nothing for so long that she turned away from the lake to stare at him. His eyes searched hers for a long moment.

"You can't forget, either, can you?" he asked softly.

"No," she replied huskily, knowing immediately what he meant. Images of that night at his new house flooded her with a golden heat.

Ben put out a hand to smooth her windblown hair away from her cheek. His fingertips grazed softly against her skin in a slow, caressing gesture. She looked into his eyes and felt the force of his desire clear through to her feminine core.

"Ben, this—"

He silenced her, at first with gentle persuasiveness, and then with increasing demand. Their bodies flowed together as they sank slowly back onto the grass. A fire storm of raw, primitive passion engulfed them. Last time, there had been great tenderness; now the power of their mutual hunger swept it away.

Even as their lips and tongues dueled erotically and nipped at sun-warmed flesh, their hands were busy, slipping beneath T-shirts to find soft curves and hard planes that trembled in response.

He stripped off his shirt with an impatient gesture, then lifted hers, more slowly, pressing his lips to her stomach, trailing them slowly upward until he reached the thin barrier of her bra and dispensed with that, as well.

His arm slid beneath her, lifting her to him. She clutched his head with a moan as he took first one nipple and then the other into his mouth, leaving achingly sensitive nubs that pressed against his hair-roughened chest when he claimed her mouth once more.

The breeze shifted and carried to them voices and laughter from the inn, and they both slowly became aware of their surroundings, as though realizing for the first time that they shared this world with other people.

Ben propped himself above her. "What's going on here, Jenny?"

It was his tone she heard, more than his words. That wondering, plaintive note touched the same emotion in her, bringing back the tenderness between them, a tenderness that had been absent until now. But his words also reached deep into her fears.

"We can't let this happen, Ben."

"Do we have a choice?" he asked in a voice that was only half-teasing.

She took a deep breath and moved away from him, then reached for her bra and T-shirt. "We're both adults, and we have a lot of work to do. I think we'd better concentrate on that."

He said nothing, but when her trembling fingers refused to fasten the front clasp to her bra, he did it for her, then hooked a finger beneath her chin and forced her to look at him.

"You still don't trust me, do you?"

"I don't trust *either* of us."

"ARE YOU STILL planning to open up that tower room for her?"

Ben was surprised by Harry's question—especially since his uncle hadn't shown enough interest in the work to come out and see it. They were sitting on the front porch, drinking beer. Ben had been telling his uncle about Jennifer's herb garden.

"She hasn't mentioned it lately, and to tell the truth, I'd forgotten all about it. But, yeah, I'll get around to it one of these days."

"You're being a damned fool, Ben, doing all that work, when she owns the place."

Harry had said that before, and Ben gave him the same reply as before. "I'm being paid for it. Even if I don't win the lawsuit, it'll still be a great showcase for what I can do."

Harry eyed him suspiciously. "Are you getting soft on her, Ben? I'll admit she's a damned good-looking woman. Like her mother was."

Ben was surprised at Harry for taking that cheap shot. He drained his beer and stood up. "You know how it is with me, Harry. They come and they go."

Then, wincing at his own show of macho bravado, Ben announced that he was going in to take a shower.

But Harry's words followed him, taunting him, twisting through his guts. He wanted her so bad that it had become a constant, nagging pain. And he knew she wanted him just as much! All that garbage about a lack of trust between them was nothing more than a smoke screen. This had nothing at all to do with their battle over the inn. Let the lawyers fight that one out. This had to do with *them*.

He continued to think about her as he got of the shower and toweled himself dry. Okay, so maybe she had a point. He *had* set out to seduce her in the hope of persuading her to hand over Victoriana. But things had changed, and she ought to know that by now. He was content to let that battle play itself out in court.

When he dressed and went back downstairs, Harry was gone—probably over to visit his neighbor, a recently widowed man who was an old fishing buddy. Ben switched on the TV, then sat there and clicked his way through the channels, looking for something to take his mind off her. When he failed to find it, he thought about going out to get a video, then gave up that idea in favor of a Ludlum novel he'd just bought. He could lose himself in books far better than he could in TV or videos—and tonight he needed to get good and lost.

It worked for a time, but when Harry returned and started flipping through the channels to find a "Bonanza" rerun, Ben was unable to concentrate on the novel. He went out onto the porch and began to review the work schedule. They were making good progress, and they should be able to start painting tomorrow. Then he remembered that he hadn't shown Jennifer the samples. He'd have to do that first thing tomorrow morning, and then go get the paint.

He sat there in the quiet darkness as thoughts of work faded into thoughts of her—of the two of them down at the lake. He thought about the way she'd trembled slightly beneath his touch, her body only confirming what he already knew. He thought about her smooth, sun-warmed skin. He thought about the taste of her, the smell of her.

He was on his motorcycle almost before he realized what he was doing. He rode slowly and carefully in town, but when he reached the road that led to Victoriana he let out the throttle. The powerful engine throbbed beneath him, matching his pounding need.

JENNIFER WAS SMOOTHING the second strip of wallpaper into place when she heard the sound. It was distant, but growing steadily louder. Within seconds, she knew what it was.

By the time the single headlight swept past her window and vanished toward the back of the inn, Jennifer was completely immobilized by her tangled emotions. It was too late for him to be coming here to work; he *had* to be coming to see her.

She'd made a very big mistake when she'd told him she didn't trust *either* of them. She'd seen the evidence of that mistake written in his eyes, both down at the lake and several times during the afternoon. She'd made herself vulnerable.

The motorcycle's engine was cut off abruptly, and a few seconds later she heard the back door slam. All sorts of scenarios ran through her mind: highly rational explanations he would surely accept, accusations that he was still trying to seduce her into giving him the inn, even a cold insistence that she had no interest whatsoever in any relationship other than the one they had.

Then she heard his footsteps in the hallway, and the scenario shifted. Her gaze strayed toward the bedroom, and her thoughts simultaneously flew back to that afternoon at the lake. When he knocked on the door, her mind went blank, but her shaky legs still carried her across the room, and her clumsy fingers somehow managed to undo the two locks.

For a moment, the Ben Walters who stood there was the man she'd first encountered: dark and dangerous. His hair was disheveled, and he wore a dark brown leather jacket with brass zippers that gleamed in the light. His blue eyes devoured her. She actually took a step back, recoiling from the force of his gaze.

He reached into a jacket pocket and withdrew some paper strips. "The paint samples."

She dragged her eyes from his and stared at them, then looked up at him again to see the amusement in his eyes, the mocking look that told her that it was a stupid excuse, but they seemed to need one.

"Wouldn't it be better to look at them in daylight?" she asked.

He nodded. "It would."

A few seconds ticked away as she refused to pick up the implicit challenge. Then he gestured toward the wall. "Would you like some help with that?"

She nodded quickly, eager to find a reason for him to be here before they were both forced to be honest. "Thank you. I realized after I got started that wallpapering at night isn't a very good idea—especially with dark colors. I just wanted to get it done."

They worked smoothly together, cutting and fitting the paper. In the corner of the living room, the big grandfather clock ticked away the minutes. Their conversation was minimal, restricted to the job at hand. She kept waiting for him to demand an explanation of her statement at the lake, but he didn't.

With his help, the job was finished quickly, and they both stood back to admire the results. She picked up a catalog of fabric samples.

"Look at this. It's not a perfect match, but it's so close. I'm going to have the seat of this chair reupholstered in it, and have a cushion made for the window seat, too."

Even to her own ears, her voice sounded too rushed, too eager. He smiled. It was a surprisingly gentle smile, one she hadn't seen since that night at his house.

"I like what you've done with this place. Not just the apartment, but the rest of the inn, too."

"Thank you." She looked around at the lovely antique furniture, the jewel-toned Oriental rug, and her new plants.

"It's my first real home. Before this, I lived in hotel suites." She stopped abruptly and turned away to start cleaning up the mess they'd left. It wasn't really her home—it would be only if she lost him.

When they had finished cleaning up, she offered him some of the lemonade she'd made to celebrate the warm weather. When he said that would be fine, she went to the kitchen to get it.

"I didn't really come here to talk about paint samples."

She turned to find him standing in the kitchen doorway. Her legs felt shaky, and she leaned against the counter.

"Then why *did* you come?" she asked, striving for a light, teasing tone. Her heart was pounding crazily in her chest, and her words came out with a husky breathlessness.

"I wanted to see you." Then he shook his head. "No, that's not true. I just *want* you, period. And you want me."

She opened her mouth to say something, although she wasn't sure just what.

He held up a hand to silence her. "Don't tell me all the reasons it shouldn't happen. I don't want to hear them. We've both wanted each other from the beginning. Dammit, Jenny, I won't wait any longer for you to admit it."

They stood there for what seemed an eternity, his words hanging in the charged space between them. The faucet dripped, and she thought irrationally about how she'd forgotten to mention that to him. The old refrigerator clicked on noisily.

His impatience fed into her desire, stripping away her doubts and laying bare the truth of what he'd just said. She didn't move, because she wasn't sure her legs would support her, but finally, slowly, she nodded.

He came to her slowly—or so it seemed to her, because she was measuring time by the rapid beating of her heart. Then he raised a hand and rested the fingertips lightly against her cheeks. His thumb brushed softly over her lips. She felt them tremble slightly—or were those tremors coming from Ben?

"Tell me," he ordered softly.

She looked into those eyes that had captivated her from the beginning. "I want you, Ben," she whispered, her lips moving against his thumb.

She turned her face and kissed his fingertips and the callused palm of his hand. Now she *knew* he was trembling from the force of his need. He drew in his breath sharply and expelled it with a long, low groan that echoed in the silence as he picked her up and carried her to the bedroom.

The room was dimly lit by the light from the hallway as he lowered her onto the thick flowered quilt, then dropped down beside her. His lips came to hers softly, with all the sensual promise of carefully controlled desire. The soft quilt beneath her contrasted with his male hardness as his body covered hers.

Time spun out in a whirling kaleidoscope of sensations as his hands traveled slowly over her, searing the flesh beneath her suddenly constricting garments. Her nipples grew taut and chafed against the lace of her bra and the thin cover of her T-shirt. His fingers quickly discovered them, and his mouth followed, bringing her pleasure that bordered on pain.

She slid her hands beneath his shirt and felt tiny ripples run through his smooth, hard body as it reacted to the touch of her fingers and nails. And then it was she who was trembling as he lifted her T-shirt and let his lips and tongue roam over her heated flesh.

Suddenly, impatiently, he sat up and stripped off his shirt, then, more gently, removed hers. There was a moment of soft, shared laughter when he fumbled for a front clasp that wasn't there before reaching around to her back with hard, sure fingers. When the shirt and bra had been dispensed with, he propped himself up on one elbow and stared down at her, his thick, dark lashes half hiding eyes that were dark with passion.

"We've waited too long, Jenny," he said, in a low, husky voice that spoke of the torment of that waiting.

She murmured her agreement and, unwilling to wait any longer, reached up to pull his face down to hers for a long, hungry kiss. His hair-roughened chest met her satiny breasts and crushed the hard nubs that were already aching for his touch.

Jennifer arched to him as he trailed his mouth with exquisite slowness down along her neck and shoulders, taking forever to reach a rosy crest and tease it with his teeth and tongue. Need roared through her, demanding satisfaction now—and still he took his time.

When she finally reached in frustration for the waistband of his jeans, he pushed off the bed in a quick movement, then stripped off his remaining clothes, exposing to her fevered gaze the extent of his desire. He had a lean, hard body of sculptured muscles and curling dark hair that ran in a thin line from his broad chest to the swollen evidence of his manhood. A small, involuntary cry of primitive need escaped her lips as she stared at him.

"Yes...oh, yes..." he whispered as he sat down beside her and began easing her jeans and panties down over her hips, taking an excruciatingly long time about it as his lips followed his hands all the way to her toes. Then he tossed her clothes on the floor and continued to sit there, not touching her with anything but his gaze, which traveled slowly along her length.

When his eyes met hers again, white-hot passion flared between them, drawing sounds from them both. She pulled his mouth to hers and arched her body, bringing soft curves to hard muscles, silken skin to bristly hairs, female passion to male desire.

They were both fierce and gentle, demanding and giving. He filled her and she surrounded him, and they moved easily into the ancient rhythms, and together reached for and found that ultimate, shattering ecstasy.

"Do you really hate the name Jenny?" he asked huskily as he drew her against him afterward.

She laughed, surprised by the question. "Most of the time, yes. But I'm willing to consider making an exception."

He kissed her softly and smoothed her tangled curls. "Good. Jennifer's fine for my partner, but Jenny's the woman who's here now."

"Are we going to regret this in the morning, Ben?" she asked, feeling safe with the question now, as she lay there in his arms.

"Maybe. We can always tell ourselves that we fought it for as long as we could."

It was an honest answer—and probably an accurate one, as well. But morning seemed very far away, and regretting the magic they'd brought to each other seemed an impossibility.

Chapter Seven

Jennifer awoke to soft darkness and a memory of pleasure so intense that it rippled through her whole body. Ben's arm was curved across her, the hairs tickling the soft undersides of her breasts, and his hard, bristly leg lay heavily over hers, claiming a possession she could not deny. The only sound in the deep silence of the night was his slow, regular breathing, which fanned lightly against the back of her head.

It all felt so right. She closed her eyes, wanting to hold on to this feeling and then wake up to it all over again. But sleep wouldn't come; she was too aware of him now. She moved carefully, slipping away from him, half wanting him to awaken and half wanting to escape for a moment into her thoughts. He sighed softly, the sound bringing a smile to her as she climbed quietly from the bed to stand there and stare at the dark, gloriously male body tangled up in the softly glowing satin sheets.

After a few minutes, she put on her robe and went out to the living room, not wishing to disturb his sleep just yet. Later, perhaps, when the glow of past lovemaking rekindled the flames, she would slip in beside him and tease him awake.

The drapes were open, and bright moonlight poured liquid silver into the room, picking out the intricate pattern on the wallpaper they'd hung hours before. The room looked complete now, she thought happily. Then she realized that part of what she felt wasn't the wallpaper at all, but rather his presence here. She'd dreamed of having him here, but the dream had fallen far short of the reality.

She sank down onto the window seat, which was bare now, since she had thrown away the old cushion and hadn't yet replaced it. *Have I really fallen in love with him?* she asked herself wonderingly. *Is that why I have this ridiculous feeling that it will all work out somehow?* Or was it nothing more than a powerful chemistry between them, perversely made even stronger by the knowledge that it couldn't last?

All she knew now was that, whatever lay ahead, she would not, *could* not, regret this night that had brought magic into her life. A magician in a leather jacket had roared into her life on a motorcycle and shown her a passion she'd never felt before, laying claim to her body with a gentle fierceness that left her weak even now as she thought about it.

She turned around to stare out the window, where the full moon hung over the lake, bathing its dark waters in a bright, glowing light. Her mind drifted as she prolonged the moment before she would return to the bed, and to him. Morning, and everything it might bring, seemed very far off.

She drew in a sharp breath. It was there again! That strange, thin column of mist was moving slowly over the surface of the lake. She held her breath, as though merely by inhaling and exhaling she might disturb it. It stopped for a moment, before once more beginning its slow, sinuous movements, drifting briefly out of her line of vision and then reappearing. She stared at it, transfixed, then cried out as two arms circled her from behind!

"Sorry," Ben muttered thickly into her hair. "I missed you."

He slipped a hand beneath her robe, then started to turn her toward him. But she resisted, and pointed out the window.

"Ben, it's out there—on the lake! See?"

He leaned past her to peer out the window, his hand still lazily caressing her breast. "It's probably just mist," he said uncertainly after a long moment.

"But what if it's her, the ghost?"

He yawned and kissed the top of her head. "What do you want to do, go out and say hello?"

"Yes, now!"

He laughed. "I wonder where all this sudden bravery is coming from. Would you go out there if I weren't here?"

"No—but you are."

"I just wanted to hear how much I'm needed," he said dryly. "Is that the only way I'm going to get you back into bed?"

She got up and grabbed his hand, dragging him along behind her to the bedroom. "Where's your sense of adventure? Hurry, before it disappears!"

"I had a different sort of adventure in mind," he muttered as he began to pick through their discarded clothing. "It could be dangerous for me out there, you know."

"Why?"

"Well, if she's been wandering around for a hundred years looking for a man..."

"I see your point." Jennifer grinned. "But don't worry. I'll fight her off if necessary."

"That's what I like." He paused after zipping up his jeans to give her a kiss. "A woman who stands by her man. Do you have a flashlight?" he asked as they started out of the apartment.

"Yes, but we don't need one. The moon is bright enough. Besides, we don't want to scare her away."

"Right. It never pays to scare ghosts. I'm sure I must have read that somewhere," he responded dryly as they hurried down the stairs.

"Don't you realize what a boon to business it would be if there really *is* a ghost out there?" she asked. "Victoriana could become famous."

"Maybe we'd better ask her how she feels about that. She might be shy."

They left the inn and hurried along the path into the woods. In spite of the full moon overhead, it was dark beneath the trees. For the first time, Jennifer began to have some doubts about the wisdom of this nocturnal excursion.

"Oh, no," he said when she slowed down. "You don't drag me this far and then get cold feet." He tightened his grip on her hand and pulled her along. "Here come the ghostbusters!"

"I'm not sure you have the proper attitude, Ben. We should be approaching this from a business standpoint. What we want to do is persuade her to *stay,* not chase her away."

Their lighthearted banter came to an abrupt end when they

emerged from the woods into the clearing at the lake's edge. They stood there, staring, their grips tightening on each other's hands.

Moonlit water rippled slightly in the night breeze. Across the lake, close to the other shore, the thin, pale column still drifted slowly along the surface of the water, standing out in stark relief against the dark forest beyond.

They remained silent as they crept slowly toward the water's edge, hands still gripped tightly. Was the shape human in nature? It certainly seemed to have feminine curves—but it was so insubstantial, blurring at the edges now that they had gotten closer.

Jennifer felt awe rather than fear—although she knew that if Ben weren't there she might feel very differently. His hand gripping hers felt very reassuring.

They stopped near the old dock, their eyes still glued to the strangely luminous figure as it meandered along the far side of the lake, seeming barely to skim the dark surface. Then it moved in their direction, and they both tensed, the sensation traveling through their linked hands. Neither of them moved.

In the next instant, it was gone! There was no slow dissolution; the apparition was there one moment and gone the next. Still, they waited in silence for several minutes before either of them spoke.

"It *has* to be fog," Ben proclaimed, but his uncertain tone belied his words.

"How could it be fog, when there isn't any anywhere else?" she demanded, speaking, as he had, in a low, urgent tone. "Fog isn't that...specific."

"We don't know that for a fact. We're not meteorologists."

"I suppose it *could* be some sort of optical illusion," she admitted, still clinging to some skepticism herself. "Something brought on by certain weather conditions. You know, like those wet spots on the road in summer that aren't really there."

"That makes sense." Ben nodded. "I can buy that."

But their doubts were evident in the looks they gave each other. "Let's go back to bed. I prefer a real woman to a ghost anytime."

She laughed. "Thanks—I think."

BACK IN HER BEDROOM, Ben watched Jennifer as she undressed with just a hint of self-consciousness. When he'd awakened earlier to find her gone from the bed, he'd been sure that self-recriminations had begun. Now, as she cast him a quick glance, he wondered what was going through her mind.

She was probably thinking just what he was: that it would be better for them both if morning never came. He had no regrets, regardless of what happened in the future, but he *was* beginning to worry about a future without her, and he didn't like that thought at all.

He forgot about that future as she slid off her jeans and stood there somewhat uncertainly, clad only in a pair of lacy bikini panties. Completely naked himself, and totally aroused, he reached out and drew her to him, breathing in the soft scent that clung to her silken skin.

They tumbled together onto the disheveled bed. He held his pounding need in check as he covered her with kisses, moving slowly down across her firm breasts to her flat stomach, then pausing for one tormenting moment before going on to the firm warmth of her thighs. He could feel the heat and the wanting that arose from her, and the tension that thrummed through her like a bowstring drawn taut.

His own need was beating an incessant tattoo along his nerve endings, threatening to shatter his self-control at any moment. He wondered how long it had been since he'd wanted a woman this badly—especially since he'd had her only hours before. But any memories of other times and other women had faded into oblivion. It felt as though his very soul were crying out, begging for union with hers.

She reached for the waistband of her panties, but he grabbed her hands and pulled them away, imprisoning them above her head as he pressed against her, forcing his throbbing manhood against the flimsy barrier of lace again and again, while she writhed beneath him and whimpered her need.

Then he could stand it no longer, and he stripped off the final barrier—only to find himself abruptly pushed over onto his back as she used the moment to gain the upper hand. Her aggressiveness aroused him still more, making his need painful.

She brought her moist warmth tantalizingly close, then hovered there, almost but not quite enveloping him as she leaned forward to touch his lips with a teasing kiss.

Even in the dim light, he could see the triumph and laughter in her eyes—the certainty that she could outlast him in this sensuous game. She was right; he was in an agony of need. When he finally acknowledged that fact with a groan, she took him into her and enveloped him with her womanly warmth.

There was no slow, building rhythm of love this time; they had already driven each other too close to the edge. Instead, almost the moment their bodies were fully joined, they both fell away into the sublime abyss of pure sensation.

Afterward, as they lay curled together, drifting slowly off to sleep with murmured sounds of satisfaction Ben felt strangely unsatisfied. His body had been very well sated indeed; what was missing were the words that should have been there.

He wanted to tell her that he'd never felt this way before—and he wanted to know that it had been the same for her. He needed to believe that this night hadn't been merely an accident, a momentary surrender to a purely physical attraction.

But he said nothing, and neither did she—and he finally fell asleep without any answers.

JENNIFER AWOKE to morning sunlight filtering through the pastel-printed drapes to create a soft, hazy warmth. She smiled and drifted languorously through memories of the night just past, curving snugly against Ben's warmth.

Then her clock radio clicked on, and as the announcer's voice began to recite the first of the day's news, the memories began to fade. She tried to cling to them, but all she could remember clearly now was her own poignant question: "Are we going to regret this in the morning?"

Ben stirred beside her. "Turn that damned thing off," he muttered against her ear as his hand slid down across her stomach.

She wanted to. Oh, how she wanted to. She wanted to turn off the radio, and the day, as well. But it was too late. All the thoughts she'd held at bay so easily in the magic of the night were battering at the door of her consciousness.

She pushed his hand away and sat up in bed, smoothing her tangled hair away from her face. "Your crew and the kids will be here soon. Maybe we could say that I heard a prowler and you came over to stay in case he returned."

Total silence greeted that suggestion, so she finally turned to look at him. His darkness contrasted sharply with the pale peach sheets, emphasizing an essential maleness that needed no further definition. She felt herself sliding back into enchantment, away from the insistent voices of reality. His hooded gaze locked on to hers, and he shook his head.

"Why not?" she asked. "After all, there *was*..."

"We don't have anything to hide, that's why." His voice was still thick with sleep, but his tone had an implacability to it that separated him from the tenderness of last night.

"We don't?" she repeated incredulously. "Ben, you're not thinking clearly. The kids might not know about...the lawsuit, but surely your crew does. Everyone in town knows."

"So what?" he asked challengingly. "What does that have to do with *us*—with our being here."

"It's not right!" she stated angrily, unable to believe his obtuseness.

"Isn't it?" he asked harshly as she got out of bed. "Then why was it right last night, Jenny? And don't try to tell me it wasn't. The only thing that was wrong was how long it took for us to admit what's going on here."

He sat up in bed and ran a hand through his tousled hair. "Look, I know we've got some problems, but..."

She hurriedly put on her robe. "You're right about that at least," she said tightly. "We definitely have problems—and last night changes *nothing*."

BEN SLAMMED the back door of the inn and climbed onto his motorcycle. He was halfway to town before he began to think clearly. So last night changed nothing? Who did she think she was kidding? Was she planning to write it off as a little mistake—a one-night stand?

He knew damned well what had happened last night. Two people had found something neither of them had had before.

He'd been ready to admit that, too—before she cut him off. Hell, he'd almost been ready to tell her he *loved* her, and he'd never said that to any woman.

Right now, she was probably busy convincing herself that he'd seduced her. And even if he *had* once intended that, she should know better.

Ben didn't know yet what he was going to do about this situation, but he did know that she wasn't going to get away with kicking him out of her bed like that. He remembered how her body had quivered with passion, how his touch had ignited her— and he'd make damned sure *she* didn't forget it, either.

"THE HEARING has been set for two weeks from today."

"Do I have to be present?" Jennifer asked as a knot of dread formed inside her. It seemed surreal to her that the law could have been grinding away while she and Ben were making love.

The attorney said that although her presence wasn't mandatory, it would be expected. She made a note of the date and set up an appointment with him the day before to go over the details.

"Have there been any problems with Walters?" the attorney asked.

"No, everything's fine," she replied, stifling a bubble of near-hysterical laughter. Problems, Mr. Wexford? No, of course not— unless you count the fact that we just spent the night making love.

She hung up, wondering how on earth she could possibly face Ben as an adversary in two weeks. How could he deal with this? Was he really capable of separating this from what had happened between them?

She wondered if he knew about the hearing yet. The knot in her stomach became bigger and colder. Wexford had told her that the date had been set three days ago. He'd left a message for her earlier, and she hadn't returned his call, since she'd been toying with the notion of offering Ben a half interest in Victoriana. So Ben almost certainly knew about it—and had probably known before he came over here two nights ago.

Images of that night flashed through her mind. She couldn't believe that what they'd shared had been a sham—an attempt on his part to get her to give up Victoriana. She couldn't believe it now, even though she'd been convinced of it earlier. She couldn't believe it, even though she knew many stories of women being deceived in such a manner.

She couldn't believe it...and yet, she couldn't *not* believe it.

Ben had clearly been avoiding her for the past two days. She'd discovered that he was showing up early, before she went downstairs in the mornings, issuing instructions to his crew—and then vanishing. One of his crew told her he was working on his house, but she knew that what he was really ''working on'' was staying away from her.

She ate her lunch unenthusiastically, planning to spend the afternoon working on the herb garden. It was hard, demanding work that kept her mind off Ben and her tangled feelings for him. But by the time she had finished lunch, it was raining.

Casting about for something to keep her very busy, Jennifer thought of the crystal chandelier. She'd opened the box, and she knew that each piece would have to be cleaned before it was put together again. It sounded like a perfect rainy-day project, so after checking in with her cleaning crew, she went out to the carriage house with a supply of cloths, a pail of ammonia water and a bottle of polish for the brass frame.

She was about halfway through the tedious project when she heard the door behind her open. Ben! Surely it was him. Surely they could talk about this.

But it wasn't Ben. Such was her state of mind that for a moment she didn't recognize the man who stood there. Then she realized that it was Mr. Collins, Win's executor and old friend. She managed a smile that she hoped looked welcoming and started to get to her feet. He waved her back again.

''Don't let me interrupt you, Jennifer. I hope you don't mind me calling you that. It's a lovely name. We gave it to our own daughter.''

She assured him that she didn't mind at all. When he saw what she was doing, he began talking about the chandelier and about the work in general.

''I just spoke to Ben, and he said that the agreement between you two is working out just fine.''

Jennifer came very close to laughing about that, covering it by coughing and pretending to be bothered by the ammonia fumes. "Yes, it is," she said, lying for the second time this day.

"He said you've made some wonderful choices for redecorating. That's high praise coming from him, I must say. He's a very opinionated young man—especially when it comes to this place."

"We want the same things," she said, forcing down laughter once again. "After I'd chosen the wallpapers for the rooms, he told me that several of them were nearly identical to ones that had been in those rooms in his grandfather's time."

"Ah, yes, his grandfather. Now *there* was an interesting character. There's a lot of him in Ben. They were very close."

"Yes, Ben told me that."

He shook his head. "That man didn't mind making enemies, I can tell you that. In fact, there was a time when some folks thought he'd gone too far." He paused. "Well, I'd better be going. I just wanted to stop by to see how the work was progressing."

Jennifer had been paying scant attention to his words. She remembered how she'd hoped that Mr. Collins might be able to shed some light on the question of her inheritance.

"Mr. Collins, did Win—Edwin, that is—ever tell you why he left Victoriana to me, instead of to Ben?" She hurried on to explain that she hadn't known about Ben until she came here. But, to her disappointment, he shook his head.

"No, he never told me why. Edwin was my friend all our lives, but I won't pretend that I really understood him. He was a very complicated man. Also, I think, a very unhappy one. I always thought that something had happened when we were children—something he wouldn't talk about that had a very bad effect on him. I assume you know now that Ben and his father weren't on speaking terms for the last years of Edwin's life. They're both very stubborn men, but Edwin *did* try to reestablish contact with Ben. Ben, unfortunately, wasn't ready to listen."

"It's hard for me to see Win as being a vengeful man," Jennifer said. "But that's what he was doing when he left Victoriana to me. He certainly knew how much Ben wanted it."

"Well, as I said, Edwin was a complicated man whose mind could work in strange ways."

After he had gone, Jennifer sat there wondering if she'd made an essentially simple matter into something more complicated. Win had told her that he thought of her as a daughter, and despite his attempts at reconciliation, he'd lost his son. So he'd given to her what he would otherwise have given to Ben. It must have come down to that.

And yet he must have known that he was setting her up for a confrontation with Ben.

She turned back to her work, then remembered that Mr. Collins had said he'd just talked to Ben. Knowing she should let well enough alone, she nevertheless got up and walked over to the door, telling herself that it was time for a break, anyway. But the moment she stepped outside, she saw Ben's truck driving away.

JENNIFER RUBBED her aching head and got up from her desk in the spare bedroom to get an aspirin. She stared at her reflection in the bathroom mirror as though she might find some profound truth in her own eyes.

Was she in love with Ben? How did you know when mere attraction turned to love? Where was that important line—or did it even exist?

She hadn't been sleeping well, and she often seemed to herself to be slow and dull-witted during the day, drifting off in the middle of various tasks or finding herself wandering about the inn for no reason—other than the hope of encountering Ben, of course.

He was still here only rarely, supposedly using the current spell of good weather to work on his house. She'd thought more than once of confronting him over his absence, but what could she say? She could find no evidence that the work was suffering; his crew was highly competent.

In the week since they'd made love, she'd seen him exactly twice, and both times he'd disappeared quickly. Four evenings ago, she'd thought she heard his motorcycle approaching the inn, but if it *had* been him, he'd apparently changed his mind. And it was entirely possible that she'd only imagined it, since she realized that she'd been unconsciously listening every evening. So she'd bought herself a stereo and now played it constantly.

She knew she could call him and insist that they talk, but she didn't do it, because her own thoughts were too tangled. She sighed and returned to her desk, then realized that she'd left some important data downstairs. The computer for the inn had been delivered yesterday, and she'd taken her stacks of invoices and receipts down there to begin the process of transferring records from her own small computer—another task she'd failed to complete.

Walking along the dimly lit hallways still made her slightly uneasy and too much aware of her isolation, but as the weeks had passed without further incident, those fears had diminished considerably.

The lobby was dark, lit only by a small light just inside the entrance, and by the spillover from the bright exterior lights that had just been installed the day before. Faint aromas from the kitchen hung in the still air. Sherri and Tom, the caterers, had begun working from Victoriana four days ago.

She had almost reached the bottom of the stairs when she thought she heard a sound. Her fear edged up a notch or two, but didn't become real panic. The exterminators had been here and had gotten rid of most of the mice and squirrels, but she knew there could still be a few lurking around the place.

After listening to nothing but silence, she continued down the stairs and went across the lobby to the office suite behind the front desk. Then, just as she found what she wanted, she heard a sound again.

It seemed to be coming from the rear of the inn, probably the kitchen. She told herself that if she were a mouse, that was certainly where she'd be right now. Then it occurred to her that it might be Sherri or Tom. With the stereo on in the apartment, she wouldn't have heard them drive up.

Or it could be Ben!

Still, she was uneasy enough to move cautiously from the office to the short hallway that led to the desk. It was a dark area, since there were no windows, and the desk itself was tucked into a corner. When she reached the end of the hallway, where it opened out to the space behind the desk, she stopped—and then she heard what she was sure were footsteps.

She felt silly hiding there in the shadows, certain that at any moment Sherri or Tom or Ben would appear. But as she listened, she decided that the footsteps, which were coming closer now, were entirely too quiet. With the old, worn carpeting removed from the lobby, the wood floor made even the sound of sneaker-clad feet noisy.

Then the footsteps began to fade away. She was sure that whoever it was wasn't going upstairs, though. The stairs were bare, too, and several of them squeaked loudly. From the fading sounds, she thought he might be going toward the bar and library.

Could it be Ben? She knew he intended to begin work on those rooms soon. But why would he come so late, and why would he be sneaking around? He couldn't be worried about disturbing her, because the lights in her apartment were plainly visible. She could even hear the faint sound of the music from her stereo down here.

She thought about going back into the office and calling the police. But the lock on the office door wasn't working, and she knew how easily sound traveled in this huge, silent house. Anyway, what if she was wrong? What if all she'd heard were the usual sounds of an old building as it cooled down in the night?

She waited and listened and heard nothing more. Finally, she decided that she must have been mistaken. She stepped out of the shadows, slipped through the gate at the desk and hurried across the lobby to the stairs.

Halfway up, she heard another sound—and this time she *knew* it was coming from either the bar or the library. There was a strange sort of grating sound, followed by a muffled *thunk*. There was no way she could convince herself that it was either mice or simple building sounds.

Galvanized by fear and anger, she flew up the remaining stairs and down the hallway to her apartment. After closing and double-locking her door, she ran for the phone.

The police dispatcher assured her they would be there as quickly as possible and advised her to stay where she was, safe in her apartment. But after she hung up, anger got the better of her fear. What was the intruder up to? She thought about the old and possibly rare books in the library. Could he be planning to damage them this time? She was filled with rage that someone could want to wreak destruction on this place she loved. Then she thought about the gun she'd bought for just such an occasion.

Propelled by her anger, and secure in the knowledge that the police were on their way, Jennifer took the gun out of the drawer and then opened the apartment door cautiously. Seeing no sign of anyone, and hearing nothing now, she slipped out quietly and hurried down the hallway.

Angry as she was, she wasn't foolish enough to confront the intruder. But she knew he would attempt to flee as soon as the police showed up, and his only means of escape was the rear door—which meant he would have to come back across the lobby. There was a side door at the end of the hallway, where the bar and library were located, but it was still boarded up, as were the front entrance and the doors that led outside from the dining room.

She reached the upstairs landing and dropped into a crouch, knowing that she would be fairly well hidden by the railing. From there, she should be able to get a good look at him when he came through the lobby. She'd told the police to come around to the back, but it was certainly possible that he'd be able to escape before they got around there. In that case, at least she'd be able to provide them with a description.

The gun felt reassuringly solid in her hand, even though she had no intention of using it. She crouched in the shadows, waiting and listening. Then, after a few moments, she began to wonder if he might have left while she was in her apartment. It was a very frustrating thought. She wanted this person to be caught. She wanted to confront him and demand to know why he was invading her home.

Then she heard sounds again—footsteps, she thought. But it almost sounded as though they were coming from one of the rooms at the far end of the second floor. No, that was impossible. Or was it? He could have come upstairs while she was in her apartment.

She clutched the gun more tightly, aiming it in that direction and holding it with both hands now, in the grip she'd been taught to use. The dry, metallic taste of fear was in her mouth as she kept her eyes on the dimly lit hallway.

After a few more minutes, she heard faint footsteps again, then more sounds. They seemed to be coming from the library or the bar once more. She lowered the gun and relaxed a bit. She must have been mistaken about those other sounds. Given the fact that her heart was thudding noisily in her chest, and the fact that sounds tended to echo strangely in the big old inn, she decided that she must have been wrong about his being on the second floor.

Then, suddenly, the lobby was lit by headlights approaching in the driveway. Even though there were no sirens or flashing lights, she assumed it was the police. The lights grew brighter, then abruptly vanished as they drove around to the rear.

Jennifer kept her eyes glued to the dimly lit spot where the hallway from the bar and library opened into the lobby. She heard another sound—that same *thunk* she'd heard before—and she expected to see someone run out into the lobby at any moment. He had to have seen those lights or heard the car.

Soon there was a loud pounding at the back door, and a voice shouted, "Police!"—and still no one appeared. She ran quickly down the stairs and through to the kitchen, remembering her gun only at the last moment. Before opening the door, she hurriedly stashed it in a drawer. She wasn't sure what the police would say about her having it.

She let them in and led them quickly back through the lobby, confident that the intruder was about to be captured. They told her to wait there as they headed for the hallway, guns drawn, loudly announcing their presence.

Jennifer waited impatiently, but heard only the voices of the two officers. They returned to tell her that no one was there, and that the windows and the door were still boarded up.

They searched the entire place, top to bottom, after instructing her to wait in her apartment. She paced about impatiently, certain that they would find him hiding somewhere. But when they finally returned, they were alone.

"Well, Ms. Stansfield, I don't know what to tell you," the

younger one said. "We've searched the entire place. Maybe it was just mice or something. Old places like this can make strange noises."

"Did you check the locks on the windows upstairs?" she asked. "Maybe he escaped by jumping out a window onto the porch roof." She knew someone who had done just such a thing.

He nodded. "Checked every one of them—even the third-floor ones. They're all locked from the inside."

They were kind, but by the time they left, it was clear to Jennifer that they thought she was just a hysterical female.

She let them out the back door and thanked them, but offered no apologies. She knew darned well she hadn't overreacted, just as she knew those sounds couldn't have been mice or a creaky old building.

She returned to her apartment both tired and frustrated. She tried to think through everything that had happened, to see how he could have escaped—but after she'd gone over it too many times without an answer, she decided that she needed a clearer head than she had at the moment.

At least, she thought with a wry smile, they hadn't suggested that it might be a ghost. But how else could the intruder have escaped—unless he was capable of walking through walls?

HE COULDN'T FIGURE OUT how she had known he was there. He'd seen the lights on in the apartment and had heard her music playing. He was damned lucky he hadn't been caught by the police, although he supposed he could have talked his way out of it somehow.

For a while, he'd thought maybe he wouldn't have to do anything to get rid of her. The situation had seemed to be on the way to resolving itself, which suited him just fine. But lately things seemed to have changed.

From what he could see, he'd have to find some way of getting her out of there soon. Next time he'd just have to be more careful.

Chapter Eight

"Why didn't you call me last night?"

Jennifer turned and refocused her rather bleary eyes from the computer screen to the darkly frowning man who stood in the office doorway. How on earth had he found out? She'd decided that she wasn't going to tell him. She didn't need someone else thinking she was crazy—and she certainly didn't want him moving in.

Her gaze shifted briefly to the large canvas bag he was carrying, but he spoke before she could ask about it.

"I went to the diner for breakfast this morning and ran into Tim Stallworth. He's an old high school buddy, and he was just coming off duty."

Jennifer recalled that that had been the name of the younger officer, and belatedly remembered just how difficult it was to keep secrets in a small town—especially from someone who seemed to know everyone in it.

"I didn't see any reason to call you. They searched the place thoroughly and didn't find anyone." Her gaze flicked back to that bag, and she felt pulled in two directions at once. She wanted him here, but she feared the consequences.

Then Sherri suddenly appeared behind him. Her face was pale, and she held in her hand—with exaggerated care—Jennifer's gun.

"I found this in a drawer!" she cried. "It wasn't there yesterday!"

Ben took the gun from her, since it was clear that she expected it to fire of its own volition at any moment. Jennifer considered denying any knowledge of it, even as she cursed herself for having forgotten to take it back upstairs. But she was sure Ben would take it to the police, and then it would be traced to her.

"It's mine," she said, as casually as possible, avoiding Ben's gaze. "I'm sorry I scared you, Sherri. I thought I heard an intruder last night, and I had it with me when I went to let the police in. I was afraid they'd give me trouble about it, so I hid it in the drawer, and then forgot about it."

She continued to avoid looking at Ben as she made her explanation. But Sherri turned from Jennifer to him, and then apparently decided that her immediate presence was required in the kitchen. As soon as she left, Ben set the gun on Jennifer's desk then planted both hands on the desktop and glared at her. His eyes were glittering chips of blue ice, and it was all she could do to keep herself from backing away.

"Dammit, Jenny, I told you I'd move in here if you were afraid. Why did you go out and buy a gun?"

She considered telling him that she'd had it for years, but he probably knew the owner of the gun shop, too. Besides, it was obviously new.

She shrugged. "I bought it because it makes me feel more secure—and I *do* know how to use it. The man I bought it from showed me."

He made a sound of disgust. "Right. A half-hour lesson from Sam, and suddenly you're the reincarnation of Annie Oakley. Maybe you should have bought an Uzi. Were you planning just to blow this guy away yourself before the police got here? I'm surprised you even bothered calling them."

"Don't patronize me, Ben. I had no intention of going after him myself. I took it with me after I called them, because I figured that as soon as he heard them coming, he'd try to run out through the lobby, and I wanted to feel safe while I got a look at him."

She wouldn't have thought it possible, but his expression became even grimmer. "You mean you didn't stay in the apartment until they got here?"

"No, I didn't. I was afraid he'd escape before they got around back, and I wanted to be sure to get a look at him so I could give them a description.''

He backed away from the desk, but his expression didn't change. ''It really bothers me that you'd get a gun and not even tell me.''

''When I bought it, I wasn't sure that the intruder wasn't *you*,'' she stated angrily—and without thought.

''What are you talking about? You know damned well it wasn't me. You said so.''

She groaned inwardly, only now remembering that she'd never told him about the time she'd thought she saw someone in the driveway. So she explained what had happened, while he stood there frowning.

''Great, just great! Now is there anything *else* you haven't told me because you thought I might be working overtime as a burglar? Or are you *still* thinking that?''

''Don't be ridiculous, Ben!'' Her protest came quickly, because she didn't want to think it could have been him. But when she'd gone over the whole thing this morning...

''I want to hear this from the beginning. Tell me exactly what happened.''

So she recounted it all in careful detail, hoping he would be able to find the explanation she couldn't find—the one that would drive away her ugly suspicions.

''So, the only way he could have gotten in and out was through the back door, which requires a key to open it from either side. You locked it when the crew left, and then you locked it again when you let the police in, and took the key with you. I have my key, and Tom and Sherri have one. Maybe I'd better check to be sure they didn't lose theirs, or leave it lying around somewhere.''

He got up and left, and Jennifer found herself absurdly grateful that, unlike the police, he seemed to believe her. He was back in moments.

''They have theirs, and they definitely took it with them yesterday, because it's on the ring with the keys to their van.''

Jennifer sighed. ''Maybe it *was* just mice, or the inn itself, creaking.''

"You don't believe that, do you?" he asked, watching her intently.

She shook her head. "But I don't believe in ghosts, either—and that's the only other explanation I can come up with." Except, she thought, for one I don't want to think about.

"I'm moving in as of tonight, Jenny." He gestured toward the gun. "Now go put that damned thing away."

"Don't you think you might be overdoing the protective-male bit, Ben?"

He stood up, then planted his hands on the desk once again and leaned toward her. "Yeah, maybe I am. I tend to get that way when I've made love to a woman." Then he straightened with an exaggerated shrug. "It's probably just hormones. You'll have to humor me."

He turned and walked out before he could see the flush that had crept into her face. But then he suddenly reappeared, and she saw something flash briefly in his eyes.

"I'll be taking that suite next to your apartment, by the way."

"JENNY, IT'S BEN! Don't get trigger-happy!"

Guiltily she drew her hand away from the desk drawer and called out to let him know she was in the office. She'd been so lost in her work that she hadn't even heard him drive up. Or maybe she'd actually dozed off, she thought as she glanced at her watch and then saw how little she'd accomplished.

Then he was there in the doorway, smiling at her, and she felt that warm, curling sensation, which was certainly enhanced by the knowledge that he would be staying here—so close, so *dangerously* close.

"Still crunching numbers?" he asked, glancing at the computer.

"Yes. You're doing a good job of staying within your estimates. I wish I could say the same for myself." She paused. "We need to talk about that."

"Talk about what?" He shrugged. "It's your money."

"Yes, but it could be yours to pay back if you win your suit." She didn't want to talk about this—not now, not ever. But the hearing was drawing ever closer. Besides, with him moving in, she needed some way of keeping their relationship on a professional basis—and of holding her wayward thoughts at bay.

"Have you had dinner yet?" he asked, ignoring her words.

"No, I—"

"Good. Let's go get some pizza. Get yourself a jacket or sweater." He was gone before she could respond.

She went upstairs and did as he'd told her. It seemed warm enough inside, but perhaps the evening air hadn't cooled the place down yet. She told herself that she was going along with this because she was determined to raise the issue of the lawsuit. But the truth was that after days of catching only brief glimpses of him and knowing he was avoiding her, she wanted to be with him—period.

He was waiting for her in the lobby, and they walked through the silent inn to the back door. Then she saw his motorcycle parked next to her car.

"We'll take my car," she stated firmly.

He unfastened one of the helmets attached to the motorcycle and handed it to her. "No, we're taking my bike."

"Ben, I don't like motorcycles. They're not safe."

"Living out here alone isn't safe, but you've been doing that. And sneaking around with a gun instead of waiting for the police isn't exactly safe, either," he said, plopping the helmet on her head before donning his own.

"Do you promise not to go fast?" she asked, not budging when he took her arm.

"Motorcycles fall over when they go too slow," he said as he lifted her off her feet and settled her onto the back of the bike.

It took perhaps two minutes for Jennifer to forget her fears. With her arms wrapped around his waist and her face pressed close to his back, Jennifer forgot about everything except the pleasure of being close to him and flying through the darkness. When they came to a stop at the intersection with the main road, he looked back and grinned at her.

"Well, you haven't crushed my ribs yet. Does that mean you like it?"

She laughed and nodded, but didn't tell him what it was that she *really* liked about it. Being close to Ben made her feel whole again—a feeling she'd known only once before, when they'd made love.

He took a series of back roads unfamiliar to her, largely bypassing the town itself. She clung to him and felt his warm, hard body and relived every moment of their lovemaking. Motorcycles were dangerous, all right—but in a different way from what she'd imagined.

The pizza place turned out to be a noisy, crowded bar on the edge of town where classic rock blared at nearly painful levels. Ben seemed to know everyone in the place, and they were quickly invited to join a group at a large table. He introduced her, but she wondered if they already knew who she was. Surely they must.

Although she was convinced that Ben had deliberately brought her here to avoid any serious discussion, Jennifer herself was only too eager to go along with his scheme. The pizza was good, the people were interesting, and it had been a very long time since she'd allowed herself to relax like this.

When Creedence Clearwater Revival's "Bad Moon Rising" poured from the huge speakers, Jennifer found herself moving with the heavy beat, and Ben pulled her up from her seat and led her to the dance floor. Pressed together by the crowd, they moved to the pounding rhythms, staying there through another Creedence song and two Fleetwood Mac tunes. Jennifer hadn't danced like this in years. She'd nearly forgotten how good it felt, how sensual the heavy rhythms could be as they vibrated through her.

As they touched, moved apart, then touched again, Jennifer was aware of nothing but the music and their bodies. When the slow, sad rhythms of the Righteous Brothers' "Unchained Melody" came on, Ben drew her into his arms.

"The perfect song for two people who went chasing after a ghost in the middle of the night," he murmured against her ear.

She laughed softly against his shoulder. *Ghost* was a dumb movie, but she'd liked it. She thought about the plot—lovers separated forever—and felt tears welling up in her eyes. She loved him; she couldn't deny that any longer. But who was this man she loved? Was he being torn apart by their situation, as well, or was it all part of a scheme?

She felt his mouth on her hair, gliding slowly toward her ear, then teasing it softly with lips and tongue. The dance floor was still so crowded that they could do little more than sway in place, which was probably just as well. Jennifer felt heavy with desire, and too weak to stand on her own, let alone dance.

"Tired?" Ben asked when the song had ended. His arm was still around her as they made their way back to the table.

"No," she said quickly. In truth, the pizza and beer and the music and noise *were* making her tired, but she needed some time to think before they left here and went back to the inn. She needed to persuade herself that making love with him again would be a very big mistake.

"Good," he said, glancing at his watch. "We can leave in about a half hour."

When she gave him a confused look, he gestured toward the pitcher of beer on the table. "I want to be sure I'm safe," he explained. "I lost a good friend a few years ago in a drunk-driving accident."

She had noticed that he'd switched to soda some time ago, and was grateful for that. For all that she'd heard about him, she had yet to see any sign of irresponsible behavior on his part. Somehow he preserved the image of wildness without the reality—and that, she knew, was part of his appeal.

The reformed rake, she thought with a smile, recalling all the romances she'd once devoured. Every woman's dream. *Dangerous* was the first word she'd applied to him, and it still fitted. But he made her feel something she'd never felt before—something she feared she could no longer live without.

The ride home through the cool night temporarily banished her tiredness, and clinging to him with the engine throbbing beneath them only heightened her own throbbing need. When they reached the inn, Ben pulled up in front of the carriage house.

"I'm going to park the bike in here—and my truck, too, when I get it tomorrow. That way, if he comes back, he'll think you're still here alone."

Such was Jennifer's state of mind at the moment that she didn't immediately understand what he was talking about. But thoughts of the intruder led to thoughts of their situation, and she felt herself drawing back from the edge of insanity.

Still, when they paused outside the door of her apartment, she was remembering that hard, bronzed male body entangled in her pale satin sheets.

"I'd like to have the gun."

She stared at him, startled by the words that brought her erotic thoughts to an abrupt end. His expression became grim.

"Dammit, Jenny, I just can't believe that you still don't trust me, after—"

"I *do* trust you, Ben," she said hurriedly before he could make another reference to their lovemaking. "I was just surprised you'd want it, that's all. I'll get it for you."

She unlocked the door and went in, going directly to the bedroom. When she retrieved the gun from the drawer of the night-stand and turned, he was standing in the doorway. His eyes met hers, held them for a long moment, then shifted very deliberately to the bed beside her.

Hot desire roared through her. Her flesh tingled with the memory of his touch, the way his hands and lips had turned her entire body into a sensual playground, the way his own hard body had trembled.

He put out his hand, and she had taken a few steps toward him before she felt the weight of the gun in her hand. She handed it to him.

They both paused at the apartment door. Jennifer knew that one word from her and they would be in there again, lost in that world he'd created for her.

"Good night, Ben—and thank you. I had fun."

He reached out to comb her tangled curls with his fingers. The intimacy of the gesture made her catch her breath. "I know you did."

His gaze slid toward the bedroom, then came back to her again. In his eyes she saw her own desire reflected back at her. Then he leaned forward slowly, letting his lips hover just inches from hers for a heart-stopping moment before he claimed them with soft persuasiveness.

They were standing in the open doorway, and his arms were braced on the frame, his body surrounding but not touching hers as his lips and tongue teased hers. It was, she knew, a very deliberate torment—giving her only part of what she wanted, while withholding the rest until she acknowledged her need.

And then, just as she was about to arch into him, to ask him to stay, he withdrew, his eyes glittering with the knowledge that he'd broken through her resistance.

"Good night, Jenny. Sleep well."

BEN PUT THE GUN in a drawer, wanting to get it out of his sight. He'd inherited his father's dislike of guns—an unusual feeling in an area where most men hunted. No weapons had ever been kept in their home, and Ben's only experience with them had come from target shooting with friends in high school. The truth was, he thought with a chuckle, Jennifer was probably a better shot than he was.

He stared at the wall separating them. Did he want her more than he wanted Victoriana? That question kept sneaking up on him lately, ever since his lawyer had called to tell him they were about to start the legal battle.

All he knew at this point was that he didn't want to talk about it, while she apparently did. He'd shut her up effectively tonight, but only for tonight.

What was really bothering him—apart from the fact that he was here and she was there—was that he now realized just how much Victoriana meant to *her*. He hadn't expected that. He'd thought she saw it only as a challenge for her talents. But now he was sure that when she saw the inn, what she was really seeing was a home, in the deepest sense of the word.

That certainty had forced him to wonder just why he wanted it so much. He'd never questioned that before—it was his heritage, after all. But now he thought that maybe the real reason he was fighting for it had less to do with Victoriana itself than with his father.

He stripped off his clothes and got into bed—plain white sheets, not those pale satiny ones on her bed, sheets that were as soft as her skin and smelled faintly of flowers.

He lay there tormenting himself with images of her climbing naked into that bed, or maybe wearing some lacy nothing he could take off very slowly while he—

He started to get out of bed again, seeing himself pounding on her door, demanding that she let him in because he knew she wanted him as badly as he wanted her.

Then he fell back with a groan. No, dammit, surely he could control himself better than that. The next move was up to her. *She* was the one who'd said it had been a mistake—so she was the one who would have to correct it.

BEN WAS FITTING the final piece of the intricately carved trim around the corner of the porch when he heard a car approaching. He turned to see an unfamiliar vehicle come to a stop in the circle.

The man who got out was tall, lean and gray-haired, and looked as though he'd just stepped out of an executive boardroom in his conservative pin-striped suit. He even had a handkerchief in his breast pocket—something Ben couldn't recall ever having seen except in magazines and movies. As he started to climb down from the ladder, he had a sudden premonition about the stranger's identity.

"Good afternoon," the man said, in a smooth, polished voice that had traces of a British accent. "Could you tell me where I can find Jennifer Stansfield? I'm her father."

Ben wiped his hand on his jeans before extending it. He doubted she was expecting this visit, since she hadn't said anything.

Ben introduced himself and saw a quick flicker of recognition in the man's eyes. But his grip was firm, and his smile was pleasant.

"Ah, yes, you're Edwin Walters's son, then?"

Ben nodded, belatedly remembering that the man was a professional diplomat. "Jennifer went into town to pick up some wallpaper. She should be back soon. Is she expecting you?"

"No, I just decided to pay her a visit, to see how her project was coming along." He gestured toward the inn. "A wonderful old place, just as she said. Do you mind if I have a look around while I wait?''

Definitely a diplomat, Ben thought. "No, go right ahead. Things are still pretty much of a mess inside, but we're making progress." He couldn't quite resist putting just a hint of emphasis on the "we." He assumed that since Stansfield knew who he was, he must also know about the lawsuit.

When he'd gone inside, Ben climbed back up the ladder and finished his work. Then he went into the house. He was curious about Stansfield, since Jennifer had said so little about him, and the few things she *had* said had painted a pretty grim picture.

The lobby was empty. After checking the dining room and kitchen, Ben found him in the library, examining the old books in the glass-fronted case. He turned when he heard Ben approaching.

"This looks like an interesting collection. I wouldn't be surprised to find that some of these books are quite valuable."

Ben nodded. "We've talked about them. I think Jenny plans to have someone come to appraise them."

Stansfield looked surprised for just an instant, and at first Ben couldn't imagine why. But then he realized that he'd called her Jenny, and she'd said she hated that name.

"I have an old friend who's a collector. We went to Andover and Yale together. I'll speak to Jennifer about him. He has a home up here somewhere, so perhaps he could drop by when he's in the area. That way, you'd be sure to get an honest appraisal."

Ben noticed the man's use of "you," instead of "she." Andover and Yale. Well, what had he expected? He became even more uncomfortably aware of his own appearance, then got mad at himself for even thinking about it. He wasn't auditioning for anything with this guy.

Stansfield was staring up at the frescoes. "Those are very good. It's too bad that one in the corner has been ruined."

"I plan to restore it, and clean the rest of them," Ben told him.

The older man turned to him in obvious surprise. "You've done that kind of work before?"

Ben nodded.

"Well," Stansfield said, appraising him as though for the first time, "that's quite a talent. Jennifer told me that you specialize in restoration work, but I hadn't thought it would extend to something like this."

"You learn to become a master of all trades in this business. That's what I like about it."

They returned to the lobby, where, to Ben's surprise, Stansfield displayed what appeared to be genuine interest in the other repairs, and also showed a fair amount of knowledge as they discussed Ben's woodworking equipment.

"I'll be retiring in a few more years," Stansfield told him. "And I've been thinking about buying an old place like this and trying to fix it up myself. Of course, it would take much more than my present readings on the subject to make me as skilled as you are, but I can understand how this work appeals to you—and to Jennifer, too, of course."

As they continued to talk, Ben could sense that he was being sized up, though very discreetly. It became obvious to him that Stansfield was trying to elicit information from him regarding his relationship with Jennifer. At one point, he asked if Jennifer was living in the apartment yet, and Ben said that she was.

"I hadn't realized how isolated this place is," Stansfield said. "It seems to me that it isn't good for her to be here alone at night."

"I'm living here, too," Ben said. He thought about adding that he was staying in one of the suites, but decided instead to see what sort of response his admission got from the man.

"Oh? Well, I'm glad to hear that. Not that Jennifer isn't capable of taking care of herself, of course. She always has been."

A silence fell between them, and Ben could almost hear Stansfield's wheels spinning as he tried to think of a way to find out if they were living together. Before he could decide whether or not to answer the unspoken question, Jennifer appeared.

"BEN, wait until you see this wallpaper! It's—" Jennifer stopped and stared in disbelief. "Father!"

She was stunned, not just to find her father here, but also to find him deep in conversation with Ben. Furthermore, they appeared to be on very friendly terms.

The next few moments consisted of awkward conversation on her part as she tried to offset the looks Ben was giving her by behaving as though they were no more than the business partners her father believed them to be. What would he think if he knew the truth about her relationship with a man she'd told him was practically a criminal—and who was trying to take Victoriana from her?

But it was clear that Ben was not about to cooperate. Between the looks he gave her and his use of the name Jenny—a name her father knew she hated—he undermined her efforts to whitewash their relationship at every turn. And yet she knew that if she was to confront him about it, he would claim in perfect truth that he'd said nothing.

When she had gotten her father up to her apartment, he took the first opportunity to bring up the subject of Ben. "He doesn't seem to be quite the ne'er-do-well I'd understood him to be, dear. In fact, he's a very talented young man."

"Uh, yes, he is." Not to mention devious, and a few dozen other things, she thought, wondering just what Ben had done or said to impress her father.

"Is there any chance you can work out your legal differences amicably?"

That was a loaded question if Jennifer had ever heard one. As the daughter of a diplomat, she'd learned long ago to read between the lines of conversations like this.

"That doesn't seem likely," she told him. "In fact, we have a hearing coming up in two days."

"Oh? Well, I must say that the two of you seem to be getting along rather well under such circumstances."

"We've just learned to separate our working relationship from the lawsuit," she replied, then quickly changed the subject.

They went out to dinner, and Jennifer found Ben's name creeping into the conversation several more times. Even her father's reference at one point to her "settling down" here seemed to have a double meaning.

She simply could not believe that her father would approve of

Ben, even if the lawsuit didn't exist. In the past, he had on a number of occasions introduced her to young men who were carbon copies of himself: rising young stars on the diplomatic circuit. She hadn't been interested, but it had seemed rather clear to her that he expected her to marry such a man someday. Fathers, she knew, had a tendency to think their daughters would surely want to marry someone much like themselves. And she could think of no one *less* like her father than Ben Walters.

He had chartered a plane to carry him back to Washington, where he had meetings the next morning, so they parted outside the restaurant, and Jennifer drove slowly back to the inn. As always, she felt anger with him for his very belated interest in her, and then anger with herself for feeling that way. How many times over the years had she vowed never again to let anything either of her parents did upset her?

By the time she got to Victoriana, her thoughts had shifted back to Ben. Seeing the two of them together, even for those brief moments, pointed up the contrasts between the two men and made her realize why Ben appealed to her so strongly.

They were complete opposites. Her father was distant, never openly affectionate, seeming always to live in his mind. Ben, on the other hand, was earthy and passionate in every way, a man like no other she'd ever known—and a man she quite possibly loved.

As she went upstairs, she thought about confronting him and demanding to know what he'd talked about with her father. But no good could come from that. It didn't take much guesswork to see just where such a conversation *could* lead.

But before she had unlocked her apartment, Ben opened the door of his suite next door. He was shirtless and fresh from the shower, his dark, wet hair curling against his head. The scene could scarcely have felt more intimate if she'd found him in her bed.

"Where's your father?"

"He left. He had to be in Washington in the morning, so he chartered a plane." She stopped fumbling with the lock, even though what she wanted to do was to run into her apartment and put a solid door between them. "You certainly must have impressed him," she said coolly.

He gave her that lazy half smile of his. "I've gotten better at that over the years."

"What's that supposed to mean?"

"Just that there was a time when fathers definitely weren't impressed. Not that I can blame them." He chuckled. "If *my* daughter got involved with someone like I was, I'd be anything but pleased."

"Just why did you find it necessary to try to impress *my* father?" she asked, knowing that she was doing exactly what she'd just been telling herself she wouldn't do.

He leaned against the door frame and continued to smile at her. "Maybe because I thought it was important."

She had no intention of asking him why. Instead, she put the key into the lock. But before she could open the door, his hand closed over hers.

She could feel the heat from his body, could smell the shampoo he'd used. She stared at the corded muscles of the arm that rested against hers.

"Don't you want to know why I thought it was important?" he asked, his voice low and teasing.

"No, I don't." She turned the doorknob and pushed the door open, then stepped past him. "Good night, Ben."

Before she could close the door, he added one last torment. "Sleep well, Jenny. If you can."

SOMEHOW, she'd thought this day would never come, and now that it had, she was completely unprepared for it. It seemed unreal to be sitting here in her attorney's conference room, with Wexford at her side and Ben and his attorney across the polished table.

Neither she nor Ben spoke at all. The attorneys dueled politely, going over various points of the suit. Wexford had explained to her the day before that the purpose of this meeting was for each side to "discover" what the other had in the way of evidence.

Wexford presented the deposition from Win's attorney and friend, and Win's medical records, including a statement from his primary doctor to the effect that his mental functions remained unimpaired. He'd warned her that Ben's attorney might have evidence that disputed that, and he did.

Jennifer was given a copy of a deposition from one of Win's nurses, in which she stated that she had observed him to be impaired in his thinking and unable to communicate clearly several times. She also attested to the fact that Win had said Ben's name on numerous occasions, including at least once in the presence of Jennifer's mother, who had said to him, "Don't think about Ben now."

On and on it went. Ben's attorney said they were prepared to bring in expert medical testimony regarding the effect of strokes on the mind that could counter the statement of Win's own doctor. And he cited case law showing that in such cases, judges and juries often accepted the word of nurses over the word of doctors, because of their greater knowledge of the patient's behavior.

Jennifer felt sick—literally sick. At one point, she thought she would have to excuse herself and leave the room. And when Ben's attorney raised the subject of her mother and her previous marriages and divorce settlements, she felt ready to explode.

She had been looking down at the papers before her on the table, and she belatedly realized she must have missed something, because suddenly Ben and his attorney got up, excused themselves and left the room. She turned questioningly to Wexford.

The attorney shrugged. "A disagreement between attorney and client, it seems. That happens. Are you all right, my dear? I know this is hard on you."

Jennifer could hear voices in the hallway, though she couldn't make out any words. But Ben sounded angry. The only word she *did* hear clearly from him was "No!" repeated several times.

"I've seen young Tony get carried away before," Wexford said of Ben's attorney. "It appears to me that Ben didn't want the subject of your mother raised."

There was a question implicit in his words, but Jennifer didn't respond. At some level, she felt gratitude toward Ben—if in fact that was the case—but she was too sick over the proceedings to pay much attention.

They returned to the room and took their seats, and for the first time since they'd walked in here, Jennifer's eyes met Ben's. A chill went through her. She felt as though she were staring at a stranger. She'd become so used to seeing the unmistakable gleam of desire in those blue eyes that its absence made him into a different person.

Somehow she got through the rest of it. The subject of her mother was not raised again. Wexford asked her to stay when the other two left, then went into his office to take a call. Jennifer got up from her seat, not at all surprised to find her legs shaky as she walked over to the wide windows.

In view of what she'd learned today, and knowing that Ben knew all about her mother's less-than-exemplary past, she understood far better than she had before how Ben could believe that his father had been pressured into leaving Victoriana to her. She was half willing to believe it herself, despite the fact that Win had tried to persuade her to come here for years.

Ben and his attorney appeared in the parking lot one floor below. The attorney was gesturing and talking, and Ben was shaking his head. Finally the attorney got into his car and drove off, but Ben stood there for a moment, then raised his head and looked up at the window where she stood. For a long moment, they stared at each other—and then he got into his truck.

JENNIFER WALKED into her office and nearly collided with Ben, who was just leaving. They backed away quickly, glancing at each other and then averting their gazes.

"I left some invoices for you," he said, gesturing toward her desk.

She merely nodded, making as wide a circuit as possible past him to the desk.

"I should have the plasterwork around the chandelier finished by tomorrow or the next day," he went on. "Then I can hang the frame for you, and you can start putting it together."

She nodded again, although she was surprised. He had told her earlier that he had several other things to do before he would get to the plasterwork in the lobby.

"I'm going to start on the gazebo next week," he said.

"Oh? I thought you said that could wait until everything else is finished."

"Uh, well...I changed my mind. I figured I should take advantage of the good weather while we have it."

He left hurriedly, and she sat there, staring after him. The chandelier and the gazebo were the two things that interested her most. Was that why he'd moved up the schedule on both of them? Was this some sort of peace offering?

The week since the hearing had been pure hell, filled with polite, stilted conversation when it was absolutely necessary, and careful avoidance when it wasn't. Somehow they managed not to see each other for entire days, including the evenings. And when they were together, the tension was so powerful that it seemed a tangible presence in the air between them.

But their avoidance of each other seemed to have created a sort of telepathy between them, making each of them more aware than ever before of the other's attention.

Two days before, Jennifer had been watering the herb garden, for once not thinking about Ben at all as she happily tended the growing plants. And then, suddenly, she'd felt his eyes on her, igniting that self-awareness and aching desire that only he could create in her. And when she turned, she'd seen him on the porch roof.

For a long moment, they'd stared at each other, too far away to see into each other's eyes. The safety of distance.

And yesterday, when she was in one of the rooms upstairs, she'd looked out the window to see him standing in the driveway, talking to the electrical contractor who was installing the driveway lights. Believing herself to be safe, she'd let her eyes feast on him: his thick, dark hair, ruffled by the breeze, his long, lean body, his characteristic pose, with his hands jammed in the pockets of his jeans.

Without warning, he had turned and lifted his head to stare directly at the window where she stood—caught, it seemed, by the force of her thoughts.

It couldn't go on like this. Perhaps he knew that, too, and that was why he'd changed his mind about the chandelier and the gazebo. If he was attempting to give her a peace offering, it was time for her to make one, too.

But what did she have to offer? Her thoughts went back to the notion of trying to end this impossible situation by offering him half of Victoriana. Before, she'd been afraid he'd reject both the offer and her. But she had nothing to lose now.

She was still thinking about it that evening as she sat on the porch. The lovely wicker furniture she'd ordered hadn't yet arrived, but she'd bought an inexpensive chaise so that she could enjoy the pleasant evenings.

The truth was that even if she retained sole ownership of the inn, it would never be truly hers. Ben would always be here—in the work he had done. She had only to raise her eyes to the freshly painted gingerbread trim to know that. To be sure, she had made her mark on the place, with her careful selections of wallpaper and paint shades, and the herb garden that was rapidly becoming her pride and joy.

It belongs to *us*, she thought. She could only hope that he would see it that way, too.

It was nearly dark when she heard and then saw his motorcycle, but she didn't know if he'd seen her in the shadows on the porch as he roared past and parked in the carriage house.

She got up from the chaise and started down the steps, her heart thudding noisily in her chest and her brain still struggling to find the best way to approach the subject. Despite her earlier statement to herself, she *did* have something to lose. His rejection would still hurt—probably worse than she could imagine right now.

"Ben."

He had started toward the back of the inn, and he stopped when she called out. She stopped, too, frightened now that she'd taken the first step, but determined to go through with it.

"There's something I'd like to talk to you about."

He hesitated just long enough for her to feel the force of rejection, then nodded. "Okay. Let me grab a quick shower first and I'll be down."

The longest fifteen minutes she'd ever spent ended when he

appeared, seating himself on the edge of the porch, a beer in his hand.

"What did you want?" he asked in a neutral tone.

She took a deep breath and fixed her gaze on the porch post just above his head. She'd rehearsed a speech, but what came out wasn't what she'd intended.

"I can't take any more of this, Ben. We've been treating each other like strangers."

If she was embarrassed by her plea, she was reassured by the bleakness in his tone when he responded. "Yeah, I know." He hesitated. "Jenny, I'm sorry about that business with your mother. I'd told Tony I didn't want to get into that, but he brought it up anyway."

She didn't want to talk about the hearing; she couldn't stand to think about it.

"I know you said that you wouldn't settle for less then full ownership, and I can understand that. But I love this place, too. Couldn't we compromise?"

"Compromise?" he echoed, his expression unreadable in the shadows.

"Yes. Would you accept a half interest?" When he said nothing, she hurried on. "We've proved that we can work together, and I can't imagine that you want to run the place when it reopens. Victoriana belongs to *both* of us, Ben."

She held her breath as she waited for his response, and with every second that passed she became more and more certain that he was going to reject her offer. But when he finally did speak, his voice was low and musing, and his words were unexpected.

"I've thought a lot about why I'm fighting for it. Part of it is because it's always been in the family. But I think that mostly it's because I wanted to get back at Dad for what he did, whether he knew he was doing it or not."

He sat there in silence for a moment longer, then got up. "Let me think about it." He walked down the steps, then stopped.

"I know how you feel," he said.

He disappeared into the darkness, but his final words lingered in the night air against the backdrop of the ever-present katydid symphony. What had she *really* offered him...and what feelings did he understand?

Chapter Nine

Ben had become so good at avoiding Jennifer these past couple of days that he was startled to see her come out of the back door just as he came around the corner of the inn. She glanced his way briefly, then got into her car and drove off. He frowned. Where could she be going? She was too dressed up for shopping.

Until now, jealousy had been a stranger to Ben Walters. But the green-eyed monster took up residence on his shoulder as he went upstairs, and it refused to budge. Tony, his attorney, came to mind, because he'd made some remarks about her. But he knew Tony, and couldn't believe he'd make a move on a woman he'd be opposing in court. Neither could he see Jenny accepting a date with him.

Thoughts of her much-married mother crept into Ben's mind. Maybe he'd been wrong about Jennifer Stansfield all along. What did he know about her, anyway, except that she was sure great in bed? Maybe she was playing games with him, trying to make him jealous so that he'd grovel at her feet and agree to her offer. She knew now that he had a good case.

He should have let Tony hit her with that stuff about her mother. It hadn't taken a genius to see that she'd been shocked by what they had—especially that nurse's statement. She might be worried now that she was going to lose.

He showered and changed, then went down to the kitchen, where Tom and Sherri had left him some dinner. He carried it into the dining room and ate while his unpleasant thoughts ate at him. Then he went off to a local bar to have a few with some old friends. Tony hung out there, too; of course, that was just a coincidence.

But what was intended to be a way of keeping his mind off his problems fell flat. One of his buddies had seen Jennifer around town and wanted an introduction. Tony wasn't there, and Ben's suspicions grew.

He left the bar before he could give in to the urge to get roaring drunk. Instead, he stopped by to spend some time with Harry, but his uncle wasn't home. He drove back to the inn, already making excuses for Jennifer's failure to be there, none of which involved Tony or any other man.

He pulled the motorcycle into the carriage house, then started around to the back of the inn, convinced that her car would be there, even though he hadn't seen any lights in her apartment. She was probably working in the office, as she often did in the evenings.

When her car wasn't there, he continued to stare at the spot as though sheer willpower could make it appear. Then he went inside and up to his suite, cursing the fact that the cable hadn't been put in yet, so he didn't even have the brainless diversion of TV.

He turned on the radio to listen to a ball game, keeping it low as he paced about, imagining all sorts of satisfying scenarios if she showed up with some guy. He hadn't been in a fight since his high school days, but his fists clenched in anticipation of beating the guy to a pulp—even if it meant getting a new lawyer.

Finally he heard the sound he'd been listening for: footsteps in the hallway! He crossed the room and reached for the doorknob, but before he could open the door, she knocked on it.

She was clearly startled by the speed with which he opened the door—but she was alone. He was relieved for all of a half second, until he became rational enough to realize that she was unlikely to bring anyone here.

Damn, but she looked great. Her soft, silky green dress brought out the green in her eyes, and her hair was hanging loose, the way he liked it. He caught a whiff of what had to be one of the sexiest perfumes he'd ever smelled.

"Sorry to bother you," she said politely, "but I have to plan the girls' work for the next few days, and I was wondering when you expect to have the plaster repairs done in number 8.''

Plastering was definitely not high on his list of priorities at the moment, but he told her that he'd probably be finished in another couple of days.

He was doing just fine up to that point. But then he blew it by commenting too casually that he hadn't seen her dressed up in quite a while. The moment the words were out of his mouth, he wanted to take them back. He was probably playing right into her game.

She laughed and kicked off her high heels in a series of movements he found almost unbearably erotic. More perfume drifted his way.

"It's definitely been a while, since I can hardly walk in these heels. I may have to spend the rest of my life in sneakers."

Ben was staring at her long, slender legs when she looked up and caught him at it.

"Well, I'll let you get back to your ball game," she said in a kind of breathless rush. "Good night."

He didn't slam the door. He didn't kick the wall. But he came very close to going over there and kicking in her door. What he *did* do was develop X-ray vision. He could see her over there, shrugging out of that dress. Underneath it, she was wearing one of those lacy teddy things, cut low so that when she bent over to take off her stockings, her firm, full breasts all but spilled out.

Music came on—some romantic classical stuff—so he amended his vision to see her moving around the apartment in that scrap of lace and satin, the soft lamplight reflecting off her pale curls.

It was a very long night.

JENNIFER TURNED from her computer to find Ben standing in the office doorway. By this time, she was no longer surprised at the sixth sense that told her when he was watching her.

"Number 8 is turning into a real project," he announced.

"Oh? What happened? I hope the ceiling didn't fall in." There was gray dust in his hair and on his shoulders.

"No, but the damned wall almost did. I'm probably going to

have to rebuild the whole thing, and maybe part of another wall, too. They aren't the original walls, that's for sure. The workmanship is pretty shoddy, compared with the rest of the place.''

Number 8 was the smallest of the second-floor rooms. "Maybe it was created at some point by dividing up a larger room.''

"Yeah, I imagine that's what happened, but it must have been a long time ago. I'll have it ready next week sometime. The rest of them will be finished by this afternoon.''

He hesitated, then added, "I'm, uh, going to be away tomorrow and tomorrow night. Jim Thompson has asked me to help him with a house near Montpelier that he's restoring. He doesn't really have anyone who's all that good with plaster moldings. I thought I could ask Tracey to stay over, if you want.'' Tracey was the Willises' daughter, and a member of Ben's crew.

"That won't be necessary. I don't mind being alone. After all, we haven't had any more problems.''

The truth was that she'd welcome being alone. Having him next door, hearing him come and go, knowing that when she crawled into her lonely bed he was just a short distance away—all of it was driving her crazy.

He left, and she sat there thinking about the night before. His behavior had been really strange. He'd actually seemed angry with her. At first, she'd thought it was because she'd interrupted his ball game, but later she'd wondered if what she'd seen could have been jealousy. She hadn't told him that she was going to a meeting of the local innkeepers' association. He might have thought she was out on a date.

On the other hand, maybe she just *wanted* him to be jealous—wanted him to care so much about her that he'd accept her offer.

BEN WAS GONE by the time she came downstairs the next morning. She found out that he'd issued orders to his crew as soon as they arrived, and then had taken off quickly.

It was amazing how much work she got done when she wasn't spending her time trying to catch glimpses of him or thinking up reasons to talk to him or hoping to run into him in the hallway. She spent the morning doing a thorough inventory of the inn's linens, then called a supplier recommended by several people at the meeting.

In the afternoon, she checked on the progress of the cleaning crew, who had by now begun to work on the third-floor rooms, and then went outside to see what the boys had accomplished. They had finished digging up a corner of the lawn next to the woods, and were about to start planting the lovely ornamental grasses she'd discovered at the local garden center. The varieties she'd selected grew quite tall, and would provide a perfect backdrop for the wildflower garden to be planted in front of them.

She turned to look at the inn, which was sparkling in its fresh coat of creamy beige paint with white trim. The foundation beds had already been planted with a variety of evergreen shrubs. In front, between them, clusters of marigolds were starting to bloom. The big circular bed enclosed by the driveway had been planted with a colorful mixture of annuals, as well.

The Victoriana of her imagination was taking shape before her eyes, and she'd been so preoccupied that she'd barely noticed it.

That evening, after working late in the office, Jennifer stood in her living room and stared out at the darkness that threatened to swallow the inn, despite the new exterior lighting. There was no moon and the lake was just barely visible as a lighter patch in that all-encompassing blackness. Thoughts of the ghost flitted through her mind—and that, unfortunately, brought thoughts of the night she and Ben had gone down to the lake, two lovers on a whimsical midnight adventure.

She turned away and closed the drapes. It was strange how empty the inn seemed without him now. She wasn't really concerned about the return of the unknown intruder, but she felt Ben's absence very keenly, as though part of the very soul of Victoriana had gone with him.

To keep herself busy during the long evening, she cleaned the apartment thoroughly, even though it scarcely needed it. Exhausted from the long day, she finally crawled into her lonely bed and fell asleep quickly—only to be awakened just before one o'clock.

Still half-asleep, she thought that perhaps Ben had made some noise. Then she remembered that he wasn't there, and she sat up quickly, her ears straining to catch any sound. Her heart pounded crazily. Surely she'd just been dreaming. And yet she knew she hadn't. From somewhere in the inn came faint but very definite sounds. The intruder was back!

She switched on the bedside lamp, then picked up the phone. When there was no dial tone, she gaped at it for a few seconds in disbelief before depressing the button and trying again. It remained dead. Her anger turned to terror.

She got out of bed and ran to the kitchen to try the other phone. Again, there was no dial tone. Now she was certain that the line had been cut. Every horror film she'd ever seen replayed in her brain as she ran back to her bedroom and dressed hurriedly, then opened the drawer to get her gun.

It wasn't there. She simply stared stupidly at the empty drawer until she remembered that she'd given it to Ben. The gun was locked in his suite, and while there was a spare key, it was in a cabinet in the office downstairs.

She went to the apartment door and listened, then opened the door quietly. Suddenly she heard the sound of breaking glass. A window? She couldn't be sure where the sounds were coming from, but it seemed to be the far side of the first floor: the library and bar area, where he'd been before.

Her anger roared back, mixing explosively with fear as she stepped out into the hallway and went to check Ben's door on the slim chance that he'd left it unlocked. But he hadn't. She heard yet another crash of breaking glass. It occurred to her that there was quite a lot of glass in the bar—several shelves filled with various types of glassware, and a huge mirror, as well.

Gun or no gun, she was sorely tempted to go down there and confront him. But, fortunately, reason prevailed before she'd gone more than a few steps, and she ran back into the apartment instead, to get her car keys. With all the noise he was making, it was possible that she could get away without his hearing her and bring the police back before he left.

She hurried down the narrow back staircase that led to the kitchen. The phone there, a separate line for the caterers, was also dead. There could no longer be any doubt that he'd cut the phone lines to guarantee that she couldn't get the police this time.

The back door was locked, as she'd left it, with no sign that it had been tampered with. She fitted her key into it, unlocked it, and ran out to her car. But when she put her key into the ignition, the car wouldn't start!

She tried again, but the gesture was futile. Whoever was in there not only had cut the phone lines, but had also disabled her car. She locked the doors, then sat there trembling. Should she stay in the car or go back to the greater safety of her apartment? Setting out on foot to try to find help was just too risky.

A dim light flickered in a second-floor room on the far side of the inn, and for one panicked moment, Jennifer thought of fire. But as it moved to another room even farther from her apartment, she realized that it must be a flashlight. She made a quick decision to go back upstairs. Perhaps she'd be safe in the car, but she knew she'd be safer behind a heavy door with strong locks.

Within moments, she was back in the apartment, catching her breath as she leaned against the locked and bolted door. Never in her life had she felt so helpless, or so terribly angry. It was probably a good thing she didn't have her gun. She could easily envision herself as some would-be female Rambo, hell-bent on protecting her beloved Victoriana.

When her breathing had returned to normal, she pressed her ear to the door and listened intently. After a time, she heard faint sounds directly beneath her in the dining room. She opened the door quietly and stuck her head out, and a moment later she heard what she thought was the back door closing. She had relocked it, and the key was in her pocket.

After closing and relocking the apartment door, she hurried to the windows that faced the front of the inn and peered out between the drapes. The new lights mounted on the outside walls of the inn didn't cast much light on the driveway, and the lighting along the driveway wasn't operational yet. But she tried very hard to see into the darkness. She was sure he would come that way; it seemed unlikely that he'd use the woods as a means of escape on such a dark night.

Then she saw him, moving swiftly just beyond the reach of the spotlights—a tall figure dressed in dark clothing. Either he had dark hair, as well, or he was wearing a cap of some sort.

Within moments, he had vanished down the driveway into the night.

She remained at the open window, listening. After a while she heard the faint sound of an engine turning over, but there were no headlights, and the sound died away quickly.

Certain now that he had gone, Jennifer left her apartment once again and ran down the main staircase to the office. The inn had three separate lines: her private line in the apartment, the line for Sherri and Tom in the kitchen, and one for the inn itself. At present, the only phone hooked up to the inn line was the one in the office, and she was hoping that it might not have been cut.

When she found that line dead, too, she went back out into the lobby. A part of her wanted very much to go back upstairs and crawl into bed, but a stronger part wanted to get it over with now. After a brief mental tug-of-war, she walked toward the hallway that led to the bar and library. Recalling those sounds of shattering glass, she turned into the bar first and reached for the wall switch.

The shelves surrounding the big antique mirror had been swept clean of glassware. Shards and slivers littered the floor and the bar itself. The mirror was intact, but written on it in crude black letters was a very clear and chilling message: GET OUT.

Jennifer stood in the doorway, trembling as she stared at the words. There was no doubt in her mind that the message was a very personal one—directed at *her*.

She switched off the light and went across to the library, prepared to find the glass-fronted case containing the old books shattered, as well, and the books torn apart. But, surprisingly, no damage at all had been done to the library.

Next she checked all the windows on the first floor and ascertained that they were all locked, as they had been when she checked them earlier. Then she went to the kitchen.

The back door was locked. Jennifer stared at it with a frown. The intruder *had* to have a key; there was no other way he could have gotten out. But how had he managed to get a key after all the locks had been changed? It made no sense.

She walked slowly back upstairs, mulling the situation over.

The police had told her the locks were good, but they'd also said that a professional could get through any lock.

She had turned toward her apartment when she recalled the lights she'd seen on the second floor and reversed her direction. This time, she was more or less prepared for what she found: the same chilling message had been sprayed on the freshly painted walls in both guest rooms.

Fighting tears of frustration and rage, Jennifer made her way back to her apartment. Who could hate her so much—and why? Angry as she was about the senseless damage, the most frustrating part was not knowing why it was being done. Surely there *was* a reason. Surely this wasn't some sick mind's idea of a few evenings of fun.

On the other hand, when she thought about all the senseless acts of violence that filled the news, she had to admit that the intruder might be nothing more than a crazy local who knew the inn was being restored and had decided to have some sick fun.

The only problem with that theory was that he had to be a crazy who was also a professional at lock-picking.

She made herself a cup of herbal tea and sat in her dark living room, sipping and thinking. One question emerged that she hadn't considered before. Was it only coincidence that the intruder had returned on the one night that Ben wasn't here? She thought about that—and found herself looking into the deepest, darkest chasm imaginable.

The intruder had to have a key. He'd come when Ben wasn't here. Her gun was locked away in Ben's apartment. And the man she'd glimpsed as he ran down the driveway was about Ben's size and build.

"No!" she cried to the empty apartment. She refused to believe that he could be responsible for this, no matter what the evidence. There *had* to be another explanation.

But by the time she dragged herself off to bed, she hadn't succeeded in finding one. Her dreams were tormented by a tall, dark figure that was and wasn't Ben: a warm, smiling man whose eyes gleamed with desire, and a grim stranger with eyes the color of a winter's sky.

OKAY, HE TOLD HIMSELF, that was it—his one last attempt to drive her out of there. If it didn't work this time, he would just have to let the chips fall where they may. He didn't like what he'd done, but after that conversation the other day, he decided to give it one more try.

He didn't think it would work, though, because she didn't seem to scare easily. Besides, he knew by now how she felt about the place.

JENNIFER WAS AWAKE when Sherri and Tom arrived the next morning. Their hours were somewhat irregular, but on days when they had a luncheon to cater, they often arrived before the work crews.

She didn't really know if she'd slept at all. The dreams that had tormented her had the quality of waking dreams, rather than nightmares haunting the deeper regions of sleep. And if she had in fact slept, she certainly hadn't gained any benefit from it; one look at her pale, drawn face in the mirror told her that.

She dressed quickly and hurried downstairs. Her appearance must have shocked Sherri and Tom as much as it had her, because their cheerful greetings were cut off in midsentence as they stared at her.

She explained what had happened. Sherri asked where Ben was as Tom picked up the phone and pronounced it still dead.

"He wasn't here last night," she told Sherri, hoping desperately that it was true.

Tom went outside to check the phone lines and her car, while Sherri handed her a cup of coffee and commented that Ben was going to be very upset to find that the intruder had returned and he hadn't been here to protect her. Jennifer merely nodded, wishing she could believe that. In fact, she'd never in her life wanted to believe anything so badly.

When Tom returned, he informed her that the phone lines had indeed been cut. But no real damage had been done to her car. The plug wires had simply been pulled loose, and he'd already replaced them.

Jennifer drained her coffee cup. "I'd better go back upstairs and make myself presentable so I can go into town to talk to the police.''

"You don't have to do that," Tom told her. "We have a phone in the van."

She went out to their van and called the police, then went back inside and got the phone directory to check the number for the phone company. After contacting them and getting a promise that someone would be there by early afternoon to repair her lines, she leaned back in the seat and thought about the other call she knew she should make. She looked up that number and hesitated, then punched it out with trembling fingers.

"Thompson Construction Company," a cheerful voice answered.

She asked for Jim Thompson, then identified herself when he came on the line.

"Hello, Ms. Stansfield. I hear that things are going well over there. I ran into Ben a few days ago, and he invited me out to see the place."

"Please *do* come, Mr. Thompson. I'd be delighted to see you again. I'm calling about Ben, as a matter of fact. I understand that he went up to Montpelier to do some work for you. Is there a way I can reach him?"

The brief silence on the line answered her question even before Thompson spoke.

"You must have misunderstood Ben, Ms. Stansfield. It's true that I put in a bid for the renovations on a big old farmhouse up there, and I told him I'd sure like his help if I get it, but I haven't heard from the owners yet."

It took every ounce of her willpower to keep her voice light, but Jennifer told him that she must have been mistaken, then repeated her invitation to come out and see Victoriana. Then she hung up the phone and rested her forehead against the steering wheel as she fought a wave of nausea and dizziness.

After a few moments, she raised her head and stared out at the woods, where the lake shimmered in the morning sun. How much more proof do you want? she asked herself angrily. Would you believe it even if the police find evidence that he was here?

Isn't it time you stopped believing your treacherous heart—and started to trust your brain again?

To think she'd actually believed herself to be falling in love with him! And she was bitterly angry over her foolish offer to give him half of Victoriana.

When the police arrived, she was still sitting in the van, seething with rage.

BEN DROVE SLOWLY up the driveway, then stopped his truck when the inn came into view. Victoriana gleamed in the bright morning sun, and from this vantage point, at least, it looked ready to welcome guests again. Jenny hadn't mentioned a new sign yet, but he'd done a few sketches and was eager to show them to her.

He drove around back and waved at a couple of his workers, who were up on ladders painting the eaves, the only part of the exterior painting not yet finished. Then he went inside to find Jennifer.

It had taken him some time to recognize the feeling he'd had since he woke up this morning, but by now he knew what it was. He'd found peace—the peace of a good decision, finally and irrevocably made. It was strange how easy coming to that decision had been, when he'd finally forced himself to think about it seriously.

When he opened the back door, delicious aromas greeted him, reminding him that he'd had no breakfast. But when Tom and Sherri both turned toward him, their expressions grim, his interest in food vanished.

"What's wrong? Where's Jenny?"

"She went upstairs to get some sleep. She's okay, Ben, don't worry," Sherri said soothingly. And then she told him what had happened.

Ben cursed and slammed his fist into the unyielding steel door of one of the big refrigerators. "What did the police say?" he asked, ignoring the pain in his hand.

"Not much. You know how they are. They're going to send someone from the state police who can look for fingerprints, and they found where he left his car. But they said that the tire prints weren't good enough to help them.

"Ben, you should see those...those messages he left. I know they're just words, but they look so threatening. Jennifer is scared to death, even though she's trying to hide it."

Ben started toward the dining room, and Sherri called after him to remind him not to touch anything until the state police got there. He merely nodded and strode through the dining room and lobby, then stopped in the doorway to the bar.

When he saw the mess—and the warning—Ben clenched his fists in helpless rage. It was all too easy to imagine how terrified she must have been when she saw it. He went upstairs to see the two rooms. The crudely sprayed black letters had dripped down the walls, making them look like something from a horror film.

He kept thinking how she'd faced this alone—just as he suspected she'd faced things for most of her life, packed off to boarding school and ignored by her parents, then traveling the world with no permanent home until she'd come here.

He went to her apartment, raised his hand to knock, then let it drop again. He wanted desperately to see her now; he needed to see her. But what *she* needed was sleep.

Instead, he headed into town to buy a sealer to apply to the walls and some solvent to clean the mirror with. He was determined to erase every last trace of the damage as soon as the police had done their work. His next stop was the police station. Since he knew most of the local cops, including the chief, he hoped he could get more information. But they had little to offer. There was no sign of a break-in, and there had been no reports of similar incidents in the area. Their only hope was that the intruder had left behind his fingerprints.

"Where's the motive, Ben?" the chief asked in disgust. "Since it all started with that wallpaper business in her apartment, we've got to think this is directed at *her.*"

Ben thought about that on his way back to the inn, and then his thoughts turned quickly to the other evening, when she'd gone out somewhere. Was there something she was keeping from him—something possibly connected to her past? Maybe even someone she was afraid of?

When he got back to the inn, the phone-company crew was there. The state police crime-scene experts came soon after. It was late afternoon of a very frustrating day before he heard Jennifer's voice as she spoke to Tom and Sherri in the dining room.

She must have used the back stairs. He was at work in the lobby, repairing the intricate plaster moldings around the fixture for the chandelier. It was delicate work that required total concentration, but he'd decided that was exactly what he needed now. Besides, he knew she was eager to hang the chandelier again.

He'd already given up the idea of confronting her about the possibility of someone from her past being responsible. If it was true, and she'd kept it from him and from the police, she must think she had good reasons. All he could do was hope that she'd come to trust him enough to tell him. And in the meantime, he'd just wait to see if the guy tried anything else. His state of mind was such that he almost hoped the S.O.B. *would* show up here again.

He was about to get down from the ladder when she walked into the lobby. His gut wrenched at the sight of her pale, drawn face. If she'd gotten any sleep, it sure hadn't helped.

He climbed down quickly, wanting nothing more than to take her into his arms. But the look in her eyes stopped him in his tracks. As clearly as if she'd spoken the words, her expression telegraphed a message: "Stay away!" It was his fault; he knew that. He hadn't been there for her.

"I'm sorry, Jenny," he said helplessly.

She merely nodded and averted her gaze. He struggled to find something to say. But before he did, she asked in a flat, dead voice he barely recognized if the police had found anything.

Ben shook his head. "They found fingerprints all over the place, but they probably belong to all of us. They fingerprinted everyone who'd been in those rooms, and they'll want yours, as well. I've already cleaned up the bar, and we got one coat of paint on the walls upstairs. It'll take at least one more—maybe two."

Once again, she just nodded. He couldn't think of anything

else to say, so he told her that he needed to go clean up, and then they'd talk. He was hoping for some quick inspiration.

When he returned, she was sitting on the stairs, staring at the plasterwork he'd just finished. He wasn't sure she even saw it, but he used it as an opening, anyway, telling her that he'd be able to hang the chandelier for her in a few days. Then he went on to say that he'd get to work on the gazebo tomorrow. He knew she wanted that done, as well.

He started over to join her on the stairs, but she stiffened and slid into the corner next to the railing. Was he wrong about the reason for her withdrawal? She appeared to be blaming *him* for what had happened!

He stopped as though he'd been punched in the gut. Could she really believe that? What if she'd called Jim Thompson and found out that he'd lied about where he was going?

For a moment, he was angry that she could even consider such a thing. But then he thought about his own suspicions that she was keeping something from him.

Great, he thought. Just great! Here we are suspecting each other, when what we *should* be doing is—

He broke off his bitter thoughts and told her that he'd talked to the police. "They went over the place pretty thoroughly. They're convinced that whoever he is, either he's got a key or he's a real pro. They said they checked all the windows, too. Are you satisfied that they were all locked?"

"Yes. I checked them all as soon as the crews left, and I was especially careful because you...weren't here."

Her slight hesitation confirmed his worst fear: she *had* called Thompson. He took a deep breath.

"I lied to you about where I was yesterday and last night, Jenny."

She'd been looking everywhere but at him, but now her face turned quickly in his direction. The pain and anger he saw in those beautiful eyes made him wince.

"I know," she stated coldly. "I called Jim Thompson this morning."

"I went fishing."

"Fishing?" she echoed scornfully. "At night? I know you

must think I'm pretty stupid—but how can you expect me to believe *that?*''

''I meant that I went fishing yesterday, and then I camped out there last night. I went to this spot where Dad and I went for years. I hadn't been there since...since he left.''

He wasn't sure if her expression had changed, but he thought maybe it had a little bit. He hurried on.

''I sort of made up the story about doing some work for Jim. He does want me to help him if he gets the contract, so it wasn't a complete lie.'' He didn't need to look at her to know how dumb that sounded.

''I just needed to get away to do some thinking. I knew there were things you'd been wanting me to do, so I thought you'd get mad if I told you I was taking time off to go fishing.''

She just continued to stare at him, and he started to get mad as he listened to the echoes of his pathetic pleas for understanding. He glared at her.

''Let's get this straight, lady! I wasn't here last night—and I had nothing to do with this!''

She got up and returned his look, measure for measure. ''You just admitted that you lied, Ben. I imagine it must get easier with practice.''

She walked up the stairs, while he stood there staring at her, not at all certain who he was madder at—her or himself.

JENNIFER SLIPPED quietly out of her apartment, hoping the sound from Ben's TV would mask any noise she made. She had to get out of here. She couldn't stand hearing him next door—a very big change from last night, when the place had seemed so empty without him.

She ran down the back stairs and then out through the back door into the soft twilight. Then she hesitated. She'd intended to go around to the front porch, but now she changed her mind and started toward the lake instead. If he *had* heard her, or if he came out on his own, he'd be less likely to look for her there.

It was already very dark in the woods, so she switched on her small flashlight, hoping he wouldn't come out and see it. As soon as she came out of the woods, she turned it off—and then stopped with a frown.

Sitting on the grass at the lake's edge was a shiny new rowboat. Still frowning, she walked up to it. She knew it hadn't been there yesterday, because she'd come down to the lake for lunch. She ran her hand along the curved bow, recalling how Ben had mentioned getting one for them.

She got into it and sat down, staring out at the dark water, which was lightly dappled with the last of the day's light. It would be nice to be out there now, just drifting along over the water. But the image that came to her mind included Ben.

Did she believe him? Oh, how she wanted to—but she'd been there before. Wanting to believe something was dangerous.

She got out of the boat and went to the bow to see if she could pull it into the water. Then she decided it might be easier to push from the stern. She had managed to get it to the water's edge when a voice spoke from behind her.

"Are you taking any passengers, Captain?"

She jumped and cried out involuntarily, then turned around to face him. "You scared me," she said angrily.

"If you scared easily, you wouldn't be out here alone—especially right after a break-in."

"I just wanted to get out of the apartment," she said coldly. And away from *you*, she added silently.

"Boat theft is a serious offense," he remarked, a smile in his voice.

"I wasn't stealing, I was just borrowing it. You said you were going to get one for...us." She faltered on the final word.

"Right—for *us*. So I guess you won't mind if I come along."

She minded, all right. What she'd wanted was to drift around the lake peacefully, but there was no peace to be had now.

"Get in," he said, extending his hand to help her. "That is, unless you think I'm planning to drown you."

She avoided his outstretched hand, but climbed into the boat. "I'm a very good swimmer."

"Well, then, I guess I'll just have to whack you with an oar first," he responded dryly.

In spite of herself, she smiled. "In that case, I'll come back to haunt you. There'll be *two* ghosts on the lake—and one of them is going to be *very* angry.''

He chuckled—that wonderful sound she hadn't heard for so long. She was sure she couldn't possibly feel the way she did right now if she didn't believe him—and trust him.

He dragged the boat into the water, then climbed in and began to row in silence. It was dark by now, and the moon hadn't risen, so the only light was the faint, distant glimmer of the stars. They reached the middle of the lake, and he locked the oars in place, then settled into the bow, facing her as she sat in the stern.

''Is your offer still good?'' he asked suddenly, breaking the long silence.

''Yes.'' The question was unexpected, but she didn't have to think about it.

''Then I accept.''

''You do?''

''Yeah. I've been telling myself all along that my wanting this place had nothing to do with us. But once I admitted to myself that there was no way to separate the two things, I knew that was the only way out.''

''So that's why you went fishing.''

He nodded. ''I can be pretty stubborn sometimes, so every once in a while I need to sit myself down and have a serious talk.''

''Well, I'm glad you had your 'talk.' This place belongs to both of us, Ben.''

''So now we're *really* partners.''

''We are.''

''And all we have to do now is to learn to trust each other.''

''I think maybe we can—now.''

They drifted for a while longer, in a silence that was indeed peaceful. Desire whispered in the night breeze and in the soft lapping of the water against the boat, but its sound was strangely muted.

When they returned to the shore, they walked hand in hand back to the inn. By the time they reached her apartment, that soft whisper was growing louder, but while she heard it, Ben seemed not to. He bent to kiss her softly, quickly. His lips were gone almost before she could register their touch.

"Good night, partner."

Chapter Ten

They were seated on the leather sofa in Wexford's office. The attorney had spread the papers out on the table before them, and was explaining each one in great detail. Jennifer glanced sideways at Ben, who rolled his blue eyes and adopted a long-suffering look. When the attorney turned to her, she was afraid she hadn't quite gotten the smile off her face. He frowned slightly before continuing.

Wexford was not happy with her, although of course he hadn't come right out and said it. And his behavior toward Ben was icily formal.

Finally they were permitted to sign the numerous documents and escape the attorney's disapproval. The moment they were out of the office, Jennifer laughed.

"I think it would be safe to say that he doesn't approve."

Ben chuckled, then drew her into his arms and gave her a deliciously slow, tender kiss. "I hope he's looking out the window right now."

He got onto his motorcycle and pulled her up behind him, then revved it up and waved at the office. "That should bring him to the window—and raise his blood pressure a bit."

They roared off to the inn. Jennifer wrapped her arms around him and pressed her face against his back. It was done. They were full partners in Victoriana now. Her fear of losing him was over.

Something had changed between them in these past few days since he'd accepted her offer. While she often caught the gleam of desire in Ben's eyes, his behavior toward her was carefully restrained. He was affectionate toward her, taking her hand or dropping an arm casually around her shoulders or kissing her as he had just now. But there was no suggestion of anything more— or rather, there was a very strong suggestion that he was keeping his desire on a very short leash.

She wondered about his behavior, but didn't question it, because she felt the same caution herself. Maybe so much had happened that they both needed to slow down a bit. They had time now—and they had Victoriana to keep them well occupied.

On the road to the inn, they came up behind a car that turned into Victoriana after hesitating for a moment.

"That must be Professor Jenkins," she shouted over the noise of the motorcycle. "He's early." Her father's friend was stopping by today to examine the old books in the library.

Ben pulled up just as the professor was getting out of his car. Jennifer hopped off, smiling at the older man's expression as he belatedly recognized her. She could just hear him reporting to her father that she was now riding motorcycles.

She introduced him to Ben and then took him into the library while Ben went to check on his crew. She'd removed the books from the shelves earlier, and she had them spread out on two of the tables. When he accepted her offer of some iced tea, she left him there and went upstairs.

"Most of these are in remarkably good condition, Jennifer," he told her when she returned. "And they are unquestionably of great value—some more than others, of course, but on the whole a quite wonderful collection.

"I can give you the name of a very reputable dealer who can handle the actual appraisal and sale. Completely trustworthy. I've dealt with him for years."

"We've decided not to sell them for now," Jennifer replied. "But I *will* need to get an appraisal for insurance purposes."

"'We,' you said?" The professor looked up with a puzzled frown. "But I thought I understood from your father that *you* owned this charming place now."

"Um, well, I do—technically. It's a bit complicated, actually." She didn't want to tell him about her partnership, in case he happened to talk to her father before she did. And she was in no hurry to have *that* conversation, either. Her father had seemed to like Ben, but she doubted he would approve of what she'd done.

"Oh, yes." The professor nodded. "Now I recall that James said something about a son who's challenging the will."

He looked down at the book that was open before him. She saw a name written there in bold, masculine script. "Ezekial Walters. The young man you introduced me to was a Walters, wasn't he?"

"Yes, his great-grandson."

"Then he's the one who's challenging the will?"

Fortunately, Jennifer was saved from having to reply to that by Ben's arrival. She told him what Professor Jenkins had said about the books.

"Well, I guess I'd better plan to get up to my attic and do some digging around, then," Ben said. "I'm sure there are a couple of cartons up there, too."

After the professor had gone, Jennifer picked up an armload of books to put them back into the bookcase. "Ben, we'd better get the locksmith back out here so we can lock this. I can't find a key."

"How did you get it unlocked?" he asked.

"I didn't have to. It was already unlocked." She frowned and set down the armload of books. "That's strange. Why didn't I think about that?"

"Think about what?"

"It was locked the first time I saw it. I remember now that I went through the keys, looking for one that would fit, but couldn't find one. Then I just forgot about it." She shrugged and picked up the books again.

"I guess it must not have been locked, after all. Maybe it was just stuck, although it opened easily enough this time."

She started to replace the books on a shelf just above eye level. The afternoon sun was streaming in through the library windows, and she thought she saw something in the bright light. She stretched up on tiptoe. There was some sort of carving in the rich, dark mahogany at the back of the bookcase—but only in that one corner, as far as she could see.

"Ben, come here and look at this."

With Ben's added height, he could see it more clearly. He made a sound of surprise.

"That's weird. Why would someone carve a lion's face into the back of a bookcase, where it couldn't even be seen?"

As he reached out to touch it, she bent to check the lower shelves. "I don't see any other carv—"

Her words were cut off abruptly by a very familiar scraping sound. And then the entire bookcase seemed to be falling on her! She screamed, and Ben grabbed her, and the two of them stumbled away from the suddenly moving bookcase.

It swung away from the wall with a groan and a *thunk* as they stared in disbelief. In the shadows behind it was a dark, narrow staircase. For a minute, they were both too stunned to do or say anything, and in the silence they heard one of Ben's crew upstairs, calling out to someone else.

"What's that noise?" the worker asked. "It sounded like something in the wall here."

"Ben, that's the sound I heard when the intruder was here that one time. I know it's the same noise."

Ben went over to the staircase, paused to test the first step, then started up slowly. She followed him, but stopped partway up. It was very dark, and barely wide enough for one person. Up ahead, Ben spoke out in an unnaturally deep voice.

"Who is it who disturbs my rest?" he thundered, his voice echoing in sepulchral tones.

"What the hell? Holy sh—Hey, Len, did you hear that?"

Jennifer began to giggle, and quickly covered her mouth.

"Leave me in peace, before I *really* get mad!" Ben thundered.

"C'mon, let's get out of here!" one of his crew shouted.

Then she heard Tracey's lighter voice. "Hey, you guys, since when do ghosts say they're mad? Get real!"

There were some loud thumps against the wall. "Ben Walters, I know that's you! It's just your kind of trick. That's the same voice you used to scare me years ago."

"How can he be in the wall?" one of the others asked. "I'm getting out of here."

"Okay, okay, I give up," Ben called out in his normal voice.

"That's what I get for hiring someone I've known since she was in diapers."

Explanations followed. Jennifer stood there behind Ben, laughing. The two men were going to be hearing about this incident for a long time. Tracey would be sure to put it to good use the next time they gave her any grief.

When they were back in the library and could stop laughing, Ben told her the staircase came out in room 8, the one where they were rebuilding a wall.

"I'll bet that was an apartment at one time," he said, "and then the living room was broken up into two rooms."

"This explains how the intruder was able to disappear, Ben. He must have hidden in there until after the police had gone. Since my apartment's on the far side of the building, I wouldn't have heard him open the bookcase again." Then she remembered something else from that night.

"You know, while I was hiding up there on the landing, I thought I heard noises on the far end of the second floor for a few minutes before I heard him back downstairs again. I was right, after all. He must have gone up the staircase then. Maybe he didn't know it had been blocked off."

Ben frowned. "That staircase had to have been blocked off a really long time ago, Jenny. I didn't know anything about it, and Dad never said anything. Neither did Granddad."

"Why is it there?"

He shrugged. "Maybe room 8 was originally the family apartment. The staircase could have been put in as a convenience for them—a way to sneak down to the library whenever they wanted. Builders in those days liked doing crazy things. And maybe my ancestors liked the idea of being able to sneak around and keep an eye on the help."

"I wonder why they moved the apartment."

"Who knows? It could have been because of the noise. Maybe they put the bar in later, and that bothered them. And the carriage house is on that side, too. Or there might have been two apartments for the family."

"I'm surprised that your family didn't keep detailed records of this place, and any changes they made over the years."

"They did—or so I was told. But no one has been able to find them for years." He pushed the bookcase lightly, and it swung back into place smoothly. "Great workmanship."

"Ben, how could anyone else know about that stairway if you didn't even know? And why would the intruder go in there, anyway?"

"He probably went in there intending to convince you that there's a ghost in the place. It worked pretty well a few minutes ago." He grinned. "And then he used it as a hiding place when you called the police."

He paused and frowned at the bookcase. "But your other question is the important one. Who could know that that staircase is there? I've got no answer for that one. The only person I can think of who might be able to help is Harry. Neither he nor Dad ever mentioned it to me, but maybe they did know about it. And maybe Harry can think of someone else who would've known."

He leaned against a table and stared at her. "This changes things, you know."

"What do you mean?"

"What I mean is that maybe we were wrong to think someone was out to get *you*. You don't know anyone who could possibly have known about that staircase."

She nodded slowly. "Then he must have hoped he could prevent me from reopening the place."

Ben nodded. "That sounds like it to me." He ran a hand distractedly through his hair. "I keep thinking that we're missing something here. The intruder hasn't done any real damage. Let's face it—if what he wanted was for the inn not to reopen, he could have set fire to it."

"Maybe he's working his way up to that," Jennifer said with a shiver.

BEN PARKED in the carriage house and started toward the rear door, then reversed direction and instead walked across the lawn to the once and future site of the gazebo. He saw the deep ruts in the lawn made by the cement truck, and cursed himself for not having had the concrete base poured before the kids began their work on the lawn. No doubt he'd be hearing about that little blunder from Jennifer.

She was a perfectionist in her work. Everything was highly organized. Her approach was methodical. He, on the other hand, often chose his projects according to his moods.

Taking his time and really getting to know Jenny was kind of nice—although it *did* have its drawbacks. It was going to be pretty tough to keep up their present relationship. Still, he didn't want to mess things up by getting too pushy with her again. He was playing for keeps this time. Maybe she didn't know it yet, but when he'd signed those papers making them partners, he'd had a whole lot more in mind than just business.

You're down for the count, fella, he told himself. The love bug bit you good. It was still a little hard to believe.

He walked around the concrete base, examining the contractor's work in the waning light. He was really looking forward to this project. It'd be like building a gigantic toy. And as he stood there envisioning the rebuilt gazebo, it occurred to him that it might be a great place for a wedding.

"I thought at first I might be seeing a ghost out here, although I don't know many ghosts who wear jeans and baseball caps."

Ben spun around to see Jennifer walking toward him, wearing a pale, gauzy sort of dress that looked as though it would have been right at home at the old Victoriana. Then he took another look and decided he might be in serious trouble.

"How many ghosts do you know?" he asked her teasingly. He opened his arms to her, then lifted her half off her feet and kissed her. She smelled like a flower garden.

"You're the one who looks like a ghost," he told her as he set her back on her feet. "That dress looks like you found it in an old trunk somewhere."

She laughed. "I did, actually. It was among some things that had belonged to my grandmother, and it's perfect for warm summer nights."

He tilted his head to one side and ran his eyes over her. "I'll bet Grandma didn't wear it with nothing underneath, though."

He saw her flush slightly as she laughed. "Of course not.

Gram was a prude. This is my father's mother we're talking about.''

The inn's exterior lighting came on at that moment, and they both turned to look at it. ''I'm not sure I want to share this place with a bunch of strangers,'' he said. ''It'll destroy some of the magic.''

''So would poverty,'' she replied dryly. ''Besides, I want to show it off.'' Her voice became soft. ''But it *is* magic, isn't it? I felt it the first time I saw it, even as awful as it looked then.''

He wrapped his arms around her from behind and kissed her ear. ''Have you forgotten what else you saw that day?''

She twisted around to face him, frowning. ''What? Oh, you mean *you?* Of course I haven't forgotten. I thought you were some crazy bum who'd moved into the place.''

''Thanks a lot. Maybe I should have staggered outside with a bottle in a paper bag, just to complete the picture for you.''

''The 'picture' was already impressive enough, thank you. You were half-naked.''

''I wasn't wearing a shirt,'' he told her. ''That's only half-naked if you're female. I was up in the attic, and it was hot up there.''

Arms around each other, they started back to the inn. Ben wondered how he could persuade her to invite him into her bed, but she apparently still had business on her mind.

''The man the Willises recommended stopped by just after you left. He said he could repair or re-create the weather vanes, but there's just one little problem.''

''What's that?''

She grinned. ''He's afraid of heights.''

Ben laughed. ''Seems like that could be something of a disadvantage in his business.''

''Actually, he's a metal sculptor and a blacksmith. He has his own forge. Weather vanes are just a sideline. So if you'll just scurry up there and...''

''I thought *you* were the expert at crawling around on roofs.'' He paused at the back door to kiss the soft nape of her neck.

''Only in moments of desperation, when I'm being stalked by a killer,'' she said, laughing. Then she turned to him with a more serious expression. "Did you have a chance to talk to your uncle?"

"Yeah, but he didn't have any idea who it could be. He didn't even know about the hidden staircase, and he can't remember whether the bookcase was kept locked or not."

"Oh, Ben, what if the intruder tries something else? I know he hasn't done any real damage yet, but..."

He hugged her. "If he comes back, I can guarantee you it'll be the *last* time."

They went upstairs, and Ben loitered in the hallway while Jennifer unlocked her apartment door. A lamp was on in her living room, and as she stood there, silhouetted against the glow, her dress appeared almost transparent.

"Would you like to come in? I made some lemonade."

She could have offered him split-pea soup and he'd have sworn he was addicted to it. He started to follow her to the kitchen, then stopped, remembering the last time he'd done that. He'd just stay safely in the living room, drink the lemonade, and then leave. Maybe this place was getting to him. He felt as if he were in the middle of a Victorian courtship.

She came back with the glasses, walking between him and the lamp. His hand shook when he took the glass from her.

"I've got to ask you something," he said, not even knowing how much it was bothering him until he spoke.

She frowned—*still* standing in front of the lamp.

"That night you went out all dressed up...where did you go?"

She stared at him blankly and finally took a seat. "Why?"

"Because it's been bugging me, that's why."

"Then why didn't you ask me before?"

"Because I didn't—now I am. Are you going to tell me?"

She smiled. "I went to the meeting of the local innkeepers' association. The Willises invited me."

He tried not to let his relief show too much. She was still smiling.

"Okay, so I was jealous," he admitted reluctantly. "But it was more than that. I got to thinking that whoever is breaking in here might be someone from your past, someone you were afraid of who's been hanging around somewhere."

She was silent for a long time, and then she got up and went to sit in the window seat, drawing her legs up and resting her face against her knees as she stared at him. "There hasn't been a whole lot of trust between us, has there?" she said plaintively.

"No, there hasn't," he admitted. "That's why I thought we should...take things slow for a while, really get to know each other."

"You're right. We have time now, and we don't have that lawsuit hanging over us."

He wished she hadn't agreed with him. He'd hoped she'd say they trusted each other now, so...

"But we still have whoever he is," she went on.

"Yeah, I know, but there's nothing we can do about that unless he shows up again."

He drained his glass and stood up. If he didn't get out of here in the next ten seconds, he'd be dragging her into the bedroom and ripping off that see-through dress.

"Thanks for the lemonade. I think I'll go watch the ball game."

She didn't move from the window seat as he walked to the door. He was just opening it when she said something, but he didn't hear what it was, because he was too busy telling himself to put one foot in front of the other and make tracks.

"What?" He half turned toward her.

"Nothing," she said quickly. "Go watch your game."

Was she blushing, or was it just the light? He took a few steps back into the room. "What did you say?"

"I said you don't have to leave. But, of course, if you want to watch the——"

"The only thing I want to watch is you taking off that dress."

She smiled and got up from the window seat, then took about a half hour walking around the living room, drawing the drapes, while his blood pounded through his veins. He didn't blink. Maybe he didn't even breathe.

She began to unbutton the couple of hundred buttons on the dress, taking only about another hour or so. The dress had buttons to just below the waist, and when she'd finally finished with them, she wriggled out of it, letting it fall in a heap at her feet.

It took him about a tenth of a second to cross the room and sweep her into his arms.

There would be a time when he could enjoy taking it slow, claiming her by small degrees—but that time was not now. Need roared through him as they fell onto the bed, and the tremors that ran through her told him she felt the same.

"Jenny," he groaned, "I can't wait. I want to, but I can't."

"Then don't," she whispered against his ear.

With another groan, Ben lifted her and slid into her warm, welcoming softness, and within seconds drove them both over the edge, leaving them physically satisfied but still needing more. He held her and stroked her and kissed her while she made soft little sounds in her throat.

He wanted to tell her what she meant to him, but he was afraid to push his luck. This had happened once before—and she'd regretted it the next morning. Being in love made him feel vulnerable. He didn't want to tell her he loved her, only to have her reject him again.

Instead, he just held her and kissed her. When he felt her body reaching again for that ultimate satisfaction, he trailed kisses slowly down over her soft breasts, across her belly, taking his time now as she whimpered with pleasure and need. And when her body had grown as taut as a bowstring, and she was begging for release, he gave it to her, then held her as the aftershocks quivered through her.

"I LIKE waking up with you almost as much as I like sleeping with you, which I like almost as much as making love to you," Ben murmured huskily.

Jennifer did a credible job of purring as he buried his face in the curve of her neck and flicked his tongue over her sensitive skin. It seemed to her that there couldn't possibly have been a time in her life when she hadn't awakened beside him. The thought was almost frightening.

He reached over and switched off the clock radio, then drew the satin sheet down and began to trail soft, teasing kisses along the length of her body. She shivered as the cool morning air met flesh that was already heated from his touch. Waking up like this each morning could become addictive, she thought with a sigh.

She threaded her fingers through his thick, dark hair, and arched her yearning body into him, holding her breath as she waited for that most intimate of kisses—then drawing it in with a sudden gasp when his tongue at last began to probe her secret core.

Ben had a natural ease with intimacy that she lacked—or *had* lacked, before she met him. Now she was as eager as he was, and as uninhibited. They turned their bodies into erotic playgrounds across which they traveled with lips and tongues and fingers.

Her pleasure in the moment was such that she was actually caught by surprise when she felt that swiftly gathering tension, the approach of that unique melting sensation. She shifted and moved away from him, then began to blaze her own trail of kisses down across his bristly chest and his hard stomach.

She let his impatience build as she slid her fingers along his muscled thighs, deliberately avoiding what she knew he desired most. She delighted in the knowledge that she could so easily drive him to the limits of his self-control.

He groaned, and flexed his fingers convulsively in her hair, exerting subtle pressure to force her to give him what he wanted. After prolonging it for as long as she dared, given her own growing need, she caressed his hard manhood, drawing from him a long, low groan and an eager arching of his body beneath her.

Moments later, his control snapped. He tumbled her onto her back and thrust into her. She welcomed him and surrounded him, and they both cried out with the pure joy of it all.

Afterward, they lay in bed, legs and arms entangled, trying to ignore the distant sounds of their work crews arriving. Jennifer finally got out of bed. Ben looked at her warily until she bent over and kissed him. "I'm only going to get us some breakfast."

He reached out and took her hand to pull her back down into the bed. "I have something to say first."

"Oh?" Now it was *her* turn to look wary. It seemed that neither of them was yet willing to believe that their problems were in the past. He looked so very serious and solemn that she was sure there must be bad news to come.

"I think I'm in love with you, Jenny."

His soft words bathed her in a golden warmth—and yet they came as no surprise. Hadn't they been headed this way from the very beginning? She smiled at him.

"You only *think* so? I'm glad you're not rushing into this."

"Well, I've never been in love before.... How am I supposed to know what it feels like?"

"It feels like this," she said, kissing him again and letting him draw her down against him. "I love you, too, Ben," she whispered against his chest.

EVERYTHING seemed different this day. As she hurried about the inn, making decisions, issuing instructions, checking on the progress of this and that and dealing with the salespeople who had begun to show up regularly now that word had spread about the inn's reopening, Jennifer felt as though she were wrapped in a soft gauze that kept the rest of the world at bay.

When she went out to water her precious herb garden, she saw Ben on the porch roof, positioning a ladder so that he could climb up and remove the broken weather vane. He stopped when he saw her, and she could feel the caress of those blue eyes across the distance.

"I *do* love you, Ben Walters," she murmured, still filled with wonder that what had started out so badly could have turned into the greatest happiness of her life.

She continued to think of that as she plucked weeds and watered the thriving plants, enjoying the mixture of scents that tickled her nose. Idly she wondered what Win would have thought, since it was he, after all, who had started this.

She turned back to stare at the inn and at Ben, who was now up on the ladder, struggling with the weather vane. In one of those rare, blinding moments of absolute certainty, she knew.

"Ben...oh, Ben." Her eyes filled with tears. She forgot all about the herb garden and ran across the lawn toward him.

By the time she reached the inn, he had climbed back down

from the tower and was carrying the broken weather vane over to the ladder propped up against the porch roof.

"Ben!" she called impatiently.

He walked over to stare down at her, frowning with concern. "What's wrong?"

"Nothing is wrong. We have to talk."

He left the weather vane on the roof and climbed down the ladder quickly. "What is it?"

She didn't know where to begin. "It's about your father."

"What?"

"I know why he did it."

"Did what?"

She became impatient. "I know why he left the inn to me— and why he wanted me to come here and run it."

To her surprise, he nodded, then jammed his hands in the pockets of his jeans and turned away from her.

"Ben?"

He turned back to her, and she saw tears glistening in the corners of his eyes. He nodded again. "Yeah, I know, too."

"You do?"

"He set it up for us to meet."

"When did you figure this out?" she demanded, upset that he should have kept it from her.

"When I went fishing," he said, swiping at his eyes. "I intended to tell you. I just hadn't gotten around to it yet.

"I never understood why he'd cut me off like that. I know things weren't good between us, but it still didn't seem like him. He just wasn't like that. I kept thinking about that statement Wexford had from Dad's attorney in Florida—he said that Dad thought of you as the daughter he never had. That's how I figured it out."

"I don't think he ever intended to actually leave Victoriana to me," Jennifer said. "What he *really* intended was to persuade me to come up here to run the place. Then he would have told me about you, and how you were the one who could fix it up. But after the stroke, when he knew he might not live long enough to see that happen, he left Victoriana to me, knowing that you'd show up here, too."

They both stood in silence for a moment, and then they wrapped their arms around each other. There were still things they didn't understand, but they were both certain they'd been brought together by a man who'd known and loved them both, and who had given them, however strangely, one last gift.

Chapter Eleven

Ben stood naked at the bedroom window, his hands planted on his hips as he stared out at the gloomy day. Jennifer lay in bed, admiring the view—not of the rain, but of him.

"Damn," he muttered as he turned to her. "Well, it looks like you might get to see the view from the tower today. I only have about an hour's worth of work to do on the stained glass. Then I'll start on the wall."

She stretched and yawned. "Maybe I'll just spend the day in bed."

"Oh?" He came back and sat down. A slow grin spread across his face. "Well, in that case..."

"Just kidding," she assured him hastily. "I have a meeting with the accountant, and I want to start working on some ads, and—"

"Later," he growled as he fell upon her.

It was indeed later when they went downstairs to find the accountant waiting for Jennifer, and Ben's crew awaiting his instructions.

"This has got to stop," she whispered as they hurried down the staircase.

"No way," he muttered. "We'll just have to get up earlier— or take longer lunch breaks."

He set his crew to work painting the final few rooms on the third floor, and Jennifer ushered the accountant into her office. By the time her meeting with him had ended, Ben was just completing the work on the stained glass, and they all stood there admiring the beautiful doors. The ornately carved wooden frame had been cleaned and waxed, and the panes of glass gleamed even on this dreary day.

"You've done wonders with this place," the accountant said admiringly. "I can remember coming here years ago with my parents, and it looks even better now than it did then."

They both thanked him, and then they stood there, arms around each other's waists, and stared at the refurbished lobby. After two months of disorder, it had all come together so quickly. New carpets had been installed, the furniture had been reupholstered, and the glorious chandelier was back in its place of honor.

The best part of all this, Jennifer decided, was the memories of the days and weeks spent working together to reach this point. She knew she would never look at that chandelier without remembering the hours she'd spent up on a ladder, hanging the delicate crystals. And she certainly wouldn't forget the very pleasurable massage Ben had given her when she complained of aching muscles.

"Those trees make a big difference, don't they?" Ben said, breaking into her thoughts.

The "trees" he was referring to were five huge ficus plants in enormous hand-decorated clay pots. They had arrived yesterday, adding the final touch to the lobby. Or rather the next-to-final touch, she thought.

"There's only one thing missing now," she told him.

"I know, I know. It's almost finished."

She had persuaded Ben to do a painting of the inn to hang above the big fireplace in the lobby. He'd set up a studio in the old tack room in the carriage house. She'd sneaked out there a few days ago when he wasn't around, only to discover that he'd put a lock on the door. He'd also posted a large sign in elaborate script: To Whom It May Concern—And You Know Who You Are—This Room Is Strictly Off-limits! She didn't tell him that she'd been there.

He swatted her playfully on the rear. "Well, I'm off to bust up a wall. I'll call you when it's open, assuming the stairs are okay."

But later, when she was about to go up to the apartment to

see what progress he was making, he came down, covered with plaster dust.

"The damned staircase isn't where I thought it would be," he grumbled. "By the time I finish, I'm going to have that whole wall torn down."

Envisioning the mess he must be making, Jennifer shuddered. Still, it *would* be very nice to have the tower room, although she wasn't so sure about Ben's suggestion that they put a wall-to-wall mattress up there. He found her double bed a bit restricting.

They had lunch in the dining room with Sherri and Tom, who were enthusiastic about the two private parties that had been held thus far at the inn. They said they'd received another inquiry from someone who wanted to hold a wedding reception at Victoriana.

"They might actually want to have the wedding itself here, too," Sherri said.

"The gazebo would be perfect for a wedding," Jennifer said. "Thanks to all this rain, the herb and wildflower gardens are both growing like crazy."

"I'm not sure the gazebo will be finished by then," Ben said. "Let them use the lobby."

Jennifer looked at him questioningly. He'd told her that the gazebo should be finished in another month, and the wedding date was two months away. Before she could comment on it, Sherri had gone on to talk about the elaborate party they were catering this weekend. Soon, they all split up to do their respective afternoon chores.

BEN BRUSHED AWAY the gray dust that had settled on him, then leaned into the gaping hole to examine the uncovered staircase. He could see only the first part of it, because it made a sharp turn, which was why he'd erred in his guess about where it would be.

He sniffed. It didn't smell very good up there. Maybe a mouse or squirrel had somehow gotten in and died there. The odor wasn't that strong, but he figured he'd better try to get the sealed windows out today, if possible, so that the place could air out.

He started slowly up the stairs, testing each one and finding them as sturdy as the stairs in the other hidden staircase. There was no sign of dampness or rot in the walls, either, which pleased him.

When he reached the top, he saw that the circular room was completely bare, except for an old carpet rolled up in one corner. The floor was dirty, but not warped. The domed ceiling hadn't fared quite as well, however. There were some cracks in the plaster.

The rain had stopped, but the wind was whistling through the rotted frames of the round windows. That didn't bother him, since they were coming out anyway. He walked over to one of the windows and rubbed away the dust. It *was* a great view; Jenny would love it. From this window, he could look down on her herb and wildflower gardens, and the framework of the gazebo.

He guessed he was going to have to delay the gazebo to keep her from wanting to have that wedding there. He had plans for the gazebo himself, and they didn't include some strangers' wedding.

He turned to go back down for his tools so that he could get the windows out, then stopped and stared at the big, rolled-up rug. The smell seemed to be coming from there. When he walked over to it, he realized it was bulkier than he'd first thought. He might need some help getting it out of here.

It was tied with heavy rope in three places, so he grabbed one piece and started to drag it away from the wall. Something rolled out of it and clattered onto the wood floor. Ben stared at the object in stunned disbelief for long moments before finally reaching into his pocket and taking out his knife to cut the ropes.

When he had unrolled the carpet, his disbelief turned to horror. He staggered back from it, his mind as yet unable to grasp the implications of the sight before him.

He didn't hear Jenny calling him until she was partway up the stairs.

"BEN, are you up there?"

He didn't answer, but she heard some noises in the tower and started up the dusty staircase.

"Ben, what's that—?" She stopped abruptly when she saw him. His skin was ashen, and his eyes seemed almost glazed. She ran up the remaining steps. He tried to block her way—but it was too late.

For just a moment, she was sure it must be some kind of joke, maybe Ben's way of teasing her about her interest in ghosts. Lying on an old, stained rug in the middle of the floor was a human skeleton. It was completely intact, except for the skull. And it was only when she saw the head lying some distance away that she screamed.

Ben grabbed her then and dragged her down the stairs to her living room. She doubted the reality of what she'd seen as she took in the cozy comfort of her new home.

"It...it isn't *real*, is it?" she asked, deliberately turning her back on the hole in the wall.

"It's real, all right," Ben said grimly. "It was rolled up in that old rug."

She stared at him, and saw her own shock and horror reflected back at her.

Ben grabbed her hand. "Let's get out of here!"

They left the apartment and made their way in stunned silence to her office, where both of them sat staring at each other for several minutes.

"If that...that skeleton is all that's left," Jennifer said in a choked voice, "then that must mean that it's been up there for ages." Ben said nothing. "It must have been put there before the tower was closed off, a long time ago."

She stopped as the implications began to dawn on her. "Oh, my God!" she murmured. It was Ben's grandfather who had sealed off the tower.

Their eyes met, and Ben nodded. Now she could see beyond the shock to the anguish in his eyes. Desperate to help him, she attempted to find another explanation.

"The tower could have been reopened sometime later, couldn't it? Or maybe your grandfather didn't actually do the work himself. Someone else could have—"

"I tried those excuses already," he said, cutting her off. "They just don't wash. Sure, it could have been reopened, but it had to have been done years ago. And how could it have been done without Granddad knowing about it? They were living in the apartment. And, yeah, maybe he didn't do the work himself, but it's pretty farfetched to imagine that anyone else could have gotten a body up there without his knowing about it."

"But it's *possible*," she insisted desperately.

He just sat there for a long time, his head lowered so that she couldn't see his face. She got up and walked behind him to wrap her arms around his shoulders. She could feel his pain. He had adored his grandfather.

Suddenly he broke free of her and picked up the phone on her desk. She assumed he must be calling the police, but she was wrong.

"Harry, it's Ben. I've just opened up the tower room. Get over here now!"

He slammed down the receiver and sank back into his chair. His color was ghastly. She knew that her own couldn't be much better, but she was more than ever aware that Victoriana—and all its history—was *his*. His family's heritage.

He got up again and began to pace around the small office. She went to him and wrapped her arms around him again. At first he was stiff and unyielding, but then he put his arms around her, too, and buried his face in her hair.

"Do you think Harry knows about it?" she asked after a while.

"Yes." He hugged her. "I'm sorry, Jenny. I should have kept you from seeing it."

She was touched by his desire to protect her, but *he* was the one who needed protection and comfort now.

"Ben," she said imploringly, "please don't condemn your grandfather. There could be a logical explanation."

He shook his head. "There can't be a logical explanation for a body being hidden away like that. Unless you call murder logical."

She knew he was right, so she changed the subject. "But if Harry knew about it, why didn't he tell you? He knew we were talking about opening up the tower."

"He knew about it, Jenny."

She was very confused. If Harry had known, then why hadn't he warned Ben?

Then, suddenly, the word *warning* loomed very large in her mind, as though her subconscious were trying to prompt her.

"Oh, no," she murmured, more to herself than to Ben. But when she looked into his haunted eyes, she knew he had already reached the same conclusion.

He nodded slowly. "Harry was the one who was causing the trouble."

He ran a shaky hand through his hair. "I thought about him even before this. It kept bugging me that whoever was doing it almost certainly had a key—even after we changed the lock. He must have taken my key and gotten a copy made. I even went to the locksmith and asked if Harry had gotten a key made there recently. I made up some excuse about needing another house key, because he knows Harry. But he hadn't gone there. He must have gone out of town for it.

"I kept thinking about confronting him, but I didn't do it, because I just couldn't come up with a motive. It made no sense for him to do things like that."

"So he wasn't really trying to keep the inn from reopening," Jennifer said. "He just wanted to scare me out of the apartment."

"Right. And there were other reasons I thought about him, too—like the hidden staircase, and the fact that no real damage was done. Then there was the last time he came, when I wasn't here. He knew I wouldn't be here that night. I stopped by the house to pick up my fishing and camping gear, and I told him where I was going."

"But why didn't you tell me you suspected him?" she asked, hurt that he'd kept such a terrible thing to himself.

"Because I just couldn't believe it. He never had any interest in the inn. The only thing I could figure was that he thought if he got you out, somehow the inn would become mine. So I told him right away about our partnership, and I figured if that was what he'd had in mind, he'd stop." He shrugged. "After that, there just didn't seem to be any reason to tell you. I didn't want you to hate him. He's the only close relative I have left."

"I can understand your wanting to protect him, Ben, and—"

Before she could finish, a very pale and suddenly very old-looking Harry Walters appeared in the office doorway. Jennifer was shocked at the difference in him. He actually seemed to have shrunk. Before, he'd been a very robust man who looked far younger than his years—but no longer.

Ben, too, seemed shocked at his uncle's appearance, and he quickly led him to a chair. Harry sank into it gratefully. Jennifer noticed that he was carefully avoiding looking her way.

"Who is it, Harry?" Ben asked, gesturing toward the tower.

Harry just sat there shaking his head for so long that Jennifer thought he was going to insist he didn't know. But finally he drew in a breath and looked up at his nephew.

"His name was Talmadge Alcott. Folks just called him Mudge."

"Alcott?" Ben echoed, frowning. "I remember an Alcott who was about Granddad's age. Wasn't he the police chief years ago?"

"That was his brother. You probably remember him because he and Dad didn't get along."

"Yeah, you're right. I can remember Granddad saying once that Alcott had it in for him."

"Now you know why," Harry said, nodding. "He always suspected that Dad had killed his brother, but he never had any proof, so there wasn't much he could do about it."

Jennifer looked at Ben to see how he was reacting to this, but his expression gave nothing away.

"Maybe you'd better begin at the beginning, Harry," he suggested gently.

"Right. Well, you know that Dad had quite a temper. Mudge did some work for him here at the inn. He had a drinking problem, and I guess he didn't do a very good job at whatever it was, or maybe he didn't get it done by the time he was supposed to.

"Anyway, Dad was always tight with money, and he refused to pay Mudge. One night the two of them got into an argument about it down at Jack Yerby's bar. Apparently Dad told Mudge to stay off Victoriana property and threatened to take a shotgun to him if he ever showed up. Everyone in the place heard it.

"This was right before hunting season, and just a couple of

weeks later, Dad was out hunting, and he shot Mudge by mistake. It was right on the edge of Victoriana property.

"Dad knew right away what everyone would think, and, of course, Mudge was the chief's brother, which made it even worse. The ground was too frozen to bury him deep, and Dad was afraid that dogs would dig him up if he made a shallow grave. So he ended up putting him in the tower. He'd already been planning to close it off, because Mother was always complaining about drafts in the winter."

"Your father told you about this?" Jennifer asked, speaking for the first time since Harry's arrival. She was horrified at the thought that a child should have been involved in such a thing. "How old were you?"

Harry looked at her. "I was nine. But Dad didn't tell me. Eddie's the one who told me. He was thirteen, and he was with Dad when it happened."

"Oh, my God," Jennifer breathed softly, turning to look at Ben. Her mind was spinning with the implications of all this, and she knew that Ben must be having the same reaction.

"I guess I believed Eddie at the time, but we were just kids, and over the years I got to thinking that it must have been just one of those stories an older brother tells a younger one to scare him. Eddie never talked about it again, you see, and I never asked. I *wanted* to think it was just a story, even though deep down I think I always knew it had really happened."

A silence fell among them, and it was Ben who finally broke it. "*Was* it an accident, Harry?"

"Your daddy swore that it was. Nobody wore those bright colors for hunting back then, and there were a lot more accidents. He said Mudge was wearing something brown, just about the color of a deer, and it was in a real thick part of the woods, and getting on to dark, too. Eddie said that Dad was pretty upset because he hadn't gotten a deer. It was the first day, and he'd always gotten one the first day. So he might have been careless. But he would never have shot a man in cold blood like that, Ben."

After another silence, Ben said, almost to himself, "So that's why Dad wouldn't live here, and why he hated the place."

Harry nodded. "I don't think he ever got over it. He changed after that summer, Ben, and that's why, like I said, deep down I knew his story must have been true."

Harry looked at them both, then looked away again. "I guess you've probably figured out by now that I was the one who came sneaking around here. As soon as Jennifer mentioned opening up the tower, I got scared, and that's when I forced myself to admit that Eddie's story was true.

"But when I found out how you felt about her, Ben, I figured maybe you'd given up the idea of opening it up. I guessed that you'd be getting married and going to live in that house you're building."

He stopped, then turned to look at Ben. "What are you going to do?"

"I have to call the police, Harry."

"Why? There isn't even any of his family around here who'd remember him. He wasn't married, and it happened nearly sixty years ago. Think about your Granddad's name, Ben. Why can't we just take him out and bury him somewhere?"

Jennifer held her breath when Ben didn't answer immediately. She knew just how tempting Harry's suggestion must be.

But Ben shook his head. "I'm calling the police, Harry, and you're going to have to tell them what you told us. I'm not going to have this on my conscience. I don't blame you and Dad for keeping quiet, but I can't do that."

Harry nodded, resigned. "Yeah, I guessed you'd feel that way. That's one reason I didn't tell you before. And I guess you're right. God knows your daddy suffered for it. Before it happened, all he wanted to do was to take Dad's place here." He turned to Jennifer. "I'm really sorry about the trouble I caused you, Jennifer. I wouldn't blame you if you never forgave me for it."

"I think Win wasn't the only one who suffered, Harry," she said quietly. "It can't have been easy for you to do what you did."

She saw the gratitude in his eyes as he nodded, then thanked her. Ben picked up the phone and called the police. They waited in silence.

The next few hours passed in a blur of activity. After the police came the coroner, followed by a hearse. Jennifer was questioned, but only briefly. Harry agreed to lead the police to the spot where he thought the shooting had taken place, although what that was supposed to prove was beyond Jennifer.

After they had gone, Jennifer sat on the porch and thought about Win, and how he'd carried that awful secret with him all his life. She understood now why he had talked so proudly of Victoriana. Away from it, he had reverted to his old love of the place.

Most of all, she worried about Ben. She was very proud of him. If he'd decided to go along with Harry's suggestion, she wouldn't have stopped him—but she knew that she would have found it difficult to love him after that.

The men returned from the woods while she was still sitting on the porch. Ben paused long enough to squeeze her shoulder, then went inside with Harry. A few minutes later, he came back again.

"I called the Willises, and they have a room for you there tonight. If you want, I'll go up and pack a bag for you."

She hadn't thought that far ahead, but was grateful that he had. "Where are you staying?"

"I'll be at Harry's. He's pretty upset, and I think he needs to have someone around." He ran a hand through his hair. "I guess we both need to talk some more, too."

JENNIFER HAD NO IDEA what to expect when she arrived at the Willises', but she was hoping Ben hadn't told them the real reason for her sudden need of a place to stay. Mrs. Willis was a kindhearted woman, but she was also very talkative, and Jennifer did not want to spend an evening being politely grilled about what had happened.

But she soon discovered that Ben had explained her need of a room as being the result of complications during the course of his work in her apartment—a not-quite-lie that made Jennifer smile in spite of her present state of mind. He'd found a way to avoid outright lying to old family friends who would certainly know the truth soon enough, and he'd carefully preserved her privacy when she needed it.

She retired to her room, the same one she'd had before, as early as possible, hoping Ben would call. Ever since his announcement that he would be spending the night at his uncle's, she'd been fighting her own hurt feelings. He'd said that he needed to talk, and yet he'd chosen not to talk to her.

Still, even in the midst of his anguish over the grisly discovery and Harry's shocking revelations, Ben had thought about her comfort and privacy. And when he could easily have chosen to cover up his beloved grandfather's misdeeds, he'd chosen instead to do the right thing.

Exhausted by the day's events, Jennifer crawled into bed and lay there looking around the familiar room. So much had happened since she'd been a guest here before. As she thought about all of it, her hurt feelings began to drain away.

She loved Ben, and she had come to understand that a part of love was knowing when to let go. His uncle needed him now, and he needed his uncle, as well, because there were things they had shared that she hadn't been a part of. She knew he would talk to her about it at some point, but right now he needed the comfort of the old and the familiar.

Just before she fell asleep, she remembered Harry's comment about Ben's feelings for her, and his assumption that they'd be getting married. She smiled sleepily and floated away into a dream about their future.

JENNIFER WAS JUST waking up and trying to prepare herself for whatever the day might bring when there was a knock at her door. She groaned inwardly, certain it must be Mrs. Willis, full of sympathy and questions. It couldn't be Ben, since the inn had strict rules, posted in bold letters, that visitors must wait downstairs. Just for good measure, Mrs. Willis had told her about them the first time she stayed here.

But when she reluctantly opened the door, it *was* Ben who stood there, carrying a large, cloth-covered tray. He came into the room, set the tray on the small table near the window, then drew her into his arms and gave her a long, hungry kiss.

"Thank you," he murmured against her ear.

"For what?" she asked in confusion.

"For understanding about last night. I didn't want to leave you alone, but Harry needed me, and I really needed to talk to someone who'd known Granddad—the good parts of him as well as the bad."

She smiled and hugged him tight. "I *do* understand, Ben, and I know how terrible this must be for you. But there's one good thing that has come out of all this. At least now we both know why your father felt the way he did about Victoriana."

"It must have been hell for him. I doubt if a day passed that he didn't either want to burn the place down or go to the police and take his chances."

"What about Harry? Will he be in trouble for not telling?"

"I talked to the chief before I came over here, and he'd just talked to the D.A. about it. They're not going to bring any charges against Harry, because of his age and because he had no direct knowledge of it. That was the main thing I was worried about at this point."

"I think your father would be very proud of the decision you made, Ben—and so am I."

They held each other in silence for a while, content simply to be there together. Then the smells wafting out from beneath the cover on the tray became too enticing. It occurred to Jennifer that Ben had not only managed to circumvent the rule about visitors in rooms, but had also managed to persuade Mrs. Willis to provide room service.

As they sat down to eat, she commented that Mrs. Willis must like him quite a lot to have allowed her strict house rules to be broken.

"She knows what happened. It's in the newspaper and on the radio. Besides, I, uh, smoothed the way a little."

"What are you talking about?" He certainly couldn't have bribed the woman.

He picked up a blueberry muffin and began to spread it generously with butter. "Well," he said casually, "I told her that we're getting married."

Warmth began to spread through her, leaving her tingling all over. But she recalled his other little lies. "Ben Walters, you *do* have a way of shading the truth a bit, don't you?"

He stared at her, all semblance of casualness gone now. "*Aren't* we getting married?"

This wasn't exactly the kind of proposal she'd dreamed of, but Ben was Ben, and it was likely to be the best she would get. She waited for as long as she dared, then affected a nonchalant shrug.

"I suppose we are. I mean, if we're going to be partners in Victoriana, we might as well be partners otherwise, too."

"Might as well be? Wait a minute! What's more important here—Victoriana or *us?*"

She laughed. "That's a question both of us asked ourselves for quite a while, isn't it?"

"Well, answer it! *I* know which is more important."

"And so do I," she replied, leaning across the table to kiss him. "Of course, you may not think so when fall comes and the inn reopens."

Epilogue

The guests assembled on the lawn at Victoriana were talking primarily of two things: the fact that the old inn could certainly never have looked more splendid, and the sudden change in the weather that had brought clear skies after days of unprecedented August rains.

The small orchestra set up in the whimsical, flower-bedecked gazebo struck up the familiar melody from *Lohengrin*. Those who were still inside, enjoying the beauty of the lobby, thought for a moment that they had stepped back in time. Down the wide staircase came the bride, in a lovely lace wedding dress that some of them knew had belonged to her grandmother. *Radiant* seemed an inadequate description of the striking young woman.

And quite a few of them remarked, as well, on the tall, distinguished-looking gentleman at her side, who was also obviously very happy. He was a diplomat, it was whispered, and had flown here all the way from Moscow to give his daughter away.

Outside, the rest of the assemblage saw a tall, dark-haired young man who looked as much at home in white tie and tails as he did in his usual blue jeans. Together with his best man, an uncle who had recently figured in a much-talked-about scandal here, he took up his position at the entrance to the gazebo. Everyone saw his bright blue eyes watching the front of the inn, and they turned in that direction, too.

Later, as they moved through the inn and strolled on its grounds while devouring the excellent food, everyone agreed that this was the most beautiful wedding they'd ever seen. A few of the more lyrical among them had even used the word *magical*.

AND MUCH LATER, when the inn was quiet once again, the newlyweds stopped in the lobby to stare at the huge painting that hung over the fireplace. Many guests had remarked upon the talent of the artist.

Jennifer went over and touched it lightly. "I think the paint is actually dry."

"Come on. I finished it yesterday."

She laughed and drew him out onto the porch, where they stood for a moment looking at the gazebo, which was still decorated with a profusion of flowers.

"I was remembering a little while ago that when Sherri and Tom first mentioned that wedding last month, you didn't like the idea of their using the gazebo. Was it because you wanted *our* wedding to be the first to be held there?"

"Of course. I'm still not sure I want anyone else to get married there."

"Well, I'm afraid it's already booked for two weddings next month."

He groaned. "Our wedding isn't even over yet, and already you're the businesswoman."

They walked through the woods to the lake in the soft, gathering dusk. Ben wrapped an arm around her waist and kissed her cheek.

"I'm glad you wanted to spend our wedding night here."

"Where else could we go that could possibly be so perfect?" She smiled. "But please don't decide that you don't want anyone else staying in the rose suite, because it's already heavily booked, and it's a very good money-maker."

They stopped at the edge of the lake, which glistened darkly now as the stars came out. "Did you invite her to the wedding?" Ben asked, gesturing to the empty lake.

She nodded. "But it looks as though she didn't show up. Maybe it was just too painful for her. Anyway, I brought her this."

She withdrew from her pocket a piece of wedding cake

wrapped in a napkin, and walked out to the end of the dock to lay it there.

"Will you be surprised if it's gone in the morning?" Ben asked with a grin as he drew her into his arms again.

"No, I'll be disappointed if it isn't."

Their lips and bodies met in eager anticipation of a lifetime of such meetings, so neither of them noticed the brief appearance of a strange, misty sort of apparition at the far side of the lake.

American HEROES
AGAINST ALL ODDS

1. ALABAMA
After Hours—Gina Wilkins

2. ALASKA
The Bride Came C.O.D.—Barbara Bretton

3. ARIZONA
Stolen Memories—Kelsey Roberts

4. ARKANSAS
Hillbilly Heart—Stella Bagwell

5. CALIFORNIA
Stevie's Chase—Justine Davis

6. COLORADO
Walk Away, Joe—Pamela Toth

7. CONNECTICUT
Honeymoon for Hire—Cathy Gillen Thacker

8. DELAWARE
Death Spiral—Patricia Rosemoor

9. FLORIDA
Cry Uncle—Judith Arnold

10. GEORGIA
Safe Haven—Marilyn Pappano

11. HAWAII
Marriage Incorporated—Debbi Rawlins

12. IDAHO
Plain Jane's Man—Kristine Rolofson

13. ILLINOIS
Safety of His Arms—Vivian Leiber

14. INDIANA
A Fine Spring Rain—Celeste Hamilton

15. IOWA
Exclusively Yours—Leigh Michaels

16. KANSAS
The Doubletree—Victoria Pade

17. KENTUCKY
Run for the Roses—Peggy Moreland

18. LOUISIANA
Rambler's Rest—Bay Matthews

19. MAINE
Whispers in the Wood—Helen R. Myers

20. MARYLAND
Chance at a Lifetime—Anne Marie Winston

21. MASSACHUSETTS
Body Heat—Elise Title

22. MICHIGAN
Devil's Night—Jennifer Greene

23. MINNESOTA
Man from the North Country—Laurie Paige

24. MISSISSIPPI
Miss Charlotte Surrenders—Cathy Gillen Thacker

25. MISSOURI
One of the Good Guys—Carla Cassidy

26. MONTANA
Angel—Ruth Langan

27. NEBRASKA
Return to Raindance—Phyllis Halldorson

28. NEVADA
Baby by Chance—Elda Minger

29. NEW HAMPSHIRE
Sara's Father—Jennifer Mikels

30. NEW JERSEY
Tara's Child—Susan Kearney

31. NEW MEXICO
Black Mesa—Aimée Thurlo

32. NEW YORK
Winter Beach—Terese Ramin

33. NORTH CAROLINA
Pride and Promises—BJ James

34. NORTH DAKOTA
To Each His Own—Kathleen Eagle

35. OHIO
Courting Valerie—Linda Markowiak

36. OKLAHOMA
Nanny Angel—Karen Toller Whittenburg

37. OREGON
Firebrand—Paula Detmer Riggs

38. PENNSYLVANIA
McLain's Law—Kylie Brant

39. RHODE ISLAND
Does Anybody Know Who Allison Is?—Tracy Sinclair

40. SOUTH CAROLINA
Just Deserts—Dixie Browning

41. SOUTH DAKOTA
Brave Heart—Lindsay McKenna

42. TENNESSEE
Out of Danger—Beverly Barton

43. TEXAS
Major Attraction—Roz Denny Fox

44. UTAH
Feathers in the Wind—Pamela Browning

45. VERMONT
Twilight Magic—Saranne Dawson

46. VIRGINIA
No More Secrets—Linda Randall Wisdom

47. WASHINGTON
The Return of Caine O'Halloran—JoAnn Ross

48. WEST VIRGINIA
Cara's Beloved—Laurie Paige

49. WISCONSIN
Hoops—Patricia McLinn

50. WYOMING
Black Creek Ranch—Jackie Merritt

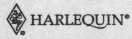

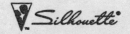

Please address questions and book requests to: Harlequin Reader Service U.S.: 3010 Walden Ave.,
P.O. Box 1325, Buffalo, NY 14269 CAN.: P.O. Box 609, Fort Erie, Ont. L2A 5X3   PAHGEN

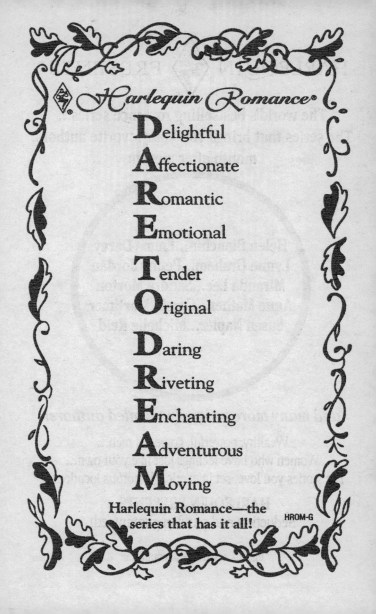

Harlequin Romance®

Delightful
Affectionate
Romantic
Emotional
Tender
Original
Daring
Riveting
Enchanting
Adventurous
Moving

Harlequin Romance—the
series that has it all!

HROM-G

HARLEQUIN PRESENTS®

The world's bestselling romance series...
The series that brings you your favorite authors,
month after month:

Helen Bianchin...Emma Darcy
Lynne Graham...Penny Jordan
Miranda Lee...Sandra Morton
Anne Mather...Carole Mortimer
Susan Napier...Michelle Reid

and many more uniquely talented authors!

Wealthy, powerful, gorgeous men...
Women who have feelings just like your own...
The stories you love, set in exotic, glamorous locations...

HARLEQUIN PRESENTS,
Seduction and passion guaranteed!

Harlequin® Historical

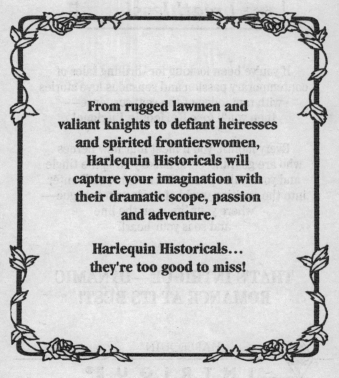

From rugged lawmen and
valiant knights to defiant heiresses
and spirited frontierswomen,
Harlequin Historicals will
capture your imagination with
their dramatic scope, passion
and adventure.

Harlequin Historicals...
they're too good to miss!

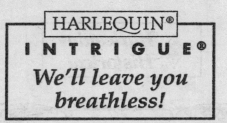

Romance is just one click away!

online book **serials**

- *Exclusive* to our web site, get caught up in both the daily and weekly online installments of new romance stories.
- Try the Writing Round Robin. Contribute a chapter to a story created by our members. Plus, winners will get prizes.

romantic **travel**

- Want to know where the best place to kiss in New York City is, or which restaurant in Los Angeles is the most romantic? Check out our Romantic Hot Spots for the scoop.
- Share your travel tips and stories with us on the romantic travel message boards.

romantic reading **library**

- Relax as you read our collection of Romantic Poetry.
- Take a peek at the Top 10 Most Romantic Lines!

Visit us online at

www.eHarlequin.com
on Women.com Networks

HEUT1

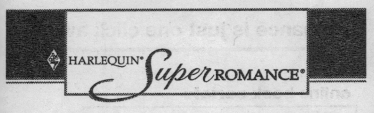